A VERY SPECIAL CHRISTMAS

Abigail Beadle has given two decades of her life to caring for her late father and preserving the family home, Ashgrove House in Wiltshire. When her loathed stepmother, Edwina, dies, Abigail is glad to be released from her bullying. She will also be able to look after the house properly, perhaps have a real Christmas at home, without Edwina's stranglehold on the finances.

But her stepmother left behind a will that casts doubt on Abigail's inheritance and raises the possibility that she will have to leave the home she loves so much. It is not until Lucas Chadwick, the man she loved when she was young, returns to the village that Abigail begins to believe her life might be able to start at last . . .

ANNA JACOBS

A VERY SPECIAL CHRISTMAS

Complete and Unabridged

a&b

Allison & Busby
London

First published in Great Britain in 2021 by
Allison & Busby Ltd
London

First Ulverscroft Edition
published 2023
by arrangement with
Allison & Busby Ltd
London

*A catalogue record for this book is available
from the British Library.*

ISBN 978–1–4448–5195–3

Published by
Ulverscroft Limited
Anstey, Leicestershire

Printed and bound in Great Britain by
TJ Books Ltd., Padstow, Cornwall

This book is printed on acid-free paper

1

Abigail Beadle walked into the church and paused to stare round. Only a few of the pews were occupied but still, that was more than she'd expected, given her stepmother's genius for upsetting people. She shivered. November could be a cold month and Christmas still seemed a long time away.

A lady was already sitting in the front pew: her stepmother's cousin, Cynthia. She was draped in very old-fashioned garments. It was what you did at a funeral, dress in black. Today Abigail would have preferred to wear red — bright red — if she'd owned any red clothes, that was. It occurred to her suddenly how outraged Edwina would have been if she'd even said that, let alone done it, and she had to turn a giggle into a hiccup.

Freedom from her stepmother's bullying had gone to her head, was bubbling out of every pore, but she had to hold it in till this was over.

As she took her seat at the front, Cousin Cynthia held out a lace-edged handkerchief, no doubt thinking she'd been stifling a sob.

Abigail shook her head, wasn't going to pretend to weep. She'd done her duty and recently kept an eye on Edwina as she grew frailer. She'd looked after her father for a few years but he had been far easier, in spite of his deteriorating health from Parkinson's. After his death, it had been even harder to deal with her stepmother, so they'd mostly avoided one another. It was a big house, after all.

1

From now on, however, she would do what she wanted and expected to enjoy the rest of her life now that her stepmother didn't hold the purse strings. She'd promised herself all sorts of small treats last night as she lay sprawled on a couch (*like a slut*), watching her own choice of TV programme (*fit only for idiots*) and drinking a glass of white wine (*real ladies only drink wine at table*).

It took her by surprise when the funeral service ended and Cynthia had to poke her in the side to remind her to stand up. She led the way outside, relishing the fresh air on her face as she followed the coffin into the churchyard. She had a sudden desire to tear off the unflattering black hat and sling it as far away as she could. It was such a horrible lump of a thing. Today, after everyone had gone home, she was going to walk down to the ash grove at the rear of the grounds and toss the hat into the highest tree. What fun it would be to see birds perching on it and, she hoped, pecking it to pieces!

In the coming weeks she'd buy some flattering clothes and get a new hairstyle. She hoped — oh, she did so hope! — that she'd make some proper friends now that she could invite them home or go out without recriminations being heaped upon her for days afterwards.

Another jab from that bony elbow made Abigail realise she was daydreaming again. That was her besetting sin, to quote one of her favourite fictional characters.

Cynthia glared at her. 'I don't know what's got into you today. Throw some earth on the coffin, for goodness' sake, and let's get this part of the funeral finished!'

Abigail did the necessary, then stood back and watched everyone follow suit. It seemed to take for ever. She didn't understand why Cynthia kept glancing at her with ill-concealed triumph. Once the funeral was over, she was never going to invite the woman to visit Ashgrove House. She wasn't a Beadle, after all, and she'd followed her cousin Edwina's example and become increasingly unpleasant to deal with as the years passed.

* * *

The mourners followed her back to the house, so Abigail still had to remain calm and solemn. There weren't many in the drawing room: the vicar, a few elderly acquaintances of the family, Cousin Cynthia and Mr Liddlestone, the family lawyer, whom she'd known since she was a child.

She hoped they wouldn't stay long. They didn't.

After they'd nibbled a biscuit or two and grimaced at the horribly sweet, cheap sherry her stepmother had favoured, which she had specified was to be the only alcoholic drink to be offered at her funeral gathering, the visitors murmured the usual platitudes and left.

Abigail had only pretended to drink. She hadn't made up her mind yet whether to pour the rest of the sherry down the sink or keep it for unwanted guests, like Cousin Cynthia. She sipped a cup of tea offered by Dot, who came in twice a week to do the cleaning and had been doing so for most of Abigail's life. Dot winked at her as she moved on. She was doing overtime today with one of her many friends helping out.

Dot did wonders with the cleaning and never

counted the extra minutes she gave so cheerfully. Why she had continued to work for such a bad-tempered woman was a mystery to everyone in the village. Abigail didn't know what she'd have done without Dot, who had been more like an aunt, comforting her after first her mother when she was a teenager and a few years later her father died.

It was ridiculous that Edwina had refused point-blank to pay for more help, given the size of the house. She'd held the purse strings in a tight grip until a few weeks ago, when she'd had a severe heart attack. She'd lingered for two more weeks in hospital but hadn't recovered consciousness.

Abigail sometimes wondered whether Edwina had been mean because they were short of money or because it gave her pleasure to make everyone except herself scrimp and manage without luxuries. Knowing her, she'd probably enjoyed it.

Oh dear! Someone was speaking to her. 'Sorry. I was lost in thought. Could you say that again, please?'

Mr Liddlestone gave her one of his gentle smiles. 'I have to go now. I have an appointment with a client in half an hour. Could you come and see me at my rooms tomorrow? We need to deal with the will. Your stepmother didn't want it read in front of everyone.'

'Yes, of course. Oh, Mr L, I'm so looking forward to having my own money and looking after this house properly.'

'Yes, I . . . suppose you are. Shall we say tomorrow at three?'

She watched him go, worried about how old and pale he'd been looking recently. Today he seemed unhappy about something, but it couldn't be because of her stepmother dying because he hadn't liked

4

Edwina either. It was her father who had been his friend.

Perhaps there was less money than expected. Well, if so, Abigail was good at managing. She'd cope, would do anything necessary to stay at Ashgrove House. Her ancestors had started building it just after King George I came to the throne in the early eighteenth century, and had added to it over the years. It wasn't a large stately home, just a small manor house. Abigail loved every brick of it.

The trouble was, you had to pay an inheritance tax to keep a house like Ashgrove and she wasn't sure there would be enough money to cover that. What would she do if she had to sell her family home and find somewhere else to live? It didn't bear thinking of. She had never lived anywhere else and was a Beadle to the core.

★ ★ ★

Gerard Liddlestone drove slowly back to the village from Ashgrove House after the funeral, feeling depressed about the mess he would have to start unravelling the following day. He rubbed his aching forehead. He'd been feeling seedy for a while and his wife was pressing him to retire.

You ought not to speak ill of the dead, but Edwina Beadle had been a horrible woman, who'd trapped a grieving widower and 'married up', as some people called it. At first she had been reasonably pleasant — never the sort you got on with easily, unlike her husband, though.

She'd persuaded her husband to write a will leaving everything to her, but fortunately Stephen Beadle

5

had had the wit to make a condition about that inheritance. She'd tried to get round that in her final will, which had left everything to her Cousin Cynthia. He was sure the latter would bring in lawyers to back up that will.

He was getting too old for these struggles over inheritance, hated to see families torn apart. After her husband died, Edwina had taken control of the estate finances and turned into a spiteful miser, treating her stepdaughter like a slave. He'd been a coward when dealing with her, he admitted, should have reminded her when she fiddled around with her will about that addendum to her late husband's will — an addendum which she had signed and which stipulated that everything should be passed on to Abigail.

The trouble was, he'd felt that her anger would have made her stepdaughter's life even more unpleasant if he reminded her, and since the house would eventually come to Abigail, it made no real difference.

He still felt guilty about letting that situation continue, though. He didn't really have another client waiting for him, but his headache was getting worse and he couldn't seem to think straight. He nodded to his secretary and told her she could go home because it was past her usual time of leaving.

He got the box of Beadle family papers out of the storeroom, set it on his desk and took the lid off. Edwina's latest will, which was on top of the pile of documents, was going to cause a lot of trouble. He ought to be working out how best to deal with it tomorrow, but instead sat scowling at it, rubbing his forehead tiredly.

Edwina had grown rather erratic in the last year of her life, changing the details of her will several times.

6

On what turned out to be her final visit to his rooms, she'd done it again. He'd tried to persuade her not to do this, of course he had, but she'd been adamant, threatening to go to another lawyer if he refused. He'd had to bring in two people from a nearby office to act as witnesses because they were the only others left in the building by that time. She'd signed it triumphantly, believing she was carrying out the threat she'd been making for years to disinherit her stepdaughter completely.

This time it was because of some imagined fault that was supposed to prove that Abigail could not be trusted with the family money or the preservation of historic Ashgrove House. Ha! Abigail had been the one looking after the house for years.

He was deeply sorry now that he'd been a coward, unable to face Edwina's fury. He should have reminded her about the addendum, but had thought she'd once again change her will again in a week or two.

He stared out of his office window, then looked back at Edwina's final will. What if . . . ? No, no, he couldn't destroy it. He just . . . couldn't. He was a lawyer. This will must be *proved* legally invalid. He was tempted, though, and who would know if he did destroy it? It wouldn't really change anything, just prevent a lot of nastiness and expense because he was sure that Cynthia Polson would try to overturn the original conditions of inheritance.

Actually, he hadn't even asked his secretary to type this new will up, because the previous will was on the computer and it had only been a question of changing the names and a couple of sentences. Even he could manage that. He switched on the computer and

7

opened the file, once again tempted to destroy that new will. Just one keystroke would do it.

No, no! He mustn't, even though it would be the easiest way to deal with this situation. He closed the file quickly and stared in horror as his fingers seemed to take on a life of their own and deleted it, then deleted the backup file too.

He jerked his hands away from the keyboard, looking at the screen, aghast. What had he done? There was a way to retrieve deleted files, he knew, because he'd had digital mishaps before. But his head was throbbing. He'd ask his secretary's help in sorting it all out tomorrow.

He shut down the computer, stuffed the paper copy of the final will back into the box, having to push down the pile of papers to get the lid closed. It was time to start a new box for the Beadle family. Only would there be any more Beadles? Abigail was thirty-eight, after all, and unmarried.

He began to pack his briefcase, stopping now and then to sigh and worry about her. She had looked happier than usual today, though she'd tried to hide it and stay solemn. But he'd known her all her life and was well aware that when her eyes crinkled slightly at the corners she was hiding a smile.

She had lovely eyes, of an unusual turquoise-blue, rimmed by long dark lashes, and honey-coloured hair like all true Beadles. She was as honest as the day was long and stubborn when she believed something was right. My goodness, how the years had flown past! Could the little Beadle baby whose christening he'd attended really be almost forty?

He was seriously considering how best to move into retirement now. Neither of his children had wanted to study law so he'd recently taken on a younger partner as the first step in disengaging. Philip Danvers was a pleasant chap, well qualified, and was settling in nicely.

Gerard began to pace up and down then stopped to stare blindly out of the window. If he gave in to temptation, destroyed the paper copy and let the final will stay deleted on the computer, he'd be breaking the law, going against all he believed in.

It occurred to him yet again, however, that what he was thinking of doing would be justice in the very best and truest sense of the word. But it was still against the law.

No, he just couldn't do it.

★ ★ ★

When all the guests had left, Abigail let out her breath in a long exhalation of relief. She switched on the radio and smiled as she heard one of her favourite tunes.

She couldn't help it. She began to waltz round the drawing room, then twirled out into the hall. From there she moved into the library and completed the circuit via the dining room at the front of the house, which was across the hall from the drawing room. She and her father had often danced round the house together. He'd loved ballroom dancing but her stepmother had not been at all musical.

As she spun round, she nearly fell for lack of a partner and laughed aloud. She was free! Free at last.

The music continued to play, so she went on dancing. On her second circuit of the main rooms, she pulled back the curtains, swaying to and fro, then starting off again, waltzing merrily till the tune changed into a tango. Oh, she loved a tango. It had been her father's favourite dance. She began moving to the new rhythm with smooth, controlled steps and impeccable turns.

* * *

Dot went into the drawing room to clear away the cups and glasses, but ducked back behind the door, smiling when she saw Abigail solemnly waltzing across the room and out into the hall. She continued to smile as the dancing took Abigail round the main rooms for a second time.

When she heard the curtains being drawn back to let in the afternoon sunlight, she nearly cheered aloud. The old witch would have thrown a fit. Edwina had always insisted on keeping the curtains drawn at the times of day sunlight fell on the windows, to prevent fading of carpets and upholstery. They were only drawn back at those times if the room was going to be used by her.

Dot had refused point-blank to keep the blinds half drawn in her kitchen, a place lazy Edwina rarely visited, and had threatened to give notice if anyone tried to make her work in such dim light.

As the music changed to a tango, Dot began to sway. She went to a ballroom dancing club for oldies in the village and loved Latin American dances most of all. When Abigail came round again, she couldn't resist it. She stepped forward and bowed. 'May I have this dance, my lady?'

Abigail swept her a curtsey. 'Delighted, my lord.'

So Dot took over. She always played the man when

she and her sister went to the senior citizens' dances in the village hall, because there was a shortage of older men her age and she was quite tall. She swept Abigail swept round in a masterful manner, swaying and swooping, holding her arms just so, and tilting her partner back a couple of times, just like they'd shown her at the club.

When the music stopped, she let go and bowed. 'That was a real pleasure.'

Abigail laughed and clapped. 'You are such a good dancer, Dot.'

'Not as good as your dad.'

'Wasn't he marvellous? He started teaching me when I was quite little, before you began working for us. But after he remarried, we only danced when Edwina was out. When he developed Parky's and gradually lost control of his limbs, he was so brave about it, never complained. We both missed the dancing dreadfully.'

'My Hilton was a good dancer, too. I miss him for that, though not for much else. He was a lazy devil round the house.'

Abigail didn't comment. Everyone in the village had known that Hilton Eakins was a drunkard and a slob, of course they had, but they'd never dared say that to Dot's face, even after he died. She changed the subject. 'I shouldn't be dancing on the day of my stepmother's funeral, should I? Please don't tell anyone.'

'If I were in your place, I'd be tap dancing on the rooftop for the whole world to see, I'd be so happy. She was a nasty person and treated you badly.'

Dot held up one hand to stop Abigail protesting that remark. 'I didn't say anything before about how

11

things were. It wasn't my place and I couldn't do anything about it, could I? But you don't have to pretend with me, love. I know what she was like better than anyone. You can dance, sing, shout, do anything you feel like from now on. You've earned it.'

To her surprise, Abigail gave her a big hug and said, 'The first thing I want to do is thank you, Dot, for everything you've done over the years, especially since Dad died. You've been a great comfort to me.'

'I wish I'd been able to do more to help you.'

'No one could. It was just a question of enduring. But the way you winked at me sometimes or made jokes about her helped. I knew I wasn't alone in the world, even after Dad had gone, not with you around. That meant so much.'

'What are you going to do now, if you don't mind me asking?'

'I don't mind you asking, but I don't actually know till I find out how matters stand financially. All I can do is start sorting out the house because I'm not living in my stepmother's clutter. I hate how she changed things around. Her ornaments will be the first things to go. Cheap, horrible tat, they are. But even before that, I'm going to bring my own books up from the cellar, then take all those mouldy, boring old tomes off the shelves in the library and put *them* in the cellar. I'll fill the shelves with my novels. *Romances*, even.'

'You daring devil!' Dot chuckled. Ma Beadle had been particularly down on romances. Abigail, on the other hand, would read any sort of novel but loved romances best, said she felt safe knowing there would always be a happy ending to the story. Reading romances had been her secret vice, that and the occasional bar of chocolate or bottle of wine. Not much of a life, poor lass.

As Dot walked back to the kitchen, she shook her head sadly. Only a gentle soul like Abigail would consider it to be an act of rebellion to put her books out on public display. They wouldn't look as nice as the old books, though, because the romances were all second hand. Over the years Abigail had bought them from charity shops or market stalls, and had smuggled them into the house with the shopping. Hundreds of them, there must be now.

The smile faded. Dot wasn't sure her job would be safe from now on and that was worrying her. Why had Mr L been looking so unhappy today at the funeral if everything was all right? There was some problem looming, she was sure of it. She knew she wouldn't be sacked unless matters were desperate, but her job would depend on how much money had been left and whether Abigail would be able to stay here. There would no doubt be massive death duties to pay. No, they called it inheritance tax these days, didn't they? Well, it didn't matter what they called it, she considered it unfair for the government to take so much of what people had left to their families. Double dipping, she called it. People had already paid tax on their money when they earned it, after all.

Surely the old house wouldn't have to be sold? It'd break Abigail's heart to do that. It'd break any Beadle's heart! It'd upset Dot, too. And let alone she would find it hard to manage on the old age pension without the extra money she earned working here, she too loved the big old house and its interesting contents. No, there must be enough to cover the inheritance tax because the old witch had been an absolute miser with money. Abigail would be all right, surely she would?

13

Dot stood still to think about it. She had a good mind to ask Mr L about the will when she went into his suite of offices to clean up tonight. If she hurried with her jobs here, she might be able to catch him before he left work for the day. He wouldn't tell her any details of the will, that wouldn't be right, but she'd know from his expression whether the news was going to be good or bad for her girl.

2

Mr Liddlestone's car was still there outside the offices when Dot drove into the car park, so she didn't need to use her door key. She walked straight in, calling cheerfully, 'It's only me, Mr L.'

'What? Oh. I was just about to leave.' He rubbed his forehead.

'Is something wrong?'

He shrugged. 'I have a bit of a headache. I find funerals and wills very depressing, don't you?'

That didn't sound good, she thought. 'I've never had much to do with wills. My Hilton didn't leave one. Well, he didn't expect to die at fifty, did he? And he didn't have anything to leave, really, what with us living in a council house and him spending all his own money at the pub.'

She looked at the big cardboard box on the huge mahogany desk. It had 'Beadle' written on the front and top in neat black letters. 'That'll contain Mrs Beadle's will, I suppose. What's she done in it to upset you?'

He shuffled some other papers together quickly. 'I can't discuss that with you. I'm just . . . thinking about what to say to poor Abigail tomorrow.' He put the lid on the box. 'I wonder if you'd mind lifting this into place in the storeroom for me? Top shelf. You'll see the gap where it goes. I feel a bit woozy, I'm afraid, and everyone else here has gone home.'

'You leave it to me, Mr L. I can do that easily enough. I lift heavier things in my garden.'

'Thank you. You're a real treasure, Dot. I don't know what we'd do without you to keep us clean and tidy here.'

She couldn't share her worries with him because he didn't look at all well. Still, it was nice to be called a treasure twice in one day. She watched him pick up his briefcase and walk slowly out to the car, shoulders drooping. Dot was quite sure by this time that the old witch must have done something very nasty in the will.

Once his car had gone from in front of the building, leaving only hers in the car park, Dot picked up the box. She hesitated then set it down on the desk again and stared at it, tempted. She had never, ever snooped here before, even though half the people in the village were clients of Mr L and you couldn't help wondering sometimes. But now . . . well, she was only human.

Why had he said 'poor Abigail' in that tone of voice? What was in the dratted will? If she knew, she might be able to help her dear girl cope with it.

She lifted the lid off the box and peered inside. There the dratted will was, right on the top. She shot a guilty look over her shoulder, which was silly when she knew she was the only person in the building at this hour.

Should she look at it or not?

Oh, why the hell not? It wasn't as if anyone would ever know. Putting the box lid down on the desk, she lifted out Edwina Gwendolyn Beadle's last will and testament.

★ ★ ★

Ten minutes later Dot sat staring at it with tears streaming down her cheeks. She had no doubt whatsoever that the old witch would be roasting in hell at this very minute, and she deserved it, if anyone did.

Mr L had been right to say 'poor Abigail'. Oh, that dear girl was going to be so unhappy! Devastated!

Dot looked at the date on the will. Only done last month. It was very brief, a mere two pages and yet it'd cause so much damage. It must have been written after Edwina's big quarrel with poor Abigail.

She'd never seen her girl so upset. Well, who wouldn't be? Ma Beadle had found a pile of romance paperbacks waiting to be read and started burning them. Abigail had fought back, for once, and shoved her stepmother away, rescuing most of her books and threatening to break all the nasty little ornaments Edwina had collected if any more books were damaged. Harsh things had been said by both women, going on from the books to a few other grievances on both sides. Very harsh. But true. On Abigail's side at least.

Dot hadn't known the old lady could shriek so loudly or that Abigail could stand up for herself so fiercely. The book burning must have been the final straw in a long litany of petty unkindnesses over the years.

She looked down at the box. There was another will underneath the first one with a date three months ago. She couldn't help it, just had to read it as well.

That one left everything to Abigail, as was only fair. It was what old Mr Beadle would have expected to happen. She groaned. There had to be something Mr L could do about the wicked, unkind will. Fancy leaving everything to the old witch's cousin, Cynthia.

Surely Mr L wouldn't let such an injustice happen?

She might just have another peep at the two wills before she finished today, in case she thought of anything she could do to help. Leaving the box on the table in the document room, she went to clean the tearoom and toilets. She scrubbed harder than usual, taking out her anger on everything she touched, banging doors, muttering under her breath, worrying.

It just wasn't fair!

And Mr L must think so too or he'd not have been so upset. Well, she'd catch him tomorrow morning and talk to him. He was always the first one in. There just had to be something he could do about it, had to. But before she put the box away she stared at the newest will, tempted all over again. She wasn't going to leave that horrible thing lying around here in case the new partner saw it. Mr Danvers had only been here a short time, didn't even know Abigail. He'd not care about upsetting her whole life like this.

There *must* be something Mr L could do about it. The fair thing would be to go back to the previous will instead. Or claim the old hag wasn't in her right mind, perhaps. Dot had definitely considered her employer to be very strange mentally, starting from when Mr Beadle passed away. By the time she died, she was full of spite and nastiness, couldn't be kind to anyone to save her life.

Decision made, she shoved the horrid new will into her bag of dusters and rags, not caring if it got crumpled — it deserved to be crumpled — then fitted the lid on the box of Beadle papers and put it back tidily in the storeroom. Tears filled her eyes. She didn't usually cry but she didn't remember being this upset for years.

18

As she was walking out, something rustled beneath her foot and she looked down to see a piece of paper lying on the floor where she'd been standing. It looked like something official. Oh dear, had she dropped something from the Beadle box? She picked it up and dashed away her tears as she read the heading.

It wasn't a will but it had the name Beadle on it. She reached up to lift the lid of the box and shoved the paper down the side. It was crumpled where she'd stood on it so she hoped they'd think it had got like that inside the box. She couldn't see clearly because her eyes would keep filling with tears. She was glad when she'd finished doing the cleaning.

By the time she got home, she was regretting what she'd done. She shouldn't have taken that will. She could go in early tomorrow morning and put it back, though. No one need ever know.

But she'd still see whether she could persuade Mr L to do something about it. She'd have to confess to reading it but she didn't think she'd lose her job, just get a gentle scolding. He was never anything but gentle, had even managed that with Edwina Beadle, heaven knew how.

★ ★ ★

At eight o'clock the next morning, Dot set off for work early, but to her dismay, Mr L's BMW wasn't in the car park, which was most unusual. He normally arrived at five to eight precisely to unlock the building, being an early morning person like her.

She waited. He'd be along any minute, then she'd speak to him about the will. The new partner turned up at ten past eight. Mr Danvers was a bit of an early

19

bird too. He saw her and raised one hand in greeting. She waved back but didn't get out of her car. She was seriously worried by now that she hadn't managed to put the will back without anyone seeing her.

During the night she'd begun to worry that even Mr L might have to sack her for taking legal documents away without permission if the new partner found out. When Mr L hadn't arrived by twenty past eight, she gave up and went on to her work at Ashgrove House, which lay further along the main street, nearly at the end.

It felt as if the will was burning a hole in her shopping bag. What on earth had got into her to take it home? She'd have to go and speak to Mr L before he found out what she'd done, which meant before Abigail went to see him. She'd ring his secretary at nine o'clock and see if he was there, then say she had to speak to him urgently. But as she was about to nip into the kitchen to make that call on her mobile phone, the house phone rang and she heard Abigail run to pick up the one in the hall.

Dot tiptoed to the door at the rear of it. You could save yourself a lot of trouble by eavesdropping, especially in a house of secrets. She never passed on what she heard, just used it to protect herself and her job, and sometimes to protect Abigail too.

'Oh, no! I can't believe it . . . Yes, he was looking rather tired yesterday . . . Yes, I perfectly understand. I'll come in tomorrow morning and see Mr Danvers instead.'

As Abigail put the phone down and mopped her eyes with a handkerchief, Dot stepped out from the servants' quarters. 'Is something wrong, dear?'

'It's Mr Liddlestone. He had a stroke yesterday

evening and he's in hospital.'

'*No!* How bad?'

'Not too bad, thank goodness, but his wife told them he has to take it easier from now on so they're not to bother him.'

'Poor man! I thought he'd been looking a bit under the weather.'

'What's this Mr Danvers like? I haven't met him yet and I have to see him about the will instead of Mr L.'

Dot considered this, head to one side. 'He's only been there a couple of months and not full-time at first, because he had to settle into the house he'd bought. I've said hello to him at the office but that's about it. He's younger than Mr L, a year or two older than you, I should think. He lost his wife a few years ago. She had MS, poor thing.'

Dot had seen the photo on Mr Danvers' desk. A nice family they looked and he had been in the centre, smiling proudly with his arm round his wife. The two children had looked to be about ten. Now they were grown up and he looked sad sometimes. He'd told her his daughter was planning to marry and live in Edinburgh, while his son was off on a gap year travelling round the world.

'Didn't Mr Danvers buy the old Renshaw house?' Abigail asked.

'Yes. There'll be a lot of work to do on it. I've seen him in the hardware store buying paint and other bits and pieces, so he must be handy that way.'

'I've seen him around the village — tall, greying hair at the temples, distinguished looking.'

'Yes. Keeps his office tidy. Hasn't gone out for a meal at the pub or my friend Jen would have seen him and told me. He went over to have dinner with the

21

Liddlestones a few days after his arrival. Apart from that, no one knows much about him.'

'Well, no doubt the local spy network will keep an eye on him and gradually learn more, which you can pass on to me. In the meantime I have to go and see him tomorrow about the will.'

Dot couldn't help chuckling at that. It was quite true. She usually seemed to find out the latest gossip before most others did. 'I expect so. Well, I'd better get on with my work. Your guests yesterday didn't know how to wipe their feet and that front hall floor is filthy.'

But when she went back to the kitchen, her smile vanished and she plumped down in a chair by the table, staring in terror at the shopping bag where the will was still hidden.

What was she going to do now?

Perhaps she could put the will back when she went in to do her hour's cleaning the next day? It was the right thing to do. No one would be any the wiser if she was careful not to be seen doing it . . . only then Abigail would lose everything. And what would happen to Abigail if Dot did put that wicked will back? Her dear girl would have no money and nowhere to live. That will was so unfair. It didn't bear thinking of.

Unfortunately, Dot couldn't stop thinking about it.

And it wasn't even Mr L who'd be dealing with it now, but *Mr Danvers*. He'd not care about Abigail. Why should he? He hadn't even met her yet. Things were going from bad to worse, but she had to do the right thing . . . she supposed. Only what was the right thing? How did you know for sure in circumstances like these? Could she bear to put it back? Trouble

22

was, she'd bet Mr Danvers would have a look at the will today. Stood to reason he'd want to be prepared for his meeting about it.

* * *

Abigail came to see Dot just before lunch. 'I've rung the hospital. They said Mr Liddlestone is as comfortable as can be expected. What does that mean, do you think?'

'It probably means he's going to recover.'

'I asked if I could take him in some flowers, but they said he'd be going home soon as long as he continued to improve. Only family to visit. When I see Mr Danvers tomorrow, I'll ask him how Mr L is. He's bound to know more about his partner than the hospital will tell me. I do hope he's approachable.'

'I find him very pleasant to deal with.'

'Good.'

'Why don't you make a start on clearing out them old books in the cellar? You know you're dying to have them out of the damp.'

'Yes, I suppose so. And we'll give the library a good spring clean before I put my own books on the shelves. Perhaps you could work another extra day this week?'

'Of course I can. I'm only doing Ashgrove House and Mr Liddlestone's office these days. I'll come in first thing tomorrow, shall I?'

'Thank you, Dot dear. Look, I was thinking during the night. Those books in the library may have some value, so I'd better not dump them in the cellar and certainly not throw them away until I find out. I think I'll phone Porfrey's, the antiquarian bookshop

23

in Medderby, and see if they'll send someone to value them.'

'Good idea. That's the way to think. Make the most of what you've got. There are some boxes of old books in the attics, too, remember. Your stepmother said they were too scruffy to have on view. Show those to whoever comes, as well.'

Abigail returned a few minutes later. 'I rang the bookshop. The woman said James Porfrey could come to make a quick preliminary assessment of the books this afternoon, because he'll be in the area on another call. Will you help me get the boxes of books down from the attic?'

'We don't need to hump them heavy boxes up and down. Take him up to the attic to look at them, why don't you? You're not your stepmother, suspicious of everyone. You can let people into any part of the house you like now.'

'I can, can't I? Oh, Dot, I don't know whether I'm on my head or my heels. Is it wrong to feel so happy . . . so *liberated*?'

'Not at all. You did your duty, more than she deserved, that's for sure, and now your life's your own. See that you make every second count.'

'I will. I definitely will.'

Dot smiled, but the smile had been forced and she couldn't keep it up as she went on with her work. She couldn't get that dratted will out of her mind. And though Mr Danvers seemed all right, what would he say if he caught her going through a client's box?

Actually, she was less and less inclined to return the nasty thing, because she hated what it would do to Abigail. But she'd have to. Wouldn't she? The thought kept creeping into her mind: who would know if she

didn't put it back? No one. Mr L wasn't likely to come back to work, from the sounds of it. Then her grandmother's voice echoed in her head: *Honesty is the best policy, Dorothy, always remember that.*

Only Dot hadn't found that to be true in real life, especially with her husband and the way he wasted their money if she let on how much she had. And then later with the old witch, who had to be managed carefully. She had a book of quotations which she enjoyed dipping into and had found one she much preferred about honesty: *Honesty is the cruellest game of all because not only can you hurt someone — and hurt them to the bone — you can feel self-righteous about it at the same time.* She forgot who'd said it, but that person had been so right. If only she could be sure no one would know what she'd done, she'd burn that will this very day. But you couldn't be sure, could you? She didn't want to land herself in trouble with the law.

★ ★ ★

That afternoon, Cousin Cynthia turned up at Ashgrove House without warning, driving her ancient car as badly as ever. While parking it in front of the building, she accidentally put her foot on the accelerator instead of the brake, and landed up with the two front wheels in the rose bed.

Dot, who'd been watching, couldn't help chuckling and made no attempt to go and help her. Cynthia Polson had been sucking up to Edwina for years and getting handouts. It was probably partly her fault that the terrible will had been written. She certainly didn't deserve to inherit Ashgrove.

Abigail, who'd been waiting in the sitting room for

the book valuer, went running out to help. Of course she did. But Dot didn't join them. She didn't feel she could speak civilly to this particular visitor.

Cousin Cynthia got out, glaring alternately at Abigail and the car. 'It wasn't my fault. The stupid car jumped forward when I stopped! There must be something wrong with it. How on earth am I going to get it out of there?'

Abigail looked at the car, sighed for the poor, mangled rose bush, and guided her visitor towards the door. 'Give me your car keys and I'll see if I can back the car out of the flower bed for you.'

She took it very slowly and it proved quite easy to do. She also did a neat three-point turn so that the car was pointing in the right direction for Cynthia to leave without hassle. She stopped to pick a rose that was hanging by one thread, then went in to join her visitor, sniffing it, enjoying the delicate fragrance. 'Would you like a cup of tea, Cousin Cynthia?' She gave in to temptation and added, 'Or a glass of my stepmother's sherry, perhaps?' Cynthia was definitely on her personal blacklist for her many unkind remarks over the years, usually saying something that would please her stepmother.

'No, thank you. I only popped in to see if Mr Liddlestone had told you what was in Edwina's will. Last time I saw her, she hinted that she was leaving me, er, something substantial, but she wouldn't say what.'

'Didn't you hear the news? Poor Mr Liddlestone had a stroke last night and is in hospital. I can't see his partner about the will until tomorrow, so I haven't found out what exactly is in it. I'll phone you as soon as I know what Edwina has left you. Now, a glass of sherry?'

Cynthia grimaced. 'No, thank you. I never did like Edwina's sherry.'

'Pity. We have several bottles of it left.'

'I'd advise you to pour it down the sink. It's rubbish. Well, I have a lot to do so I'll come back tomorrow to find out what I've been left.'

She seemed happier than usual today, which was strange, considering her 'dear auntie' had died so recently. Remembering the years of unkindness in support of Edwina, Abigail took a deep breath and said firmly, 'I shall be very busy tomorrow, so it won't be convenient for you to visit me. I'll phone you as soon as I know anything about what you've been left.'

For a moment their gazes clashed, but for the first time ever, Abigail didn't lower her eyes. She didn't intend to have anything to do with this horrible woman if she could help it.

Cynthia blew out a puff of irritation and paused by the door, a sour expression on her face. 'You should be wearing black. What on earth are you thinking about, wearing a blue blouse? I don't like that blouse anyway. It's vulgar, shows your cleavage. What little cleavage you've got.'

Abigail nearly said something to placate her, then realised she'd be making a stick for her own back if she let Cynthia take over her stepmother's role of criticising her appearance. She spoke quickly, before she could lose her courage. 'It's none of your business what I wear, so please don't comment on my clothes again.'

Cousin Cynthia gasped and drew herself up. 'How *dare* you speak to me like that? Now your poor dear stepmother has gone, I'm your closest thing to an older relative, and it's my *duty* to keep an eye on you.'

'I'm thirty-eight, and that's old enough to manage my own life, thank you very much. And you're not actually related to me.'

'*Well!* The impertinence of it.'

Abigail didn't move and after a moment, Cousin Cynthia left, muttering about the appalling manners of today's youngsters.

Youngsters! It seemed a very long time since Abigail would have described herself as young. Where had the years gone? She'd intended to go to university, had wanted to study history, but then her father had been incapacitated by his illness and her stepmother was no good at nursing people, so she'd postponed going. She hadn't regretted it for a moment, either. She and her father had always been close and grew closer as the years passed.

Oh, what was she thinking about that for? She'd got over her disappointment years ago, had even managed to do a few history units with the Open University.

She smiled as she suddenly realised she'd just succeeded in something she'd been wanting to do for ages: stood up to Cynthia, who had followed her stepmother's example in criticising her. And it hadn't been as difficult as she'd expected. A tiny triumph, but still, it was a start. The new Abigail wasn't going to be a meek and colourless mouse.

She caught sight of herself in a mirror and scowled. She was going to change her appearance dramatically, buy some flattering clothes and some jeans, a type of garment her stepmother had loathed. She'd try a different hairstyle, too, only what? She wasn't up to date on fashion. But she couldn't do anything until she got control of the money.

★ ★ ★

When Abigail turned away from the front door, she saw Dot standing in the library doorway.

'You got rid of her, then?'

'Yes. And I told her not to come here tomorrow to ask about the will. Was that too rude of me?'

'No. She's a nasty creature, wasn't as bad till after your father died and your stepmother egged her on. In fact, she's turned into another Edwina, with never a good word to say about anything or anyone. I'm glad you didn't let her bully you.'

'It's about time I stood up for myself, isn't it?'

'It certainly is. And who's she to criticise your clothes? *She* dresses like Queen Victoria in short skirts.' Fury about the unfairness of the will speared through Dot yet again. Was that horrible woman really going to inherit everything?

Abigail looked down with loathing at her dowdy skirt and blouse. 'I look pretty old-fashioned, too, though it wasn't my choice to wear clothes like these. I only let Edwina choose them to keep the peace. You know what she was like when she got into one of her tempers.'

Dot rolled her eyes. Everyone nearby had known when Edwina threw a tantrum.

'Besides, she might really have cut up any more fashionable clothes I'd bought, as she threatened. I was also rather afraid of her having a heart attack, too, she got so red in the face.'

'Well, she had one anyway and that definitely wasn't your fault. The truth is, she didn't like to see you looking pretty.'

'Pfft! I couldn't look pretty if I tried.'

'Oh yes, you could.'

'I'm thirty-eight not twenty-one, Dot! And an old-fashioned thirty-eight at that.'

'Doesn't make any difference. You've got a pretty face. Always did have. Dowdy clothes can't take that away from you, though pulling your hair tightly back doesn't flatter you. You've got nice hair, same colour as my favourite honey — a true Beadle you are. It isn't even going grey yet, except for a few threads here and there, so you don't even look your age.'

Abigail stared in the mirror, as if she'd never seen herself before and slowly undid the tight clasp at the back, shaking her hair out.

Dot came to stand beside her, slightly taller than her, gaunt and yet physically strong. 'Look, my friend Elsa does hairdressing from her back room. She's really good, used to work for a top stylist in London till she moved back to Wiltshire. She's semi-retired now. She'll only do people whose hairstyle she approves of because she doesn't want to work full-time.'

She chuckled and added, 'Elsa says she doesn't intend to do any more snail perms, whatever people offer to pay her.'

Abigail blinked. 'Snail perms?'

'Old ladies who have their white hair cut short and tightly permed so that it sits on their pink scalps like a collection of snails.'

'Oh, what a lovely image! I'll never be able to keep a straight face again when I visit the post office. Mrs Dewton has a snail perm every three months.' Abigail leaned against the door frame, laughing heartily, then went off to do some clearing up.

She *was* pretty when she relaxed, Dot thought fondly. She definitely didn't look her age, or she wouldn't if she dressed more snazzily. As for that Cousin Cynthia, she was a nasty creature who didn't deserve to inherit Ashgrove House. Fancy coming here the day after the funeral and criticising Abigail like that! Trying to take over her stepmother's role, that's what, and she'd be taking over the money if that will was acted on, and probably try to use poor Abigail as a servant like the old witch had.

Suddenly the anger at the unfairness of it all burned so high that Dot gave way to temptation. She strode back into the kitchen, got out the will and tore it to pieces, muttering. 'There, take that! And that!'

She stopped for a moment to stare at what she'd done, then laughed and stuffed the pieces of paper into the old-fashioned Aga. She watched them burn, stirring them with the poker till the black flakes turned into ash.

She waited, expecting to feel guilty, but she didn't, not a bit. On the contrary, she felt as if she'd done the right thing. She also had the strangest feeling, as if people were cheering her on, and looked round guiltily. But of course there was no one there. How strange! What Mr L would say if he ever found that the latest will had gone missing, she couldn't guess. *If* he came back, that was.

He might or might not suspect that she'd taken it. That did worry her a bit. More than a bit.

But without evidence, no one could prove she'd removed the will, could they? And she'd just burned the evidence. Mr Danvers didn't know it even existed.

And anyway, it'd be weeks before poor Mr L returned to work. If he ever did. Oh dear, she didn't know whether to hope he would get well enough to return or give in to his health problems and never come back again.

And she wasn't sorry she'd burned the will. So there.

3

After turning off High Street into the drive, James Porfrey stopped his car to admire Ashgrove House. The building was quite delightful. Most of it was Georgian in style, the main part early to mid-1700s, he'd guess. It wasn't large, having three storeys only if you included the attic. The windows at the front were classically proportioned, the ones on the upper floor not as tall as the ground floor windows.

As he set off again, he wondered what this Miss Beadle would be like. Trish said she'd sounded nervous on the phone. A poor old spinster, he supposed, and short of money. Fluttering with anxiety about selling off the family treasures one by one.

He met a lot of elderly women like that, felt sorry for them when they turned out to have nothing of real value. But business was business. Occasionally he did find something worth the effort. He couldn't pretend, though, or the shop would make a loss, though he had never treated anyone unfairly if they did have something valuable to sell.

He rang the doorbell twice and was about to press it a third and final time when he heard footsteps inside. So there was someone at home, after all.

The door was opened by a woman a little younger than him, if he was any judge. Her face was flushed as if she'd been running, her hair was coming loose in tendrils round her face, and a long strand of cobweb was draped over one shoulder.

'So sorry . . . to keep you waiting! I was up . . . in

33

the attic,' she panted.

He presented his card. 'James Porfrey. I came to see Miss Beadle.'

'That's me.' She wrinkled her nose. 'Only the name sounds so old-fashioned, doesn't it? Beadle is bad enough, but *Miss Beadle* is worse. Ugh. Could you just call me Abigail, do you think?'

He was enchanted by her frankness and by the beautiful, innocent eyes in a rosy face without make-up. 'Of course I can call you Abigail. It's a lovely name. And I'm James. Excuse me.' He reached out to pull the strand of cobweb from her shoulder and tossed it into the flower bed.

'Thank you.' She stepped back and gestured. 'Do come in. The library is this way, at the back of the house in a sort of wing that was built on later. There are some other books in the attics. That's why I was up there, trying to sort the boxes out to show you. I think I've found all of them now, but it's absolutely chaotic up there.'

He stood in the hall, not moving because he was delighted by the interior as well as the exterior. The elegant curving staircase led up from a black and white tiled marble floor. 'This place is a real Georgian gem.'

'The house? I suppose so. Beadles have lived here since King George I's day, but this is the second house that's been built on the site.'

'Second?'

She laughed. 'The Tudor house was so badly damaged during the Civil War, it was sold cheaply and knocked down, though some of the cellars still date from that time. The buyer was Augustus Beadle and he decided to build what was then a very modern house; this one. The wing with the library in it was built later by Roderick Beadle, who fancied himself a scholar.'

'Fascinating. I'd like to see it all sometime, if you'd let me.'

'Come any time you like. To me, it's just home. I don't know as many details as I'd like about the technicalities of the building, so if you can share anything special you know with me, that'd be great. After Dad died, my stepmother would never let anyone but her touch the family papers and diaries, you see. Now she's gone, I intend to have a good old read of them, scandals and all.' She chuckled.

She had a rich chuckle, very musical, as well as that lovely smile, James decided. But why on earth did she dress so badly? She was young and slim enough to keep up with any fashion she fancied.

'I may even write it all up, make a coherent account of it one day.' Then her smile vanished. 'Only why bother when I'm the last of the Beadles?'

'People other than family might enjoy the story.'

'Do you think so? Anyway, I mustn't bore you with my embryonic plans. This way.'

'I don't find it boring to listen to people who care about the past. I've made a particular study of houses like this one. Not stately mansions, but just —'

She finished it for him, saying, 'Gentlemen's residences.'

'Exactly.' He was surprised at himself for confiding in her. He didn't usually share personal information with clients, especially new clients whose possessions he hadn't yet inspected.

He followed her into the library and stopped just inside to stare round, once again in admiration. The room was lined with mahogany bookcases — genuine solid mahogany, not veneer, and clearly original. The shelves were filled with rows of leather-bound volumes, some in matching sets.

He breathed in the smell of dusty old books, loving it as always. 'Which books did you want valuing?'

'Nearly all of them. Such stuffy old things!' She gestured with one arm. 'Not those shelves to the right of the window, but all the rest, as well as the books in the attic.'

'If you can leave me here for an hour or so, I'll be able to form a rough idea of whether there's anything worth selling and whether we should proceed to a detailed evaluation. Then perhaps we can go up to the attics and take a quick glance at the boxes there.'

She picked up a tattered paperback. 'I'll sit and read in the bay window, in case you have any questions, Mr Porfrey. I'm so glad my great-grandfather put bay windows in at the back of the house. I know they're not pure Georgian but they're lovely places to sit and read.'

She was hiding the book's cover from him, which intrigued him. What was she reading? Surely not erotica? No, he couldn't see her reading that sort of rubbish. What was making her look so guilty, then? He didn't blame her for keeping an eye on him. Some book dealers could be villains with old ladies, filching the odd book, undervaluing the better ones.

Abigail wasn't an old lady, but she wasn't young either. In fact, it was hard to judge her age. She was quite pretty, but as well as her clothing, she really should do something about her hair. Not cut it short, but get it properly styled. Or was she one of those women who didn't care about their appearance? He took his laptop out of his briefcase. 'Mind if I set this up in here? Do you have an Internet connection I can use?'

Her face fell. 'No. My stepmother didn't believe in it.' Then she brightened up. 'But I'm going to get a computer, then sign up for a connection. I'm making a list now that I'm free. There are so many things I intend to do from now on.'

She clapped one hand to her mouth. 'Oops. I mustn't say things like that, must I? It'll upset people and they'll think I'm heartless. I'm not, but I have a lot of catching up with the modern world to do.'

'Catching up with what exactly?'

'With life! I feel as though I've been trapped in a time warp for over a decade.'

Diplomatically, he didn't comment further, but he understood what she was saying. He'd met quite a few spinsters who'd cared for their parents and been imprisoned by the standards and customs of a bygone age. He hoped Abigail Beadle would manage to lead a fuller life from now on. If there was one thing that came across at a first meeting, it was that she was a genuinely nice person.

'At this stage, I can manage without getting online. I have some recent catalogues on my computer.'

After setting up his laptop, he began to inspect the shelves, occasionally making a note to check more recent prices for a particularly interesting book. His customer opened her paperback and was soon lost to the world.

He forgot about her as he found quite a few rare books, nothing of great value, but taken together they'd fetch a tidy sum. And there were still the attics to go through. He'd found some real treasures hidden away in attics.

He cleared his throat, but his hostess didn't look up, so he went across to stand next to her. 'Excuse me.'

She still didn't seem to hear him.

'Abigail, do you have a moment?'

She looked up, her beautiful eyes swimming in tears.

He was startled. 'What on earth have I done to upset you?'

She sniffed. 'You haven't done anything. I've been reading a sad part of the story. I always cry at sad bits. Don't you?'

'Er . . . no. But then, I don't read a lot of novels.' Now he simply had to know what she was reading.

'Novels have been my solace for years, especially romances like this one. Because of my stepmother, you see. She hated romances, didn't believe in that sort of love. I've been buying books secretly from charity shops and at the car boot sales in the village for years. I'm running out of new ones now, so I'll have to hunt for some more.'

He was puzzled. 'What on earth's wrong with reading romances? My cousin Trish reads them all the time.' Then he realised how he could see this woman again. 'I can let you have several boxes of paperback novels, if you like. I can't guarantee what's in the boxes, but the books are far too tatty for us to sell, so you might as well have them. They were part of a recent clearance we did on a deceased estate. We'd never have bought them specifically, because we're an antiquarian bookshop but they wouldn't let us have the others unless we took these away.'

'I couldn't impose.'

'Why not? It'll save me the trouble of taking them to the tip.'

'It will? Really? Then I accept.' Her smile was dazzling. 'How kind of you!'

'And we get similar boxes in from time to time. I'll let you know if you like.'

'Oh, I do like. How wonderful!'

His first impression of Abigail Beadle had been wrong, he decided. When she smiled, it was an effort to concentrate on business matters, she looked so pretty and vivacious. The rest of the time, she seemed nondescript, rather subdued in fact. Which was the real Abigail? And why was he wondering about that? He wasn't interested in women. His divorce five years previously had been so acrimonious he'd sworn to stay away from the marrying sort of woman for ever more. And if he'd ever seen a marrying type of woman, it was this one.

He changed the subject for safety, and began to explain his findings to her. 'So we need to schedule a time for me to go through your books properly. If you wish me to proceed with a full valuation, that is.'

'Oh, I do, I do. I want to get rid of this lot of ugly old tomes!' She flapped her hand scornfully at the old books.

'I hope you don't mind but I took a quick glance at the books you don't want to sell. You have one rather valuable book among them. It's worth well over a thousand pounds, maybe as much as two thousand if we put it in a specialist auction and advertise it online. And there are several books dotted here and there on the shelves that are worth a few hundred each. Did you know that?'

She gaped at him, clearly too shocked to speak.

He grinned and answered his own question. 'Obviously you didn't.'

'Which one is so valuable?'

He went and picked it out.

'That ugly old thing?' She stared at it as if it would bite. 'I didn't mean to put it among the keepers. I can't think how it got there. I'd better lock it away somewhere, I suppose.'

'Do you have a safe?'

'We do. But I don't have the combination. My step-mother kept that to herself. It's another thing I need to put on my list of things to do: get a locksmith in.'

Another piece of her soft hair fell down while he was watching and curled delicately against the nape of her neck. The sunlight streaming through the long windows painted flecks of gold in the honey-coloured strands and —

Concentrate, James! You're here on business.

'In that case, probably the best thing to do, Abigail, is leave the book on the shelf among others that look similar. Hide it in plain sight. How about I come over on Friday morning to do the full valuation?' He glanced at his watch. 'I'm afraid this took longer than I expected and I have another appointment now. I can look at the books in the attic when I next come.'

'Yes, that'd be fine. I'm not going anywhere for the moment, apart from the lawyer's office tomorrow to see about the will.'

'I'd better get on my way now. Is there somewhere I can wash my hands first? Those books were rather dusty. Some of them don't seem to have been touched for years.'

'We only have Dot to clean two days a week, and she works flat out to keep the areas we have been using clean. I've never had time to dust the books I don't read. Does that matter? Should we clean them up?'

40

'No, no. We'll deal with them before we sell them, if necessary. It's safer that way. You don't want to damage anything.'

'All right. Let me show you to the cloakroom. It's a bit old-fashioned, I'm afraid.'

★ ★ ★

As she watched him drive away, Abigail realised she was still clutching the valuable book, so ran to tell Dot about it, knowing her friend would keep the secret. They both looked at the worn maroon leather cover with the title and author's name embossed on it in gold.

'Who'd ever have thought it?' Dot marvelled. 'That tatty old thing. Why, the edges of the pages are all uneven and some are stuck together.'

'They used to sell books with pages folded over from the printer. You had to cut them before you could read them.'

'How ridiculous!' Dot opened the cut part of the book as if it would bite. 'Well, it can't be very interesting because no one's ever read it to the end. Over half the pages are still uncut.' She peered at the book title on the cover. 'No wonder. *A Tour of the County of Wiltshire by an English Nobleman, with Observations on the Local Industries and Vernacular Architecture.*' She read the first page. 'Ha! He sounds a right old snob.'

Abigail leaned over to look at the book with her and chuckled. 'He does, doesn't he?'

Dot looked up at the clock. 'You put that back carefully on the shelf, in case there's some fool willing to part with good money for it. I'd better get off now. Will you be all right on your own here tonight?'

41

'I'll be fine. I never feel nervous at Ashgrove. After I've eaten my evening meal, I'm going to have a drink of wine and watch what I want on the main TV, not my little old one.' She sighed happily.

It didn't take much to make that poor lass happy, Dot thought as she drove away in her old rattle-trap of a car. But Abigail really ought to get out and meet people of her own age. She had an elderly car, too, because Edwina had only wanted to be driven to church or the shops. And she said it saved paying delivery charges to send her stepdaughter out on errands. Mean old witch! Abigail shouldn't go out till Dot had taken her to see Elsa and got her to buy some new clothes. Someone had to take her in hand and bring her appearance up to date.

As she drove out of the gates, a young man walked in front of her car and she had to brake hard. He raised one hand in apology and walked on, head jerking in time to some music coming through earphones, hair gelled to defy gravity and stand straight up in the air.

'Did you ever see the like?' Dot murmured. 'Turn him upside down and you could scrub the floor with him. Them young folk's fashions get sillier and sillier.' She hoped Abigail wouldn't be drawn to buy some of the unflattering clothes younger men and women were wearing this year. That girl had a lovely figure underneath those baggy, dowdy garments and should be proud of it.

Dot shook her head at herself. What was she doing sitting here in the car when she should be on her way to do Mr L's rooms?

Mr Danvers had gone home early, the elderly secretary told her. 'And I have arranged to meet someone so I'll leave you to lock up, Dot.'

'All right.'

So she was the only one there. She could have put that terrible will back but somehow she couldn't regret burning it. When she was sure Miss Cawdell had left, she got the Beadle record box out to check that she hadn't left any incriminating evidence. No, there was just the previous will, sitting at the top of a big pile of who knew what. Lawyers never seemed to throw anything away, in her experience.

She gave a wry smile because under it were several other wills. It seemed Edwina Beadle had changed her mind frequently about who was to get what. Well, that wasn't relevant now. She couldn't produce any more nasty wills. She straightened the pile so that she could put the lid back on, then put the box away again, then went on working.

She finished quite quickly today and locked up behind her, because Mr Liddlestone's office didn't need much doing apart from dusting. She hoped the poor man would recover quickly and come back to work. A terrible thought came into her mind. What if they closed the whole practice down? Or he sold it to the new man. Mr Danvers was nice but he might change things, including who did the cleaning.

She'd really miss the money she earned from this job if it was taken over by a cleaning service. It made such a difference to have a bit of extra money coming in. She didn't sleep well, still felt guilty, but she couldn't un-burn that horrible will now, could she?

* * *

The following morning Abigail woke early, as usual, and went to stand by her bedroom window, watching

43

the sun rise slowly and gild the green of a couple of evergreen trees' leaves with a shimmery gold light as they waved gently in the breeze. The trees in the ash grove were quite bare now but she liked how they looked in winter, so graceful.

By the time she'd had breakfast, however, the sky had clouded over and the landscape had lost its colour as a grey cloak of moisture drifted across it, dimming the colours, washing away the sun's highlights.

Just before half past eight she heard Dot's old car chug up the drive and come round the back. A minute later her friend came hurrying in, turning to shake the raindrops off her umbrella. 'Heavy showers, they said on TV last night. For once, they were right.'

And yet, an hour later the rain stopped and sunshine brightened the world again. Even as Abigail watched from the bay window in the library, a rainbow formed, a great glowing arch with its nearest end coming to earth right in the middle of the bare branches of the ash grove. She could hardly breathe for excitement. She'd never seen a rainbow so close, hadn't known you could actually see where the end of one touched the earth.

It seemed like an omen.

She smiled. Perhaps there really was gold buried at the rainbow's end. She didn't know who'd have buried any gold in the ash grove, though. Her family had never been rich in anything but land and their beautiful home, and now there was hardly any land left, except for these few acres. They'd had to sell their fields and cottages one by one over the past three generations, mainly to pay the inheritance tax.

She was glad the ash grove the house was named after still belonged to her family, though. She loved

44

walking among the old trees. It had always felt like her very own magic place because no one else ever went there. And as long as she owned it, she could prevent it being chopped down. Suddenly she remembered one of her vows made at the funeral and chuckled. Now was the time! She grabbed the horrible black hat from where she'd tossed it on top of the hallstand and dashed out to see if she could walk through the rainbow's end.

Sadly, once she was under the trees she could see nothing of the rainbow, only fractured rays of sunlight spearing down between the bare branches. She found a suitable place, looked down at the funeral hat and said loudly, 'Farewell, O ugly one!'

With all her might, she tossed it up in the air, cheering when it caught first time on one of the highest branches of the tallest ash tree. She waited in case it fell back to earth, but it didn't. It stayed where it was, swaying in the breeze with each movement of the branch.

Whenever I'm feeling in need of courage, I'll come and look at that hat, she thought. *It's a symbol of the new me banishing the old ugliness, that's what it is.*

She paused. Why had she let her stepmother tell her the hat was good enough for funerals and church? That it was a waste of money to buy another one. Because she'd been frightened during the past two years of her stepmother getting too angry and having a stroke or heart attack, that was why. Though she needn't have bothered, because there hadn't been a heart attack during their worst quarrel and there hadn't been any sort of quarrel on the day a heart attack had happened.

Her stepmother had simply stopped speaking,

looked surprised and fallen down onto the rug in slow motion. Just like that, a life coming to an end. She remembered a poem she'd had to learn at school. It had meant nothing to her as a child, but remembering it now, she felt it had been a warning, and one that she'd not understood till it was too late:

> *Then be not coy, but use your time;*
> *And while ye may, go marry:*
> *For having lost but once your prime,*
> *You may for ever tarry.*

Go marry! Oh, how she'd wanted that: marriage and children, a life with someone who loved her. Which meant a life with Lucas, her only real boyfriend. She looked round bleakly. She'd given her crucial years to her father and then to this house. Had it been worth it? How could you tell? She'd just done what seemed to be right at every stage.

I'm not going to waste a moment from now on, she thought, not one single nanosecond. Who knows how long I'll live, how much lost time I'll be able to make up for?

She turned back towards the house, pausing to smile at it. Well, she might not have a family to love, but she loved the old house passionately. Only, who would love it after her?

Oh, stop being so maudlin! she told herself. Just get on with living. You'll figure something out eventually. There must be some distant cousins who would love to own Ash-grove House.

It was time to get ready for her visit to the lawyer. Dealing with the will shouldn't take all that long, surely? Afterwards she would go down to the charity shop for some new books. She'd lain in bed reading until one o'clock last night and didn't have a single unread romance left on her pile. She depended on her daily dose of love to cheer her up and give her sweet dreams. She couldn't wait for Mr Porfrey's boxes of books to arrive, but would need a book or two to keep her going in the meantime — and a couple more bottles of wine. Why not?

★ ★ ★

Dot caught Abigail as she was pulling on her coat. 'You're not going to see the new lawyer looking like that, surely?'

'Why not?'

'That's such a shabby old coat. At least put on your Sunday best.'

'I don't think that one's much better.'

'Oh, yes it is. This one's so shabby, it's not even fit to give to the charity shop. You need a whole new wardrobe, my girl.'

'I know. But I can't do anything about that until I get some money, and maybe not even then. Edwina always said we had to be economical, so there can't be a lot of money left, can there? And we'll have inheritance tax to pay.'

'Being economical's one thing; dressing like a scarecrow's another!'

'I'll think about new clothes later.'

'There's time to have a quick look at something that might suit you for now. I found some of your great-aunt Juliana's clothes in the attic a few weeks ago when I was looking for that box your stepmother wanted. I couldn't resist a peek and there was a dress on top that made me think of you. It's in a classic style and made of beautiful material, so it hasn't really dated. Come and try it on. It even looked to be your size. We'll go through the rest of the clothes up there later.'

'There isn't time. I'll be late.'

'Nonsense. It won't take more than two minutes to try it on and you always set off far too soon when you're going anywhere. You'll only be sitting waiting in the reception area for quarter of an hour if you go now.'

Dot snatched the shabby old coat out of her hand and kicked it across the hall floor. 'Never, ever wear that hideous grey rag again!' Then she grabbed her girl's arm and dragged her up the stairs, laughing.

Abigail laughed as well and gave in.

Dot didn't let go of her arm until they were in the attic. 'It's over here.' Panting slightly, she bent to open a trunk and shake out the dress.

Abigail stared at it in wonder. It was a soft turquoise blue, not garish but subtle as a shade. It probably dated from the 1930s and was beautifully cut, really elegant. Somehow you could tell it had once cost a lot of money. She stroked the soft material then couldn't resist holding it against herself and staring in the dusty old mirror with a cracked corner that had been propped against the far wall for as long as she could remember.

'Try it on. I'll turn my back if you're shy. Go on. I'm dying to see how you look in it.' Dot loved that girl and was determined to make her dress in flattering clothes from now on.

'Um . . . I'm ready.'

Dot turned round and beamed at Abigail. 'Oh, that's lovely. Just absolutely gorgeous, it is. Could have been made for you, my dear. It really brings out the colour of your eyes. You're definitely wearing it today and I'm not having any argument about that.'

'You won't get it. The dress is beautiful. But I'll still need a coat when I go out. There's a cold wind blowing.'

'I found this one while you were changing.' She passed across the simple navy winter coat and it too fitted perfectly.

When she'd waved goodbye, Dot sighed. This was the start of the transformation she was planning for her lovely girl. That was how she thought of Abigail: 'her girl', because she'd more than half raised her. She was like the daughter Dot had never had and always wanted. Life could be cruel sometimes. She'd lost her one baby, lost it at seven months, when you could see its delicate little face. A girl, it had been. Oh, how she'd wept. Something must have gone wrong inside her because after that she'd never even started another baby. But then she'd had Abigail to love and cuddle, and that had made up for a lot.

She went to grimace at herself in the hall mirror. 'You were a bit bossy today, Dorothy Mary Eakins,' she told her reflection. 'You've got to let her spread her own wings now, not take over from her stepmother and nag her to do things your way.'

Only, if she hadn't been bossy today, Abigail would have gone out looking like a ragbag yet again. On that thought, Dot put the ratty old coat in the ragbag to be made into polishing cloths. Then she rang up her friend Elsa and made an appointment for Abigail to have her hair done that very next afternoon. In for a penny, in for a pound.

She set to work cleaning the old witch's bedroom, grimacing at the lingering smell of a sickly elderly body and stripping off all the bedding. Throwing open the windows, she let the breeze freshen the air, but she didn't like to do anything about the clothes and other possessions, had to leave that to Abigail.

While she was gazing up at the sky, she said a quick prayer that Philip Danvers hadn't found out about the missing will. She added a plea that no one should ever find out, promising the deity if he was listening that she'd never do anything like that again.

She'd surprised herself by having nightmares about it the previous night. She definitely wasn't cut out to be a criminal. And yet . . . the will had been so unfair she still couldn't really regret what she'd done. Well, she wouldn't regret it if she got away with her crime. She didn't want to land herself in trouble with a bunch of lawyers. Or even with Mr Philip Danvers, the only remaining one at the practice.

★ ★ ★

Before his next client arrived, Philip got the Beadle family's box down from the storeroom and read through the most recent will. It all seemed very straightforward. Nearly everything was left to Abigail Beadle, as you'd expect.

He wished Gerard was here to tell him a bit more about the family, which had been living in the village for centuries, judging by the contents of the box, and another box with the same name on he'd noticed on the high shelf in the storeroom. Sadly, the senior partner wasn't even allowed visitors at the moment, apart from close family. And Mrs Liddlestone had made it plain that he was not to disturb Gerard with work-related business, not under any circumstances.

He got some basic information about the Beadles from the secretary, but she'd refused to comment on the lady who was coming to see him. Talk about being thrown in at the deep end! All Philip knew was that the Beadles lived in that lovely early Georgian house at the far end of High Street that he walked past regularly and sometimes stopped to admire. There was only one of them left now, this Abigail.

He'd chatted briefly to an old man out walking his dog, probing delicately about the lady who'd just died. From the tone of the man's voice, she had not been liked.

'Not a real Beadle, her!' the old man has said harshly. 'Good riddance to bad rubbish, I say. She won't be missed.'

Even Gerard, a true gentleman if ever there was one, has intimated to him when discussing the families who'd been clients for a long time, that this Mrs Beadle who'd just died had been 'difficult'. But what was the daughter like? No one had said anything bad about her, but they'd used the adjective 'poor' occasionally. He remembered the old saying: the apple doesn't fall far from the tree, but the dead woman had been a stepmother so that didn't apply.

When the secretary showed in Miss Beadle, Philip was shocked at how wrong his guesses about her had been. She hesitated in the doorway, looking nervous and much younger than he'd expected, and rather pretty too, in a quiet way. He went across to welcome her. 'Do come in, Miss Beadle. I'm so sorry for your loss. Would you like to sit here? If you feel too upset to continue, just let me know.'

Her reply surprised him. 'Thank you, but Edwina was my stepmother and we didn't get on, so I'll be fine.'

He watched her loosen the coat and clasp her hands together on top of a worn leather handbag.

'Would you like a cup of tea? No? Then we'll get straight down to business. Do you know how things have been left?'

'Not really. My stepmother was . . . um, rather secretive.'

'I see. Well, I'm pleased to tell you that she's left you everything: the house, its contents and whatever money is in the bank.'

She relaxed visibly. 'Oh, good. I expected her to do that because the house has been in our family for hundreds of years, but after Dad died, she used to threaten to leave it all to charity when she got angry at me. I didn't think she'd really do that, though, because I'm the last Beadle of the direct line left.'

She paused, frowning, then added, 'I think there are a couple of Beadles among my distant relatives but we've lost touch with them.'

'Well, fortunately the will is very straightforward because there aren't even any other bequests.'

'Really? Cousin Cynthia seems to think she's been left something as well. She said my stepmother hinted at that.'

'I'm afraid not. You are the sole beneficiary.'

'Oh. Right. And . . . what about inheritance tax? I'm a bit worried about that. How much will I have to pay?'

'Well, it's going to be quite heavy, I'm afraid. About forty per cent. Do you know how much money you have in the bank? Are there any valuable antiques you can sell, if necessary?'

She shook her head. 'Edwina would never discuss money with me. We do have some old furniture, but it's been well used for generations, so I doubt it's valuable any longer. And there are one or two paintings. I don't know what they're worth, but they can't be all that valuable because when each of the last three owners died, which includes my father, their heirs had to sell off land to pay the inheritance tax and no one even thought about selling the paintings, which are of rather ugly people.'

After a pause she added rather painfully, 'I don't think I'll be able to sell any more land because actually, there isn't much left, just the plot at the end of High Street, and I believe it's on the same title as the house.'

'Do you have an accountant to help you through this?'

Another shake of the head. 'My stepmother quarrelled with him last year.'

'He might take you back as a client.'

'I think I'd rather find a younger accountant, if you don't mind. Mr Glowder was rather grumpy. You don't know of any cheerful young accountants, do you?'

He managed not to smile at that. 'I'm afraid I'm too new to the district. I can ask around, if you like.'

'Yes, please. So . . . what do I have to do next?'

'Apply for probate, which will take a few weeks and then have the house and its contents valued.'

'Right. But I can use the money in the bank for my daily living expenses, can't I?' She flushed bright red as she added, 'I don't have much money of my own, you see, just a small annuity my grandmother left me. I've never had a job because when I was about to go to university, my father fell ill with Parkinson's and I had to look after him instead. My stepmother

53

isn't — wasn't — any good with illness, you see.'

Her eyes filled with what were clearly happy memories for a moment or two. 'Anyway, I loved Dad dearly, so it was no burden. He lasted longer than anyone had expected, but after he passed away, my stepmother's heart began to fail and she had to live quietly, so she needed me to manage the house and the everyday details. Or she was supposed to live quietly, only she got into arguments with people so rarely did.'

Her sigh was heartfelt and he began to feel sympathetic towards her. She seemed gentle and hesitant, an amazingly old-fashioned sort of woman considering how young she was, according to the family tree he'd found in the Beadles' box of papers. 'You should go and see the bank manager now, explain the situation to him and make arrangements to draw on the family account.'

Philip walked her to the door, feeling protective. How could anyone remain so naïve and innocent in this day and age? He was a good judge of character and would swear that Miss Beadle wasn't pretending about anything. In fact, she was charming in her confusion and hesitation. He smiled at the memory of that blush.

4

The bank manager was very helpful. After a satisfactory chat to her, Abigail put in an application for a personal credit card.

'There is a security box in your family's name. Do you wish to inspect the contents, Miss Beadle?'

She looked at the woman in surprise. 'Oh. Yes. I suppose so.'

She left Abigail with it in a small room and Abigail opened it hesitantly. Inside she found most of her mother's jewellery. She remembered some of it from her childhood. She grimaced as she studied the various pieces. Heavy, old-fashioned stuff. They didn't *look* valuable, but what did she know? She'd have to get them valued.

There were also a few pieces which she didn't recognise. Had they come from her stepmother or from more distant Beadle ancestors? They were lumpy and old-fashioned, mostly in silver, and included a few gold rings with jewels set in them. She'd probably have to sell them. She left the jewellery in the security box and walked out of the bank with more money in her purse than she'd had for years. She decided to join the library next — a further act of rebellion, as far as she was concerned. Minor but satisfying.

As she walked along the street towards it, her stepmother's voice echoed in her mind. 'You are *not* bringing those dirty library books into this house. I shall burn them if you do. Who knows what germs they carry or who has touched them? And you don't *need* to join. We have enough books in our own library to last a lifetime, even for someone who wastes as much time reading as you do.'

'Well, I'm joining the library now, Edwina,' Abigail muttered as she walked briskly across the street. 'Suck that up.' She'd heard that phrase on TV and it seemed appropriate. She needed to get up to date with some modern idioms. She was dying to say 'Whatever!' to someone she didn't like in a bored tone of voice, had been practising it in front of her dressing table mirror.

Oh, she was being silly!

At the entrance to the library, she stopped in disappointment because it was closed. An old woman who had been reading a notice in the doorway exclaimed, 'Oh, no!' and burst into tears. Abigail hurried forward, wondering what on earth had upset her so much. 'Can I help you? Tell me what's wrong.'

But the woman only covered her face with her hands and continued to sob more quietly — such soft, helpless mews of despair. Abigail couldn't bear to leave anyone in such distress, so looked round for somewhere to sit and talk, see if she could help. Seeing a bench in the small public garden next to the library, she guided the stranger towards it and sat down next to her.

She pushed her own handkerchief into the woman's hand and waited as the sobbing gradually abated. But even then the woman didn't speak, just sat there looking utterly miserable and mopping away further stray tears.

'Do tell me what's wrong?' Abigail begged in the end. 'Maybe I can help you.'

'No one can help me now. They're closing down our library. What'll I *do*?'

'Closing it down? Why?' Abigail knew the library was well patronised, because she'd watched enviously as people went in and out, mainly older folk or parents with small children during the daytime. Oh, how she'd envied those women having children and loving families to go home to as she walked away down the street on her own.

The old woman spoke in a dull tone. 'It's them council cuts. First they went and cut the hours the library was open, now they're closing it completely. Go and read the notice. Go on! Read it. I'd like to shoot them all, I would.' She scrubbed at her eyes. 'They don't care how they take away people's pleasures, they don't.'

'I won't be a minute. Don't go away.' Abigail hurried across to the big window beside the entrance and read the sign.

Medderby Town Council regrets to inform customers that due to funding cuts, it has been forced to close down this branch library. Customers are advised that they can continue to borrow books from any other library in the area. The main library in Medderby Town Centre has a particularly fine collection of books on all topics.

We apologise for any inconvenience caused. Please note:

* *No more books may be taken out of the Ashbury St Mary library from now on.*
* *Final closure will be in two weeks' time so all books must be returned before then.*
* *The library is closed today for a special staff meeting.*

Abigail was horrified that they'd even think of closing down the village library. It might only be a small branch, but it was a very lively place, with lots of groups, talks and activities such as computer classes. She'd been planning to attend one of the latter herself to brush up her skills but, what with the funeral and all, had been too late to get a place on it. But she'd been sure there would be another because this one had been so popular that places had filled quickly.

What philistine had decided to close this place down? she wondered. Didn't they understand how important a library was? It wasn't just for lending books, but was a focal point for the whole community, somewhere lonely people and children could safely go. No wonder that poor woman was upset.

She felt upset for herself, too. She'd looked forward so much to borrowing books and learning about computers. She walked slowly back to sit next to the old lady. 'That's terrible news. By the way, I'm Abigail Beadle.'

'Yes, I know.' The woman gave her a distinctly unfriendly look. 'It won't matter to you if they close it. You've never used it, have you? Too posh for a place like our library, you Beadles are. And anyway, you don't need to. Everyone knows that big house of yours has shelves and shelves of books.'

That personal attack shocked Abigail. 'I don't at all agree with them closing the library. In fact, I was just going to join it myself.'

'Why?'

She said it before she'd thought. 'Now my stepmother's dead, she won't be able to burn the books if I take them home.'

'Burn them? Whatever do you mean?'

'She threatened to burn any books I took home, said they would be dirty.'

'I knew the old witch was a mean sod, but I didn't know she was unkind to you as well. You were devoted to her, gave up your life for her. Everyone said so.'

'I did my duty, that's all. It wasn't through devotion, but because I'd promised my father. But most of all so that I could look after the house.'

Silence, then the woman's wrinkled old hand clasped hers briefly. 'There's not many do their duty these days. More credit to you, dear.'

'Thank you.'

'But you'll be able to drive into Medderby and join the library there. The notice says they have a fine collection of books.' Her voice was full of scorn. 'Only, some of us can't get there, can we? I don't have a car.'

'Can't you take the bus?'

'They're axing the bus service from here to Medderby. Haven't you heard? No, you wouldn't have, what with your stepmother dying and the funeral to arrange. I shan't be able to get to the library there unless my son takes me, only he's a busy man. He finds time to take me shopping every week. It's a stretch but he fits me in somehow. I can't ask him to do more. He and his wife use that big supermarket on the outskirts of town and take me with them. They don't go near Medderby town centre where the main library is.'

More tears rolled down her cheeks. 'What'll I *do* without my books? I'll go mad, I will. I'll go stark, staring bonkers.'

'Do you love reading so much?'

'It's the only pleasure I have left. My hubby has Alzheimer's and once I've got him to bed, I sit and

59

read. Sometimes Roger has a nap in the daytime and I can read a bit then as well. When he's awake, I have to keep my eye on him all the time, you see, because he's getting so confused. I'm lucky he sleeps a lot. Some of them don't.'

'That's sad for you.'

'Yes. I miss Roger. His body's still there, but he's not inside it any more. I usually read a book every two days. And now . . . now I shan't have anything at all to read. I can't buy books because I haven't any spare money, can barely manage as it is. What am I going to *do* with myself?'

They sat there in silence for a few moments, then Abigail said, 'You never did tell me your name.'

'Betty Winters.'

Abigail had a sudden idea. 'Do you like reading romances?'

'What if I do? You aren't going to lecture me about them being rubbish, are you? Because it's nothing to do with anyone else what I read and I *like* romances.'

'So do I.'

'*You* do?' She sounded disbelieving.

'Yes.' Abigail named a few of her favourite authors to prove it. 'I used to buy books from charity shops and the market, but I had to hide them from my stepmother. She threw several into the fire once. I was furious.'

'I thought a posh person like you would read the classics.'

'Oh, no. I like happy endings and stories about love. We did some of the classics at school and they were mostly miserable. Except for Shakespeare. I did enjoy some of his plays. And Jane Austen. Some of her books were amusing, though I like Georgette Heyer's

60

stories better.'

'I like happy endings, too. They make you feel good for a while.' Betty sighed and another tear escaped to track slowly down her cheek, taking a couple of detours on the way along the deeper wrinkle lines.

Abigail couldn't bear to see her so upset. 'Look, I've got a lot of romances at home. I've been hiding them in the cellar, so they're a bit damp, and some of them are rather tattered, but you could borrow some of mine if you like.'

Betty stared at her for so long, mouth half open, that Abigail didn't know what to think.

'Do you really mean that?'

'Of course I do.'

'Could I come and get some now? Would you mind? Only I've nothing to read tonight.'

'You'd be very welcome to come back with me.'

'Just let me put my library books into the returns slot. I was going to read them again if I couldn't get anything else.' She used a stick to help her walk, moving slowly and painfully.

And this woman was a carer for someone even worse off. She was a heroine, Abigail thought, a real life heroine.

As they made their way along the street together, some of the locals stared at them, as if in puzzlement. 'What are they staring at?' Abigail whispered.

Betty let out a cackle of laughter. 'Me walking along the street with you. Your grandma sacked me once, you see, said I was cheeky. I've not had a good word to say about the Beadles since.'

'Oh. I'm sorry.'

'Not your fault. And I *was* cheeky to her.'

'What did you say to her?'

'I said she should pick up her own knickers when she took them off an' her bedroom was a disgrace. Well, it was.'

'You didn't!' Abigail smiled. She could just imagine the outrage on her grandmother's face. How often she'd longed to say something similar to her stepmother.

'You should have seen her bleedin' majesty's face when she realised what I'd said. I did it on purpose because I wanted her to sack me, but I meant every word. Mum had made me go to work at the Hall, you see, but I hated it from the very first day.'

Abigail grinned. 'I'm not surprised. You'd be too lively.'

'Thanks. I consider that a compliment. After your grandma sacked me, I went to work in the cinema in Medderby as an usherette. I got to see all the films for free. I loved doing that job. But then television took over and the cinema closed. I still like watching them old films on TV.'

By the time they reached the house, Abigail had heard all about Betty's son, who lived nearby, but was too busy to see her very often, apart from the weekly shopping trip, and her two daughters, who'd moved away and phoned sometimes.

She interrupted the gentle flow of information to say, 'We're here.'

Betty stopped. 'I've never been in through the front door.'

She grinned at her companion, an urchin's grin that made Abigail suddenly see what she must have looked like as a child.

'I went *out* through the front door as I left, though. That made her high and mightiness squawk, but I wanted to make sure she wouldn't have me back, whatever my mum said to her. Eh, the things girls had to do in those days to get what they wanted.'

She hadn't managed to get what she wanted in a much later era, Abigail thought. Only, she couldn't have let her father down. She should have stood up to Edwina more, though. Oh, well, no use crying over spilt milk. She opened the front door and waited for Betty to puff slowly up the three shallow stone steps and come into the entrance hall.

'You're not like your stepma, are you?' she said as she paused.

'I hope not.'

Betty stopped to gaze round. 'Eh, how well I remember it. Have you put your own books in the library now?'

'Not yet. I will be doing that when I've rearranged things. Shall I bring you a bagful up from the cellar, then you can choose some.'

'Thanks, dear. Miss Beadle, I should say.'

'I prefer 'dear'.'

'Do you? That's nice.' Betty subsided onto a hall chair, looking weary now. 'I've another whole hour before I need to get home, so I can take my time choosing. I usually sit in the library and read the newspaper.'

'Is someone looking after your husband?'

'Yes. Social services send someone for two hours a week, see, to give me a bit of a break. But the woman who does it kicks up a right old fuss if I'm even ten minutes late going back.'

★ ★ ★

Dot had been cleaning upstairs. She heard the front door open and voices talking, so left the bedroom to peer down from the landing into the hall. When she saw Betty Winters sitting there, she was surprised and called over the banister, 'What are you doing here, Bet? You've always said you were never going to enter this house again as long as you lived.'

Betty looked up at her. 'Well, I've changed my mind, haven't I? It's all right, Dot. I'm not trespassing. Miss Beadle brought me back here with her. She's going to lend me some of her books.'

'Why would she do that?' Dot started down the stairs.

'They're closing the village library in two weeks. Today it was closed for an emergency staff meeting. They apologise for the inconvenience. Ha! As if that makes it all right.'

'They're always taking days off to hold meetings, them lot are.'

'They say we can go into Medderby to borrow books from now on.'

'*What?* How are people supposed to get there without a bus service?'

'What do they care?'

'But that still doesn't explain why you came home with Abigail.'

Betty gave her a wry smile. 'It was the final straw for me, closing the library. Roger's been a bit difficult lately, you see.' She blinked furiously. 'Miss Beadle found me bawling my eyes out, silly old fool that I am, and brought me back here to lend me some books. Only pleasure I have left now, reading is, you see. I don't like all the violence on the TV, though I do usually watch the news and the ballroom dancing.'

Dot patted her shoulder. They'd known each other since they were children. 'Alzheimer's is cruel. But

64

see you bring them books back again. She thinks a lot of her romance stories, Abigail does.'

Betty drew herself up. 'No one's ever accused me of being a thief.'

'I'm not accusing you of anything, just saying. She's too soft for her own good, that one is, so I'm keeping my eye on her, making sure no one takes advantage of her.'

'Best thing would be for her to write down what I borrow today. Or I'll write it down, if you give me some paper. Then she'll know where her books are and she can tick them off when I bring them back.'

'Good idea.'

'Do you think she'll let me go on borrowing books?'

'I 'spect so. If she can. If she's able to stay here.' She lowered her voice. 'Death duties, you see. Or whatever they call it nowadays. You have to pay the government when you inherit a place like this. We shan't know where we stand till they've valued the place and told us how much there is to pay.'

They heard footsteps coming up the cellar steps just then, so broke off their conversation.

★　★　★

Abigail had been able to hear every word of what the two women said. Because of some trick of acoustics, the sounds from the ground floor carried down into the cellar. She'd stopped to listen, deeply touched by the way Dot was trying to protect her.

Both women turned round to look at her searchingly as she came into the hall, carrying two plastic bags full of books.

'Can we go into your library to sit down and look

through the books?' Betty asked. 'I'd like to see that room again, if you don't mind, find out if it's as grand as I remember. It was my favourite room to clean. I hid in there sometimes if I finished a job early.'

'Of course we can go in there.' Abigail led the way in, plastic bags swinging in her hand. 'I'll spread the books out on the table near the window, shall I?'

'Good idea,' Dot said.

Betty paused to sniff the air. 'It always did smell musty in here. You want to open some windows and freshen it up.'

'Give us time,' Dot said. 'The old lady only just died and she absolutely hated any windows being opened.'

'I'll open the French doors this very minute.' Abigail went across to turn the big old key in the lock and pull the tall doors with their bevelled glass panes into the room.

As Betty went across to look at the books, Dot whispered to Abigail, 'Everything go all right at the lawyer's, dear? No nasty surprises?'

'No. It was what I'd expected. My stepmother left me everything . . . subject to inheritance tax, that is.'

'The government's always dipping its fingers into people's pockets, whichever party is elected. Any excuse to take our money. Even after you die they skim some off if they can.'

Betty stopped looking at books to chime in. 'You're going to be paying a fortune in death duties with a place this big. I saw a programme on the TV about it only last week. Forty per cent, you have to pay. Or was it fifty? No, forty.' She shook her head sadly. 'That doesn't seem fair to me. It's not just a possession; it's your home. No skin off my nose because I won't be leaving enough to be taxed on. But my

66

son's friend lost his parents in a car accident and you wouldn't believe how much inheritance tax he had to pay because their house was over the limit. So he had to take out a mortgage after all. He was so upset.'

'*You* never used to care about things like that, Betty,' Dot said in surprise. 'Or watch documentaries on TV.'

'I get a lot of time to think these days. Too bloody much. And having the TV on seems to calm Roger a bit, though he's not fond of loud music. Neither am I.'

Dot nodded her head vigorously. 'All that wailing and thumping they call music these days fair sets my teeth on edge. Give me the good old Beatles any day.'

Abigail joined in. 'Or ABBA. You can sing along with the songs and dance to them.'

Betty and Dot exchanged quick glances. That showed what a lonely life that poor girl had led. Then Betty turned back to the books.

Abigail had been enjoying the visitor's views about the world, but she could see that Dot was fairly twitching with impatience.

'Have you made your choice, Betty? I don't want to rush you, but I've got a lot to do today.'

'I wasn't thinking. Sorry to delay you. I'm ever so grateful. I'll borrow these four, if I may, Miss Beadle. And we'll write down which I'm taking.'

'We don't need to do that. I'm sure I can trust you.'

'Oh, I'd much rather do it. I always write down who I lend things to. Saves a lot of trouble in the long run. You should do it too.'

After the books had been duly noted, Betty looked at her watch and moved stiffly towards the door. 'Got to get a move on or I'll be late back.'

'Have you far to go?' Abigail asked.

'Other side of the village.'

'I'll drive you home.'

'I can't impose.'

'It won't take me a minute to get the car out.'

The two older women stood by the front door waiting for her.

'She's so different from her stepma and grandma,' Betty said wonderingly.

'She's nothing like them two harridans. Lovely nature, she has. I'd not have stayed on here all these years if it wasn't for her. She's one in a million, my girl is. I just hope they don't take all this away from her.' She gestured round them. 'Even if she can pay them there death duties, it's a big house for one person to look after.'

'I bet it costs a lot to run.'

'Yes, but she loves it here.'

'Well, there's no place like home, whether it's big or small. I'm very fond of my little cottage.'

Abigail brought the car round to the front and the conversation ended abruptly. Betty got in and Dot sighed at having to wait for the details of the will. She went to get her outdoor broom and used it over-vigorously on the steps that led up to the front door to vent her frustration.

★   ★   ★

Dot waited in the kitchen. Abigail often sat here in the evenings when her stepmother wasn't around, because it was the only really warm room in the house. It wasn't a cheerful place, though. Perhaps they could rearrange things, brighten it up a bit before Christmas. They could have a real Christmas this

68

year, with decorations in the front hall and library, one full of genuine love and kindness. She might suggest a little two-person party on Christmas Eve, with no grumpy aunts or cousins to be invited. She glanced at the clock. It was over an hour since Abigail had left.

She'd boiled the kettle several times, ready to make a pot of tea, and she had some of her scones set out on a plate, carefully covered to keep them fresh, when she heard the sound of a car. 'About time too.'

Abigail came in through the back door, stopping to smile at her. 'Tea break time?'

'If you fancy a cuppa.'

'I'd love one. I went shopping on the way back. I'll just bring in the rest of the bags.' She dumped two bags of groceries on the surface and went out a second and third time. 'I got all sorts of things today. Including some of your favourite chocolates, Dot.' She held out a big box. 'These are to say thank you for all your help this week.'

Dot couldn't answer straight away because she was touched and knew her voice would wobble.

Abigail looked at her anxiously. 'These *are* your favourites, aren't they?'

'Yes. You didn't need to, but thank you.' She blinked her eyes, but couldn't stop all the tears, so had to wipe some away with a piece of kitchen roll. When Abigail gave her a hug, more tears flowed.

Once she was calm again, she said, 'Little acts of kindness like that make the world run more smoothly, I reckon. Now, I'll make the tea and you can butter them scones.'

'I love your scones. And there won't be a bell ringing to summon me today, so I'll be able to eat them in peace. I haven't got used to that yet.'

When they were sitting sipping their tea, Dot couldn't wait a minute longer. 'Well? What exactly did that will say?'

'What I told you. It was all very simple. Edwina left everything to me. She *ought* to have left a few small bequests to other people . . . like you . . . for all you've done for her. Or even her cousin, Cynthia. But she didn't.'

'I never expected anything. Nor I don't need anything. It's you I'm worried about. What did the lawyer say about them death duties?'

'What could he say? We have to have the house valued and pay them what they ask. I went to see the bank manager and there isn't a lot of money left in the account. There's some old-fashioned jewellery in a deposit box, but it doesn't look very valuable.' It was Abigail's turn to struggle against tears. 'I expect the house and contents will look very valuable on paper. They forget the maintenance needed. Oh, Dot, I don't think I'll be able to pay the inheritance taxes and keep Ashgrove House.'

'I was worried about that. Are you going to declare everything?'

'What do you mean?'

'Well, that book Mr Porfrey found, for one thing. It doesn't *look* valuable. You needn't tell *them* about it, surely?'

'I shall have to.'

'No, you won't. I could take a few things home with me, like the best of the family silver, and hide them in my attic while everything's being valued. Afterwards, you could sell them gradually. They'd bring in something for a rainy day, at least.'

'I couldn't be *dishonest*!'

'Other people are. I know for a fact that Major Payton's wife hid most of his mother's jewellery and silver after he died, because I used to clean for her.' Dot struggled to keep quiet, but couldn't. 'Sometimes, Abigail love, you have to think about yourself.'

'I don't think I *can* lie and . . . and connive.'

'You could try, for the sake of the house if not for yourself.'

There was silence.

'You've never lived anywhere else and you love this place. I'm not suggesting you do this for greed, but won't you even fight for your home?'

'I still don't want to tell lies and act dishonestly.'

Dot knew that mulish look. Mr Beadle had had it too, just now and then. He'd let his second wife ride over him roughshod most of the time, because he was a gentle soul, but every so often he'd dug his heels in and that was that. Why, even a bully like Edwina had known better than to try to change her husband's mind when he got *that look* on his face. Abigail got that same expression. Dot wished she'd get it now in support of staying here, not in support of paying unfair taxes.

Well, if anything was going to be done to fool the authorities and help her girl, it'd be up to Dot to do it secretly. If she could think of anything, that was. She gasped as she suddenly realised that she might even be planning more criminal activities. Well, that will had been unfair and she could try to help protect the house, couldn't she?

'Are you still awake, Dot?'

'Oh, sorry. Just thinking about something. What did you say, dear?'

71

'I said I have to clear out my stepmother's clothes and . . . all her other personal things. I wondered if you'd come and help me.'

'Of course I will. I already made a start on cleaning her room. She wouldn't often let me do even that.'

'I'll pay you at the usual rate for any extra work you do, of course.'

'No. Not this time. I'll do that particular job as a friend or not at all. I know how hard it is cleaning out someone's personal belongings.' She got another big hug for that, and she didn't mind at all.

She wondered if Abigail would have hugged her so hard if she'd known that she was still determined to save something to help with the inheritance costs. The more Dot thought about it the more certain she felt it was the right thing to do. She'd already broken the law once by burning the will. Not for her own benefit. Never for her own benefit. It still didn't feel wrong to have done that. And now it was the same with this death duty stuff. So, whether it was legal or not she intended to do whatever she could to help Abigail, because she too loved the old house. She loved the village too.

In fact, she intended to live here in Ashbury St Mary till they carried her out of her home feet first. The only thing that worried her was that the council might try to force her to move into a smaller house or flat. They'd already offered to pay people's expenses if they did that voluntarily. Well, she would fight tooth and nail to stay. She'd been in that house for over forty years. It was her home. That was why she under-stood Abigail's feelings so well.

Then she remembered something. 'I've made an appointment for you to have your hair styled by my friend Elsa tomorrow.'

'How kind of you. But I think I can wait a little to do that.'

'No, you can't. You have lovely hair and we're going to show it off as it deserves.'

They locked glances and Dot folded her arms across her chest, trying to look fiercely determined. She must have succeeded because Abigail shrugged and said, 'Oh, very well, then. Why not?'

5

When they went upstairs, Abigail stopped in the doorway of her stepmother's bedroom, feeling as if she were an intruder. She pulled out a couple of drawers and peered into the wardrobe. Her stepmother had always been untidy and the contents were like rats' nests. Nothing had ever been thrown away and clothes had been stuffed into drawers so tightly they burst out if you opened anything carelessly.

There was her father's bedroom to clear, too. Her stepmother had refused point blank to have it touched after he died and had sat in there sometimes. She'd missed him, had loved him in her own way. There was no doubt about that. Abigail had heard her weeping sometimes at night, too, saying his name over and over.

She'd been quite sure that her stepmother wasn't fond of *her*. Well, the dislike had been mutual.

Clearing her father's room out would be much easier, so Abigail turned to Dot. 'I think we'll do my father's room first.'

The look Dot gave her said she was well aware why. He'd been a tidy man, as neat in his ways as in his appearance. There probably wouldn't be anything to shock them.

Dot turned towards it. 'Why not? We won't find any nasty surprises there, that's for sure.'

Someone rang the doorbell just then. 'I'll get that.' Abigail ran downstairs and accepted a small parcel from the postman, and a murmur of condolences.

She took it to the kitchen and checked it. Oh, dear. Something for her stepmother. She'd open it later. She looked at the view from the window. Her step-mother had been able to pay the inheritance tax when her dad died — just! — by selling off a house they'd owned in the village.

But that had been the last separate dwelling belonging to the estate. She was pretty sure the rest came under one land title, so they'd have to sell this house with the land. Unless you could get it rezoned. She wasn't sure how you did that. Or whether the council would agree to it. Besides, even if she got it rezoned, a house this big would look silly on a small suburban plot and whoever bought the land would definitely cut down the ash grove the house was named for. Her heart twisted in pain even to think of losing her special place.

Most of these ash trees had been replaced over the years, because they only lived about four hundred years, but a few had been coppiced and were thought to have been planted at the same time as the house was built. As far as she was concerned no tree had lovelier foliage in summer.

She would have to accustom herself to the idea of leaving her home. She needn't leave the village, though. There were smaller houses for sale there regularly and she'd probably have enough money left to buy one. Or would it be better to make a complete break? How did you even begin to know what was best when all you knew, your whole life and all your memories were based here? Besides, she didn't want to watch others living in her home. She loved Ash-grove, every shabby inch of it, and had been in charge of its everyday management for years. It was heritage

75

listed, so it couldn't be knocked down as easily, but she'd heard that an unscrupulous developer could simply lock it up and let it crumble, while building modern houses on the land round it, then later claim it was a danger to safety. Or it could be burned down by 'vandals'.

Oh, what was the use of worrying about the details now? Time enough for that when she'd gained probate and had everything valued. She looked at the kitchen clock in surprise. She'd been standing here like a fool for ages, leaving Dot to do all the work.

She ran up the stairs. 'Sorry. I got lost in memories for a while.'

Dot shrugged. 'There's time to do that if it helps you get used to your new situation. There's a poem says it better than I can. I've always liked it since I learned it at school.' She closed her eyes and chanted, '*What is this life if, full of care, We have no time to stand and stare* . . . Eh, what comes next? I'll have to look it up when I get home. As for you, young lady, you can just stop getting your knickers in a twist. There isn't a rush for the clearing up.'

'You're so understanding.'

'I've been longing to have a go at your father's room for years, only *she* wouldn't let anyone in. He'd be horrified at the state it's in now. Look at that dust! And she's just thrown her rubbish in the waste paper basket whenever she's come in here without emptying it. Good thing I brought up some rubbish bin liners, eh?'

A couple of hours of hard work had the job done, with no surprises. Abigail's father had been well organised. In the end there was one bag of throw-away clothing oddments and two bags of clothes that

76

Dot assured her would be welcomed at the charity shop.

'I'll have to leave it at that for today, love. I have some shopping to do. I can drop this lot off for you on my way, though. We didn't get round to your step-mother's things at all, but I'll come back tomorrow and we'll make a start on them then. Her room will take a lot longer than half a day, I'm sure.'

'Only if you let me pay you tomorrow.'

'Oh, all right. Now, you need to be thinking of putting the rest of the shopping away, then getting your tea. Will you be all right on your own tonight?'

'I'm always all right here at Ashgrove.'

'Well, I'll just check all the doors and windows, then you make sure you lock the back door carefully after I leave.'

★ ★ ★

Abigail didn't feel hungry yet, so stayed on the door-step after she'd waved goodbye to Dot. The sun was low on the horizon now and it'd soon be dusk. The days were so short in winter. She gave in to temptation and went for a quick stroll round the ash grove. How many times had she walked off her worries here?

There were no rainbows now, just long shadows criss-crossing under her feet and a chill little breeze whispering among the branches. She looked up, smiling involuntarily at the sight of her hat, still somehow attached to that high branch. All the leaves had fallen now. They were among the last trees to shed. Would she still be here in spring when the delicate leaves started to grow again? She hoped so.

A bird came and perched on the branch, taking a few pecks at the hat, then flying off again. Maybe in spring, if the hat was still there, the birds would use the felt to line a nest. She hoped so. The birds that migrated south for the winter had already left, but she'd buy a feeder and be sure to put stuff out to feed the ones who bravely stayed behind. There was no one to stop her doing that now.

The sight of the hat had cheered her up enormously and she now felt quite hungry, so went back into the house. As she locked the door carefully behind her, she rolled her eyes at her own carelessness in leaving it unlocked while she was out of sight in the grove.

She made some scrambled eggs on toast for tea, followed by a dish of frozen berries with a scoop of one of her more extravagant purchases from the small local supermarket: strawberry ripple ice cream and a few nuts sprinkled on top.

In spring there would be fruit and vegetables to buy fresh from Rob Percy's stall at the weekly market. He had a thriving market garden and nothing you bought elsewhere tasted quite as nice as the stuff he grew locally. But at this time of year, they were past the fresh berries she loved so much.

She enjoyed every single mouthful of her dessert, with the news on the old TV in the corner keeping her company as she ate.

★ ★ ★

After watching a couple more programmes and drinking a glass of wine, Abigail went up to bed, sleeping far better than she'd expected to, better than she had for ages.

She woke before it was fully light and lay listening to the house creak around her like an old friend. Then she heard a sound that surprised her. Footsteps. She stiffened. Could someone have broken in? She listened again, but heard nothing. Still, she couldn't settle, thinking of that valuable book, so easy for a burglar to steal. She would have to go down and investigate the noise. After putting on her shabby dressing gown, she picked up the poker her stepmother had insisted on her keeping beside the bed and crept down into the dimness of the hall, feeling a fool, sure now that she'd been mistaken.

But she heard the sound of footsteps again. Oh dear! Her heart sank. It was coming from the library.

'You can do it,' she muttered to give herself courage. Taking a deep breath, she crept along to investigate.

When she went in, she saw something shimmering near the fireplace and caught her breath. It looked like . . . it couldn't be. Surely what Dad had told her about the family ghosts couldn't be true? *She* had never believed it, anyway, and they hadn't appeared while Edwina was the nominal owner.

There was the sound of gentle laughter and she swallowed hard, staring at that corner. The shimmering light grew brighter and gradually took on the form of a beautiful woman in eighteenth-century clothing.

Oh, no! She didn't *want* to have ghosts to contend with. Abigail recognised the figure, of course, from the family portraits and sketches. 'Georgiana Beadle!' she exclaimed. It was her ancestor, looking just like the portrait in the sitting room, in an eighteenth-century gown with a full skirt, picture hat with ribbon bows and a shawl crossed at the front and tied at the back.

The ghost swept her a curtsey. 'At your service, Abigail. I've been looking forward to meeting you properly.'

'I'm imagining this. I must be.' She closed her eyes, willing the illusion to go away. But when she opened them again, the ghost was still there.

Georgiana shook her head and made a tutting noise. 'You're not imagining anything, great-great-however-many-it-is-granddaughter. I'm a genuine English ghost.'

'You *can't* be real.'

'Why can't I? You can see me. I can see you as well.'

'Why have I never noticed you before, then?'

'We only let the owner of the house see us, usually.'

'See *us*?' Abigail asked faintly.

Two more forms shimmered into existence: another woman and a man. Each ghost inclined its head to Abigail and took up a position on either side of Georgiana. They were all three wearing dress from different eras, but they each had the narrow Beadle face, with wide turquoise-blue eyes and soft honey-coloured hair, just like Abigail's own.

'What do you want?' she managed at last.

'We've come to meet you properly, of course,' said the man. 'I'm Roderick, by the way. I hope you'll forgive me for making my footsteps sound louder than usual to wake you up before your nice old maid comes here for the day.'

'I know who you are, too. We still have your portrait.' A Regency buck, just like those in the historical dramas on TV, wearing tight trousers, a cutaway jacket and a very high shirt collar and neckcloth. He reminded her strongly of Mr Darcy in the 1995 TV

80

show *Pride and Prejudice*, which she'd watched several times.

He smirked as if he knew what she was thinking. 'It's a good portrait, isn't it? I was a handsome young fellow in those days.'

Georgiana gave him a nudge. 'Stop thinking about yourself, Roderick. We're here to help Abigail, not talk about you.'

'Help me? What are — ? Why would — ?' She was having trouble putting a coherent sentence together.

'You need to save the house for future generations, as well as for us. If you don't, we'll have nowhere to go and no descendants to care about. There are quite a few of us who like to visit Ashgrove from time to time. You're not the only one who loves the old place, you know. We've all cared for it and looked after it as best we could when we were alive. So . . . we're going to find a way to help you save it now, if we can.'

'I have to be imagining all this,' Abigail said loudly. 'I must be asleep and dreaming.' She closed her eyes firmly, counted up to twenty and opened them again. 'Oh, no!' She shut her eyes again hastily and prayed to wake up, this time counting loudly to fifty. She only got as far as thirty-five then had to look and they were still there, patiently waiting and looking rather amused.

Georgiana waggled one finger at her in a chiding gesture. 'Your father was just the same the first time. We had to prove we were real.' She looked sideways. 'You do it, Roderick. You're the best at lifting objects in her plane of existence.'

'My pleasure.'

His voice was deep and he reminded her so much of her father it brought a lump to her throat. 'Does

Dad ever come back?' She wouldn't be frightened of her father's ghost, she was sure.

Georgiana looked at her sadly. 'He's not been able to face it yet. And he's a bit busy at the moment helping your stepmother cope with the fact that she's dead. She gets very angry, doesn't she? But as *she* isn't a Beadle born and bred, she couldn't come back here anyway, even if she wanted to, so you're safe from her nagging for ever, and good riddance to her too. Hurry up, Roderick! We're waiting.'

He pointed his index finger at an ornament and it lifted up into the air.

'Oh, do be careful!' Abigail exclaimed. 'That one's valuable and I need all the money I can scrape together.'

'Hold out your hands, then.'

'What?'

'Catch!'

The ornament sailed through the air and she reached out to catch it automatically. It slowed down and dropped neatly into her outstretched hands.

She clutched it tightly to her chest. It felt real. It was real. She definitely hadn't moved it. And she wasn't asleep. So the ghosts must be real. They were still smiling at her sympathetically.

'You're going to need your family's help, I'm afraid,' the other lady said, her voice deeper and her hair a slightly paler shade than Georgiana's with the silver threads showing clearly. She was wearing a two-piece in a lovely shade of dark rose, with its pleated skirt coming to just below the knee and a V-necked top.

'You're Juliana!' Abigail said involuntarily. This lady had featured regularly in the 1920s and 1930s photo albums. A very glamorous woman, she'd always thought.

82

'Yes. I must say you're more familiar with your family portraits than your father was when he inherited. Now that you know we're here, you can call on us any time you need advice or help,' Juliana said. 'Though it'd be better if you call us when you're alone because if someone sees you talking to yourself, they'll think you're mad.'

'Unless there's an emergency, of course,' Georgiana put in. 'Then just call out.'

Abigail was rather puzzled. 'Help me to do what?'

'You may need information,' Juliana said.

Roderick grinned at her. 'Or you may need something moving to frighten a person who's giving you trouble. I love doing that. We don't actually hurt people — well, we couldn't, we're friendly spirits — but sometimes, when they're not being kind to the owner, we are allowed to frighten them a little.'

'How do you do that?'

'My favourite is walking through walls and betting how loudly they'll scream when I slowly emerge. Remember, we're on your side. We're as keen as you are to save the house for ourselves and for the Beadles of the future.'

'There won't be any future Beadles. I'm the last one and I'm a bit past having children,' Abigail said sadly.

Georgiana frowned at her. 'How old are you? Thirty-eight? In this modern age, you've still got time to have a baby, two even. If you had twins, you could do that in one fell swoop.'

'I'm not married. No one has ever wanted to marry me and I can't see that changing.'

'Your stepmother drove the man who did away, that's why.'

'*What?*'

But Georgiana had faded slightly and didn't answer Abigail's question.

'We'll help you find someone to marry,' said Juliana. 'I like weddings. I sometimes go and watch them if they're being held in the village church. It's got lots of things to look at and you meet some charming ghosts there, keeping an eye on their own families.'

Abigail covered her eyes for a moment, but when no one spoke, she uncovered them again to see what they were doing, and found she was alone.

'There. I *was* just imagining it!' she said aloud.

Immediately the group reappeared.

Roderick's laughter echoed round the room. 'You weren't imagining it but if you need more proof, here you are! This one is definitely a fake.'

An ugly ornament Abigail's stepmother had once been given by Cousin Cynthia lifted up suddenly from a small table near the window, sailed through the air and smashed on the hearth.

Juliana chuckled. 'I always did hate that stupid figurine. Your stepmother and her cousin had no taste.' She studied Abigail and frowned. 'And by the way, you really must find some nicer clothes now, my dear girl. I don't like to see a descendant of mine dressing so badly. You're not doing any credit to the family, wearing such dreary, unflattering rags. There are several of mine up in the attic which would fit you and haven't really dated. Now, I'm a bit tired. The first time we talk to someone is always such hard work. I really must go back and rest.'

She began to fade again and as Abigail watched, the others faded too. Roderick was the last to go, waving a vigorous farewell. His hand seemed to hang in the air before gradually disappearing, finger by finger, accompanied by a happy chuckle that left Abigail smiling.

Still clutching the valuable ornament, she looked across at the shards of china in the fireplace, then tottered to the nearest chair and collapsed on it. Either she was going mad or Ashgrove House really was haunted. As her father had said. If no one else could see her ancestors, she wouldn't dare mention them to anyone — except Dot, of course. Dot would believe her.

She sat for a few minutes then realised that it was getting lighter, well past dawn. She went upstairs to get dressed. Today she needed to clear out her stepmother's bedroom and look for the key to the safe. There were all sorts of jobs needing to be done.

Oh, and she was going to get her hair restyled later today. Did she really need the bother of that? She looked in the mirror and sighed at the floppy mess of hair she usually just tied back. Yes, she did need to do something about how she looked. Georgiana was right about that.

6

Just after eight o'clock, Dot tried the back door and found it unlocked, so shouted, 'I'm here!' There were plates and a mug stacked neatly on the draining board. By the looks of them, Abigail had had a decent breakfast. Good. Footsteps sounded on the stone flags of the corridor and Abigail burst into the room, glancing over her shoulder as if afraid of being pursued.

'What on earth's the matter, love?'

She stared at Dot as if she didn't recognise her and let out her breath in a whoosh.

'Something's upset you. Tell me at once.'

'I don't know whether I should. But I *have* to tell someone. Promise to keep it to yourself.'

'Of course I will. Here, sit down.'

'I — you'll think I'm going mad. I saw — still can't believe it — but I saw . . . No, I can't say it.'

Dot studied her carefully. 'You saw the family ghosts, I suppose.'

Abigail gaped at her. 'How do you know about them?'

'Your father told me.'

'Why would he do that?'

Dot shrugged. 'Same reason you're doing it now. He needed to confide in someone. He and I were kids together, you know, though he was a few years older than me. He played cricket with my brothers and cousins, stopped them bullying me when he could. I thought the world of him.'

'So did I.'

'There was no one else he could tell, after all. Your grandmother was very strict and didn't allow herself to believe and later, well, you can't imagine any ghost wanting to speak to your stepmother even if she was a Beadle born, which she wasn't. I believed him, though.'

'You did? Why?'

'Because he never told me a lie, just as you never have. Besides, every now and then it feels as if I'm not alone. So . . . what were these ghosts like and what did they say to you?'

'Well, keep it to yourself, but . . .' Abigail told her all that had happened.

By the end of the tale, Dot was grinning. 'I like the sound of them and I've always liked their pictures. They have kind faces. They've got excellent taste in ornaments, too. I hope they throw something equally ugly at that horrible Cousin Cynthia when next she comes round and tries to interfere with your life, and I just pray I'm there to see it. Don't let her get even a toe in the door or she'll never stop nagging you.'

'I don't need warning. I can't stand her, either. She was never kind to me, even when I was little, but she got so much worse after Dad died.'

'That's because Edwina has been training her. It amused her. Oh, she used to make my blood boil at times!'

Abigail still seemed bemused, so Dot took charge. 'I'll sweep up the shards of that ornament, then we'll go upstairs and get to work on that dratted woman's bedroom. Clear her out once and for all, and good riddance too.'

★ ★ ★

It felt strange to go into her stepmother's private territory and find the bed showing only a bare mattress. Abigail felt like backing out of the room again and leaving Dot to clear it for her, but that would be cowardly and she'd promised herself to be brave about whatever needed doing from now on, so she said as briskly as she could manage, 'You take the wardrobe and I'll take the drawers.'

'Are you likely to keep any of her clothes?'

'No way!'

'Then I'll go and get those dustbin liners again. I should have brought them up with me but I was a bit distracted by the thought of your ghosts.'

While Dot was gone, Abigail took another deep breath and opened the top drawer. Makeup mainly and all sorts of bits and pieces. She'd throw all that away. Then she saw something gleaming, and lifted out the shallow tray of half-used lipsticks, little bottles of moisturiser and who knew what else.

Underneath it was a whole tray of costume jewellery, none of which she remembered her stepmother ever wearing. They must be things her stepmother had brought to the marriage; Abigail knew all of the Beadle family jewellery because her mother had worn what she liked and kept the rest in the bank. Edwina had taken possession of the jewellery almost immediately after her marriage and worn it from time to time.

'I'll just give this lot away,' she said as Dot came back in. 'It's only costume jewellery.'

Dot studied it. 'I have a friend who has a second-hand shop. I'll take it to her, shall I? She might give me something for it, more than you'd get if you tried, I'm sure.'

'Do you really think so? Garish things like these?'

Dot picked up a brooch of brightly coloured stones, studied it then shrugged. 'Might as well give it a try, eh? She'll tell me if it's not worth anything.' She found a scarf in another drawer, picked up the tray of jewellery and tipped it into the centre, tying it into a firm knot. 'I'll put this in the kitchen with my handbag, together with anything else I can help you sell.'

'Yes, all right.'

'But only if you promise to keep the money from this to yourself and not declare it.'

'Dot! That's against the law.'

'There won't be much. Think of it as going towards saving Ashgrove.'

Abigail hesitated. 'That's what the ghosts said: they need me to save the house for them as well as for myself.'

'Well, they were right and I like them even more for saying that. Just think. Where will they go if you let their home be taken away?'

Abigail looked at her in dismay and felt a trickle of doubt about her own stance. 'We-ell, it won't be much money. Will you keep it for me till everything is settled? Then I won't feel as guilty if I tell the valuers I haven't got anything else.'

'Of course I will. And any other money we make from selling the odd item here and there. I shan't put the money in the bank because people will ask questions, but I have somewhere very safe to hide it.'

For a moment all hung in the balance. 'For the house,' Dot pleaded and knew she'd won when her girl sighed and nodded slowly.

'Very well, then. But only if you take ten per cent of what you make. I mean it, Dot. You'll have expenses.'

'OK. All right by me.' They'd see about that later, she vowed. She doubted she'd be asked for a detailed account because Abigail knew Dot wouldn't cheat her — and she wouldn't, unless it was by not taking the ten per cent. Or by keeping the running total a secret. Was it still cheating when you were doing something to help a person? Banishing such worries in favour of action, Dot rolled up her sleeves. 'Let's carry on, then.'

They worked all morning, finding a lot of rubbish as well as things worth giving to charity, but no sign of keys to the cupboard-sized strongbox in an unused pantry where the silver was kept or to the safe, where the jewellery and smaller items were probably kept. They didn't know the combination, either.

'Perhaps Mr Liddlestone had the details,' Dot said.

'I'm sure they won't be lost because Edwina must never have thrown away a single thing since she got here.' Abigail stopped for a breather. 'Look, it's nearly lunchtime and — Oh, that's the doorbell. I'll go.'

* * *

Mr Danvers was standing outside. 'I was feeling like some fresh air after a morning with Gerard's clients, so I thought I'd call in rather than phoning. Is that all right?'

'Of course it is. Do come in. Excuse the mess but we've been clearing out my stepmother's bedroom.' She tried in vain to push her hair behind her ears but as usual it kept slipping forward.

Dot came down the stairs to join them, carrying two bulging plastic bin liners and talking as she moved. 'I'll put these in the rubbish bin, love. I don't think your stepmother knew how to throw . . . Oh, Mr Danvers. Sorry to interrupt.'

He nodded a greeting then turned to Abigail. 'Um, I would like to see you privately, Miss Beadle. If Dot doesn't mind. Oh, and I forgot to tell you, Mrs Eakins, that we're changing the locks at the rooms, but we still want you to clean for us, so if you call in there before five today, Miss Cawdell will give you a new set of keys.'

'Oh, good. It there any news of Mr L?'

'Just that he's improving slowly.'

'Poor man. Look, I've got some shopping to do, Abigail, or I'll have nothing to eat tonight. I'll be back in an hour or so to take you round to my friend's. I can put one of these bags in my own dustbin while I'm at it. You won't have room in yours for everything we need to throw away. Do you want anything from the shops?'

'No, thank you. I bought plenty of food yesterday. Would you like a cup of tea or coffee, Mr Danvers?'

'I'd love a coffee, if you have time.'

She led the way to the kitchen. 'I was due a break. We could sit outside, if you like. It's a lovely day and there's a sheltered spot, if you keep your overcoat on.'

'Good idea.' He went to stand in a little patch of winter sunshine outside the back door while she made the coffee, then insisted on carrying the tray across to the old wooden table and benches that had stood outside in that spot for as long as she could remember.

They seemed never to change, as if they were untouched by the weather, and the faded timber looked so pretty she had refused to let her stepmother paint the outdoor furniture white, like some Edwina had admired on the television. Abigail had only had

91

to say 'waste of money and painters always charge a fortune' and her stepmother had dropped the idea.

'What did you need to see me about, Mr Danvers?'

'Philip, please. It occurred to me that I'll be helping you with the inheritance tax and I've never even been inside the house. I was wondering if you could show me round. Not necessarily today but as soon as convenient.'

'I'd be happy to. If you drink up quickly we can do a quick tour now if you like, but I have a hairdressing appointment later so you'll have to come back another time to study the details.'

'If it's not too much trouble.'

'I love walking round. I have to make the most of the place while I've got it. I can't see any way of paying the inheritance tax without selling it.'

'And that hurts.' His voice was soft, his expression understanding.

She tried to speak calmly, but couldn't stop her voice wobbling. 'It does, rather.'

They sipped in silence then he said, 'There is one other thing that's important: the safe. Apparently there are some valuables in it.'

'Yes, there is a safe, but after Edwina took it over, she would never say exactly what was in it.'

'Could we inspect the contents, do you think?'

'We could if I had a key and knew the combination but I don't. I was hoping there would be a key left at your office.'

'There's no sign of one there. I'll have to ask Gerard about it when he's well enough to receive visitors but that could be a while. Maybe we should bring in a locksmith.'

'I don't suppose there's much in it but yes, I think

we'd better do that. I need to find out where I stand.'

'All right. I'll arrange it.'

'Is Mr Liddlestone going to be all right?'

'Yes, well, sort of, with a few weaknesses. But his wife is guarding him fiercely. She's determined no one's going to bother him and is insisting he retire forthwith.' He drained his mug and pushed his chair back. 'It's pleasant sitting out here but we'd better go and look round the house.'

He was an easy companion and seemed quite taken by the old place. 'I can see why you love it. Would it be all right for me to have a quick glance at the ash grove you love so much?'

'Does it show so clearly?' She glanced at her watch and took him there.

'You're right. It's a delightful place. Your own miniature wood. I bet you played here a lot as a child.'

'Every day I could.'

He stopped and stared upwards with a frown. 'What's that?'

She could feel herself blushing. 'It's a hat. I — um, threw it up there.'

He looked at her in mild surprise. 'May I ask why? Or is it a deadly secret?'

'Because it was a horrible old thing and I've hated it for years.'

'Why wear it then?'

She sighed. 'My stepmother thought I should keep it to wear for funerals. She said it was a sign of respect to wear black, but probably she just thought it'd be a waste of time to buy a new hat. I'm afraid I let her have her own way more than I should have done. She could be so . . . so *strident* if you crossed her.'

'Yes. I've heard other people say similar things

93

about her.'

Abigail looked down and grimaced. 'Since the rest of my clothes aren't very nice, either, it didn't seem worth making a fuss about a hat I hardly ever wore.'

'My grandmother was difficult towards the end, too,' he confided. 'She seemed to change personality after she turned eighty.'

'My stepmother didn't exactly change personality at all, just got worse. She was always difficult to live with. I could never understand why my father married her.'

'And yet you stayed with her after he died.'

'I'd promised him faithfully, word of a Beadle, that I'd look after her. There was the house to look after, too, and that was far more important to me. *She* wouldn't have looked after it. I was even able to do some of the smaller maintenance jobs.'

'Very modern!'

As they went back into the house, he said thoughtfully, 'So now you've done your duty, you're due a little relaxation.'

'Exactly.'

'How about starting off your new life by coming out for a drink with me to the Golden Rose pub tomorrow night?'

It was the last thing she'd expected him to say and she didn't know what to reply.

'*Say yes, you idiot,*' Juliana's voice whispered in her ear. '*He's an attractive man.*'

Abigail could feel herself blushing, nearly said no, then had a fit of what-the-hells and blurted out quickly, before she could lose her courage, 'That'd be nice.'

'I'll pick you up at six tomorrow, and look, let's

have a pub meal while we're at it, if that's OK with you? I'm not a good cook.'

'Um . . . yes. Thank you, Mr Danvers.'

'I just told you: my first name's Philip.' He smiled. 'I'm glad you agreed to come with me. It's a bit difficult when you move to a new area and you don't know anyone. I haven't been out to a pub for ages because I don't like going alone.'

'I used to go to the Golden Rose with Dad, but I haven't been there since the year before he died. I shall look forward to it.'

'*Good girl!*' Juliana whispered in her ear.

Surely Philip could hear that ghostly voice? But no, he didn't show any sign of it.

'*He can't hear anything I say, silly! He's not a Beadle so we haven't included him.*'

Abigail walked Philip to the door then went to grab a quick sandwich for lunch. She had a date. That felt strange, but rather nice. It had been a long time. After she'd eaten she went to stare at the safe, wondering what it contained and where her stepmother could have put the key and combination. Typical of Edwina to be still causing trouble after her death.

7

When Dot came back from her shopping trip, Abigail was in her own bedroom, going through her clothes and feeling quite desperate about what to wear for her date the following day. 'I'm up here!' she called. 'Can you help me?'

Dot stared in surprise at the bed, which was piled with just about all the clothes Abigail owned. 'Are you clearing your stuff out as well? If so, it's about time. Most of these are only fit for old women and frumps. You need a whole new wardrobe.'

'I can't afford that, though I'm definitely going to buy a few casual things.' She could feel a blush rising. 'The trouble is, Philip — Mr Danvers, that is — has invited me out for a meal at the pub tomorrow and well, I said yes.' She waited, half-expecting the sarcastic comments her stepmother had made about her rare, occasional dates, but Dot only came to pat her on her arm.

'That's great. He seems a really nice fellow to me, though a little staid. Well, he must be nice if Mr Liddlestone took him on as a partner. He's a good judge of character.'

'Yes. Only I've nothing to wear except that dress I had on when I went to his office for a business meeting. I'll have to ring him in the morning and cancel. Look at them! *Just look!*'

Dot stared at the pile of shabby clothes, eyes narrowed. 'Don't you dare cancel!'

'I daren't spend much on clothes till I see where

96

I stand.'

'No need to spend money, or not much, anyway. We'll leave the rest of your stepmother's stuff till later and go through that box of thirties clothing in the attic. If the dress you were wearing for your visit to the lawyer was in your size, there might be others that fit you. And some of those clothes are classics and look perfectly all right today.'

She shook her head and grimaced. 'Well, a lot of people don't seem to care what they wear and that's a fact. My niece goes out dressed like a tart. And my neighbour's daughter is a goth, which means she wears only black. She puts holes in her clothes on purpose, and has holes poked in her body too. Did you ever hear anything as stupid? How she blows her nose properly with a ring in it, I don't know.'

Abigail smiled. She'd heard about Dot's niece a few times. 'Perhaps I'd better wear that dress of Juliana's again. Only . . . well, it isn't very casual, is it?' She did like it, though. Had held it up against herself several times and admired her reflection in the mirror.

'You're right. That one's far too dressy for a casual meal at the pub. We have to go out soon, so I'll make us something we can eat quickly. We'll have to see what we can come up with for you to wear after we get back. You can start throwing away some of these frumpy old things while I'm doing that — no, throw *all* of them away.'

Abigail began stuffing the sad collection of garments into bin liners, but couldn't help worrying. Could she afford enough casual clothes to get by? Maybe a couple of pairs of jeans and a few tops. They'd be so practical. Her stepmother had thrown a fit at the thought of her wearing jeans, so she'd had to

97

stop. Honestly! Everyone wore them these days. Next time she went into Medderby, she'd buy a pair. Two pairs. Hang probate! Hang everything.

She gave an approving nod at her determined expression in the mirror. It seemed to say that she was taking another step towards becoming the new Abigail.

And to prove it, she had a date!

She twirled round twice on her way to the kitchen.

* * *

As she got downstairs, Dot was just coming out of the kitchen.

'Ah, there you are, Abby love. I was just going to shout for you. We need to leave for Elsa's in a few minutes so I've made a sandwich for you. She doesn't like people being late.'

'I'd forgotten. What sort of hair style shall I ask for?'

'*Ask for?* Don't you dare voice an opinion. *She* will decide what suits you, and you'll like it, I promise. She's got a magic touch with hair, my friend Elsa has.'

Before she left the house, Abigail stood for a few seconds in front of the hall mirror, staring at herself. She was looking forward to wearing more casual clothes again, but Dot was right: her hair definitely let her down. It made her face look too thin tied back like that. She did hope this Elsa would be able to do something with her stupidly soft hair.

* * *

Abigail felt nervous as she locked the car and followed Dot into Elsa's house.

The door was opened by a teenager in a pale blue overall, who led them through to the back of the cottage, where a light and airy conservatory had been turned into a small hairdressing salon with lilac and white fittings. An older woman, presumably Elsa, was just finishing a client's hair. She stood back and said, 'There you are.'

The girl moved forward to hold a mirror so that the woman could see the back.

'Oh, Elsa, it's lovely! Thank you so much. How much do I owe you?'

The customer looked poor, Abigail thought, her coat shabby, her shoes scuffed. But her pleasure at her new hairstyle lit up her whole face.

'You don't owe me anything because you let me use your head to show Michelle here a few of the basic techniques of cutting, and you bravely let her try a few snips.'

'Are you sure?'

'Of course I'm sure.'

'Well, I'll bake you an apple pie, then. Just as a thank you.'

Elsa grinned. 'I wouldn't say no to that. My attempts at pastry always turn into concrete.'

While the assistant showed the customer out, Elsa turned to Abigail. 'At last! I've been dying to do something about your hair for years. Take that rubber band out at once and never put one in again. They break the hair, especially fine hair like yours.' She walked across to hold up a lock. 'Very soft. Falls out of pins. Am I right?'

'Yes. It's always been hard to manage.'

'It won't be when I've finished with you.' Elsa gestured to a chair next to a wash basin at the side of the room. 'Take off your jacket and we'll let Michelle wash and condition your hair.'

'Oh, right. Thank you.'

It was bliss to have her hair washed. Abigail felt so tired and frazzled after the past two weeks that she lay back and let them do as they wanted. Michelle massaged her scalp and the gentle, rhythmic kneading made her want to groan aloud in pleasure, but she didn't — at least, she hoped she hadn't done.

When Michelle led her across to the chair in front of Elsa, Abigail's nervousness returned as she wondered what she'd look like when this was finished. Then she told herself not to be silly. She couldn't look much worse than she usually did, could she?

Dot leaned forward. 'Abigail's always busy, Elsa love. She can't be doing with something that needs a lot of fiddling around.'

Elsa nodded. 'It's such a lovely colour, we just want to show it off, simple and elegant.'

Dot stepped back, going to sit at the other end of the room. Michelle came to stand behind the hairdresser, ready to serve her, watching every move she made.

'Close your eyes now, Abigail,' Elsa ordered. 'And don't open them till I've finished.'

She did as asked, relaxing again.

Scissors snipped, hair tumbled softly, shorn locks tickling her face and neck as they fell to the floor. After a while, she had a desperate urge to open her eyes, but there was something about Elsa that said she was not to be trifled with, so she didn't give in to her curiosity. The snipping and fluffing of hair seemed to go on for a long time.

'You have a slight natural wave,' Elsa said. 'You've

not been letting it follow its nature, scragging it back like that. No, keep your eyes closed.'

More snipping, but no more long locks falling, it seemed to Abigail, just tiny wisps that felt like light kisses. Eventually, the movement stopped and there was complete silence in the salon.

Elsa said, 'Yes. I think that should do. You may open your eyes, Abigail.'

She did and stared in shocked delight at her reflection. She had jaw-length hair, shining now, showing the natural variations in colour. 'My stepmother always said the different colours were 'a fault in the growth'.'

Elsa looked at her in amazement. 'What? She was lying. It's lovely, your hair is. People pay a fortune to have the colour varied like this, but it never looks as good as yours does naturally. And when bad hairdressers try to do it, the hair looks stripy and artificial. Ugh. Don't ever be tempted to use a colour treatment on your hair. It's beautiful as it is.'

Beautiful! A hairdresser had just told her she had beautiful hair. Abigail met Elsa's eyes in the mirror and the older woman nodded.

'You're brilliant at your job,' Abigail said. 'I can't believe that's me.'

'Thank you. I don't do badly when I'm allowed to use my expertise as I see fit. Now . . .' She proceeded to give instructions for washing and fluffing up the hair, then stepped back and let Michelle take away the protective gown.

'How much do I owe you?'

'Pay me what you think it's worth.'

'I can't afford to pay that much. It's priceless to me.' She took out her purse and gave Elsa two banknotes.

Elsa handed one back. 'When you have your finances sorted out, you can pay more. This'll do for now. Come back every three weeks for a light trim. Michelle, give her a card so she can phone for appointments.'

'People can be so kind,' Abigail said to Dot as they slid back into the car. 'I feel absolutely wonderful.'

'Well, that's no reason to get tearful, is it?' But she blew her own nose hard. 'Bit of hay fever,' she muttered gruffly.

'I know.' Abigail hid a smile.

When they got back to Ashgrove, she said, 'I'll just finish clearing out my clothes, then we'll see if we can find something in the attic for me to wear.' But she spent nearly as much time staring at herself in the mirror as she did clearing out the last of her horrible clothes.

And she couldn't help smiling. She had never, ever had a hairstyle that suited her as much.

★ ★ ★

A short time later, Dot opened the front door and found Sam Braxton standing there, looking nervous. 'I'm sorry to trouble you, love, but I was speaking to Betty Winters and she thought . . . I wondered if . . .'

He kept twisting a handkerchief round and round in his hands, looking so nervous she guessed what was coming.

'I wondered if I could borrow a couple of books like Betty did. Do you think Miss Beadle would let me, Dot?'

That dratted library thing again, Dot thought. But she couldn't send Sam away. He had enough troubles and was a real hero where his wife was concerned, and him nearly eighty. 'I'll fetch Abigail.' She went to yell up the stairs. 'Have you a minute, love? There's someone to see you.'

Abigail came running down and Sam faltered out his request, still twisting that handkerchief, his voice husky with nervousness.

'Why don't you come inside and you can tell me what sort of books you enjoy.'

'Any sort. You've lent Betty some books and I'm in the same position as her. Only my wife's not got Alzheimer's. Janie's in a wheelchair after an accident years ago. She does a lot of reading and she likes romances best of all. Well, so do I actually — not the sexy ones, the gentle ones. But they have got to have a happy ending, otherwise I don't see how they can call it a romance. Sad endings leave you feeling down.'

'I agree. I enjoy reading that sort of story, too.'

'I wouldn't trouble you at such a time, only well, with the library closing, I'll not be able to borrow any books, because it's too hard for me to get into Medderby. I can leave Janie alone for an hour or even two, but I'd not risk it for half a day. They won't give me a respite carer like they give Betty for her husband, you see.'

As she stood listening to them, arms folded, Dot realised word had got round already. At this rate, they'd be supplying books to half the village. Only, how could anyone refuse to help lovely people like Betty and Sam?

'You want to borrow books regularly, is that it, Mr . . . um?'

'Yes, miss. If you don't mind. I'm Sam Braxton, but just call me Sam like everyone else does. I live opposite the minimart. In the cottage with the blue door.'

'Oh yes. It has such a pretty garden.'

He beamed at the compliment. 'Me and Janie both love flowers.'

'I'd be happy to lend you books, Sam, any time. And please call me Abigail, not miss. It makes me feel so old to be called 'Miss Beadle'.'

'You really don't mind lending me some?' He took a deep breath and added, 'Every week? I'll take good care of them, I promise you.'

'I don't mind at all. I've got hundreds of books but they're in the cellar. Let's go and look at them, see if we can find some stories that will suit you and your wife. Will you be all right on the cellar steps?'

He beamed at her, his whole body changing, looking younger and stronger. 'I'll be fine. I'm good for my age. I was just a bit nervous, like, coming here, but you're not like that old witch. Oops, sorry if that sounds rude.'

'It's an excellent description of what she was like.'

'Yes. Um, I could give you a house plant as a thank you, if you like. I take cuttings and pot my own.'

'I'd love that.'

Dot suppressed a sigh and while the other two were choosing the books, she went to get the notebook. He wasn't leaving the house without writing down what he was borrowing. She'd give each person a page of their own and tell them to come and get their books ticked off when they brought them back.

She sniggered. Fancy her acting like a librarian. She'd been a trouble to the librarian at school, always getting told off for making a noise. She wished she could go back and apologise for that, but the poor woman was long dead. She still didn't do a lot of reading but she knew how the books helped people who couldn't get out and about much.

'We'll go down and choose some books, and I'll bring up another bagful at the same time,' Abigail was saying. 'I'm starting to move my own books into the room we call the library, you see.'

'I'll carry a couple of bags up for you as well, miss, um, Abigail.'

We'll have people knocking on the door morning, noon, and night, Dot thought as she went back into the kitchen. *Oh well, it's a poor look-out if we can't help one another.*

As she worked, she listened for the others coming back up the stairs. At last she heard voices and darted out with the notebook. 'Write the titles of those books down, Sam, so we'll know who's got what.'

He nodded, then noticed how the hall table he was leaning on wobbled and bent closer to examine its legs. 'I could fix this for you if you like, Abigail. I used to be a cabinet maker.'

'That'd be wonderful. It's such a pretty table.'

'Eighteenth century, I should think. There's only one thing: I'll have to bring Janie with me when I do it, if you don't mind. I can't leave her for too long. She won't be any trouble.'

'I'd be very happy to meet her and if you wheel her in through the back door, you won't have to try to get her chair up the front steps. It's made for it because my father was in a wheelchair towards the end.'

'Do you have any tools?'

'A few. They're in the old stables.'

'All right if I take a quick look at them, see if you've got what I need?'

'I'll show you the way, Sam,' Dot said firmly. She turned to Abigail. 'You need to get up to the attic and

105

sort some clothes out. We want you looking your best tomorrow night.'

'Oh yes. I'd forgotten.'

'Go on! I'll be up in a few minutes to see what you've found. If I find anything useful to Sam for this job, I'll lend them to him, shall I? We'll grab a cup of tea and a piece of my lemon drizzle cake after I've finished with him.'

She watched Abigail run lightly up the stairs. That girl always thought about others more than herself, and it was going to change, Dot promised herself. Unfortunately Abigail couldn't be madly interested in Philip Danvers if she was this careless about how she dressed to go out with him. Pity. He'd make a very suitable husband. A bit quiet, though, and had grown-up children so probably wouldn't want to try for others. Surely there'd be time for Abigail to have one child at least? Dot was quite determined to find her a husband and give her the chance of a family — among other things.

'Your Abigail isn't at all what I expected,' Sam said in a low voice. 'She always seemed very cool and distant before.'

'She's a good lass. The best. She was wonderful with her father and no one else would have stayed with that nasty stepmother of hers for years. But she had to learn not to let her emotions show to that witch.'

He nodded and finished writing down the four titles then followed her meekly out to the old stables at the back. She showed him the tools and he began stroking them, muttering words like 'wonderful' and 'I never thought I'd hold one'. Then he looked at her. 'Some of these are quite valuable.'

'Really?'

He nodded. 'A few of them are worth a couple of hundred pounds each.'

She clutched his arm. 'Don't tell Abigail!'

'What?'

'She has to have the house and contents valued for them death duties. If you and I could hide these or take them home, they'd not be counted in the final total. I don't want her to be left penniless.'

'Well, I've got a very secure workshop. I'd be happy to look after the best ones for you.'

'Thank you.' And Dot, who never did such things, kissed him suddenly on the cheek and shed a few happy tears. Fate seemed to be bringing a few good things Abigail's way, and about time too.

She mopped her eyes. 'I'd better get back. You bring your van round and load it with the tools you think are valuable, then show yourself out.'

He looked at his watch. 'I'll just have a quick glance at the rest. The neighbour's sitting with Annie but she won't mind if I'm a few minutes late.'

Dot hurried up to the attic, determined to find something pretty for her girl to wear. Abigail was no longer a girl, really, but she seemed it sometimes, she was so naïve about the real world.

Christmas was coming up in a few weeks. Dot was getting more and more determined that it should be the best Christmas ever, because the last few had been absolutely miserable. A really magical Christmas, with holly and mistletoe and presents — yes, and some of the new friends her girl was making could come round for drinks. Why not? There were a few other lonely people in the village. Could she arrange a little party without Abigail finding out? Dare she do that?

She could try, couldn't she?

Abigail stared round the attic, wondering where to begin. Before she'd even taken a step forward, a light began to glow in one corner. She tensed. It wasn't . . . Yes, it was.

Juliana appeared, misty at first, but becoming clearer, though still slightly transparent, as they always were. She was dressed in what appeared to be 1930s clothing. Different garments from last time, but she looked as elegant as she had in the family photos. Ghosts must be able to change what they wore — or did they only appear to have bodies and be wearing clothes because people saw what they expected to? Oh, who knew. And what did it matter anyway?

They looked at one another for a minute or two, then Abigail blurted out, 'Would you, um, mind if I borrowed some of your clothes? Only, I've got a date tomorrow.'

'I shall be delighted. I could sense that someone had been thinking about me so I came to find out what was going on.' She frowned at Abigail. 'About time we did something about your clothes. I hate to see a descendant of mine so badly turned out.'

'I didn't choose these. It was my stepmother.'

'I know. I saw her. But you could surely have refused to wear them. Why didn't you?'

'It wasn't worth the fuss. She could make life highly unpleasant. And she was the one with the money, so she'd simply have refused to pay for anything else.'

Juliana sighed. 'You're too gentle, Abigail. You should have left her.'

'I couldn't. The house needed me. I was the only one left to look after it.'

'I suppose you're right, but we can remedy matters now. What sort of clothes are you looking for?'

'Something casual. We're only going to the pub for a meal and a drink.'

'Who are you going with?'

'Philip Danvers. He's a lawyer, new to the village.'

Juliana nodded. 'Lawyers can make very suitable husbands.'

'This is just a date and anyway — he's not my type, not in that sense.'

'Still hankering after Lucas Chadwick?'

'I'd rather not talk about that, if you don't mind.'

Juliana studied her, head on one side, and said softly, 'Then I won't tease you.' She stood for a minute at the end of a row of suitcases and trunks, looking thoughtful, then moved to stand beside a big trunk. 'I'm not Roderick, I can't move heavy physical objects here, so you'll have to open this for me.'

Abigail pushed the lid open. 'Oh, what lovely materials! I didn't know these were here.'

'You could have been wearing them for years if you'd stood up to your stepmother, but I wasn't going to let her get her hands on my things. We did *not* approve of her marrying your father, you know. She might have been tolerably pretty when she was younger, and I admit she did love him — in her own way — but she was a selfish shrew once she'd made sure of her position.'

'My stepmother was pretty?'

'Passable. Why do you think your father married her? Pretty face, pretty ways when they were courting. That soon changed.'

'I always wondered how they got together. My father never said an unkind word about her but after he died, she refused even to talk about him, got tears in her eyes. That made it easier to stay.'

'Well, let's not waste our time talking about *her*. She's gone and good riddance. My maid packed my clothes away carefully after I was killed in the car crash. I watched her do it.' She let out a musical trill of laughter. 'Don't look so horrified, dear. After all, I wouldn't be here talking to you if I wasn't dead and I'm quite used to it now, though I did think at the time it wasn't fair that I should die so young. Anyway, it was partly my own fault. Algy, my fiancé, wasn't a very good driver and I should have known better than to let him go so fast in his new car. I died, but *he* only broke one arm.'

Abigail shivered, wondering how anyone could talk so matter-of-factly about their own death.

'Now, there should be some mulberry-coloured trousers. Hurry up! No, don't drag everything out. Look down the side for the colour I tell you, then lift the top layers up and pull the trousers out carefully.'

Following the sharply issued instructions, Abigail removed two pairs of tailored trousers, the other pair a nice simple black, and several jumpers, some of them with matching cardigans long enough to be acceptable to wear again.

'There's a skirt somewhere, a flowered silk in matching cherry-coloured tones — I always loved it. Oh, I do miss eating cherries! And drinking champagne! I ache sometimes for a glass of bubbly.' Juliana sighed and stared into space for a moment or two, then drew a deep breath. 'Well, I've chosen to hang around here, so I can't complain. Come on. We have to get you looking your best.'

Abigail followed instructions and soon had a few

pieces of clothing spread out.

'That skirt will go nicely with that cardigan when you don't want to wear trousers. Well, what are you waiting for? Start trying them on.'

Abigail hesitated.

Juliana rolled her eyes. 'You *are* wearing underwear, aren't you?'

'Of course I am! Only it's . . . old-fashioned and faded.'

'Then I'm not going to see anything naughty, am I?' She chuckled. 'We don't often go into bathrooms, because we aren't voyeurs, or bedrooms, especially when it's married couples. I've seen your underwear drying on the line, though. It's probably quite warm in winter, but personally, I'd rather shiver and wear something pretty.'

Before Abigail could answer, footsteps announced the arrival of Dot, who looked at her in puzzlement. 'I thought I heard you talking to someone.'

'I was.'

'Them ghosts again?' She looked round again as if expecting something dangerous to pounce on her.

'Just one ghost this time — Juliana. She's been helping me sort out some of her clothes.' Abigail indicated the pile on another trunk.

'She has good taste, then.'

'Stop chatting to your maid and try them on,' Juliana said sharply. 'I haven't got all day. It's very tiring talking to living people, you know.'

Abigail answered Dot's unspoken question. 'She says to get on with it and try the clothes on. Please turn your backs.'

She tried on the trousers, put on a spun silk and cashmere matching jumper and cardigan and cleared her throat. 'I'm ready.'

Her two helpers turned round and nodded approval.

'There's that mirror at the far end,' Juliana said. 'The one with the broken corner. Go and look at yourself in it.'

Dot glanced in the direction of her young friend's stare, saw nothing then swallowed hard as a piece of material fluttered slightly for no reason, as if someone was waving to her. Abigail had spent too many years of avoiding looking closely at herself in mirrors so still hesitated.

'You look lovely,' Juliana said softly. 'You must be exactly my size, because everything fits you perfectly. And I love your new hairdo.'

'You do? Really?'

'Yes, really. Go on. Be brave and take a look.'

Abigail walked slowly across the attic and stared at herself in the mirror. She had never looked so good. She twisted to and fro, beaming at her reflection.

Dot came to stand beside her and finger the cardigan. 'You look beautiful. I mean it, really beautiful. And your ancestor's clothes are gorgeous, too. Tell her she has — or should I say had? — good taste.'

Juliana chuckled. 'Tell her I can hear what she says and thank her for the compliment. If I wasn't so tired, I'd show myself to her.' She sighed as she watched Abigail give Dot a big hug. 'I really miss being hugged.'

Abigail blew her a kiss.

'That's nice. Now hurry up! There are some skirts and a two-piece outfit which may be all right, now I come to think of it. You're so lucky. There's more freedom to wear what you want these days than when I was young.'

'How do you know?'

'I wander round London sometimes because I like to keep up to date with what fashionable people are wearing. You really ought to buy some jeans, you know. They're like a uniform nowadays. Everyone wears them. I wish I'd had a chance to try them. They look so comfortable.'

She broke off, turned and looked into the distance as if listening to someone, then said, 'I have to go now.'

She vanished instantly.

'Oh, my!'

Dot looked at Abigail. 'What's wrong?'

'Juliana's gone. Poof! Just like that.'

'Good thing too. Makes me nervous, seeing you talking to nobody.'

'I know you will understand if you see me doing it, but I'll have to be careful not to do it when other people are around.'

★ ★ ★

Gerard Liddlestone was glad to be allowed home from the hospital. He still felt very fuzzy-brained, but they'd told him strokes often did that to you and things would most likely get better. He hoped they were right. He let his wife fuss over him for a few moments, then said he'd love to be left alone for a while.

Renée smiled in understanding. 'You always did like having time for yourself, didn't you, love?'

He nodded because he hated the way he dribbled when he tried to speak for too long. Oh, the indignities of old age! When she'd gone, he lay quietly, enjoying a bird singing intermittently outside his bedroom window — he must ask Renée to put some feed out for them. That had been one of his jobs. Sunlight shone on the cut glass bowl on the chest of drawers, and little rainbows shimmered round the room from the crystal window pendant he'd bought Renée once when they were on holiday.

It was so good to be home!

He woke with a start, saw where he was and realised he'd dozed off. Something smelled wonderful. He smiled. Ah! Renée was making his favourite tomato soup. How delicious that would be after the ghastly hospital food.

There was something hovering at the edge of his mind, something he needed to check. What was it? No, he couldn't remember. Well, Philip was a very capable fellow. He could be trusted to deal with all the business stuff and the paperwork for it was there in the office.

He hoped he would gradually remember what had been left unfinished, and he was sure he would feel better once he could check everything with Philip. He hadn't meant to retire quite yet, just go part-time for a while, but now he'd have no choice. Renée had made him promise to do it. Let alone he wasn't having people seeing him dribbling, he was having trouble pronouncing some words properly.

They'd told him that with therapy he'd be able to speak nearly as well as before and move better, especially if he did the exercises rigorously. He was praying that they weren't just jollying him along. *He* would decide when to go out in public again, though. As for doing anything fancy for Christmas, forget it. He'd managed to get that through to Renée and she'd said she'd not force him to do anything he didn't want.

He was so lucky to have her. She'd been his best

friend as well as his wife ever since they met. Talk about a *coup de foudre*. He'd seen her across the room, and a lightning strike wasn't much faster than the way he'd fallen instantly in love with her.

He fell into a doze, smiling at the thought of her.

8

Sam drove home with the four books he'd borrowed bumping about on the passenger seat next to him in a carrier bag and the wonderful old tools clinking gently in the cardboard boxes he'd laid them in carefully.

He was still smiling at the way Dot was poking her nose into that nice young woman's affairs now that old Ma Beadle was dead. She'd manage the queen, Dot Eakins would, but even she hadn't been able to manage that old witch. That lass was going to have the best Christmas of her whole life, if he was any judge, and he and Janie wouldn't do badly, either. They had a few good friends still alive.

He braked gently as someone deep in thought looked like stepping off the pavement in front of the library. When he realised who it was he stopped the car and opened the window on the passenger side, leaning across for a chat, because this was another person going through hard times.

'Hey, Lucas. Watch where you're going, lad. Have you been arranging your next computer course after this one?'

His companion scowled in the direction of the library. 'I thought I'd done that already, but I've just been told they're cancelling the one that was supposed to start this week because they're closing the library. They might have let me know before this. It's a bit late to find anywhere else to hold one and people are going to be so disappointed.'

'You only do the course for three days and they're

116

not closing the library fully for two weeks according to the notice. Surely they could fit in one last group?'

'Apparently not. They have to start clearing out the library. All ten customer computers are going early next week unless I want to buy them. They're cheap enough, could have a lot of life left with my technical knowledge to maintain and upgrade them, but where would I put them? I haven't got room for them at home.'

Sam shook his head sadly. 'Nor have I. One or two maybe, if that's any help, but not ten of them, especially now that I'm looking after these tools for a friend. It's a terrible thing for the village, this library closure. So unfair. I'd booked a place on your course and my daughter was all set to look after her mother for me during those three days, then I could teach Janie what I've learned. I'm sure she could manage a computer with a bit of adaptation.'

'She could have attended a course herself, surely?'

Sam scowled. 'That mean old devil who runs the library said it'd be too risky, Janie being in a wheelchair and all. She might roll it over, get hurt and sue them in her wild excitement. As if I'd let her do anything risky. And she's had years to learn to handle that wheelchair. Eh, the library has gone steadily downhill since he was put in charge, it has that. He seems to despise his customers.'

'If I can find somewhere else to hold courses, your Janie will be welcome to attend.'

Sam nodded but sighed. 'If only.'

Lucas leaned one arm on the side of the car. 'How are you going to get your supply of books now, Sam? I could run you into Medderby about once a week, if you could find someone to stay with Janie. I could fit Janie into the car but I know she finds the jolting of vehicles hard to take for long. My business there will take me a couple of hours or more each time, I'm afraid.'

'I can't afford to spend that much time hanging around, and we don't like to impose on people's generosity. Anyway, there's no need. Abigail Beadle's letting me borrow her books and she has a lot of them, so me and Janie are fixed for the time being. Actually Abigail was wanting to come to your course so she'll be disappointed as well. She's planning to buy herself a computer now the old lady isn't there to smash it up.'

Lucas gaped at him. 'Smash it up?'

'That's what Dot told me the old witch threatened to do if Abigail brought one into the house.'

'She'd never have done it.'

'She would, you know. She could be vicious. You ask Dot. It's a real shame about that computer course, though.' Sam's voice softened. 'We'll not only miss the course but you'll miss the company.'

'I will. I also enjoyed feeling useful again when I ran the first one. I may not be able to hold down a full-time job —'

'*Yet*,' Sam corrected.

'OK, yet. But I could manage part-time if I'm careful. The ME is a lot better now.' He might not need the money but Sam was right: he did need the company.

Lucas shrugged and started to move on, but Sam had a sudden idea and yelled, 'Hang on, lad. If you had somewhere to store those computers, could you afford to buy them?'

'Yes, easily.' The people here had no idea how much

he was worth since he'd sold his business and he was keeping that to himself.

'They've got some new industrial units just off Brompton Road. I don't think they're all let yet. You could get one of those.'

'Thanks for the tip. I'll look into it.'

'And Ashgrove House is hardly used these days. Why not ask if you can hire one of the rooms there?'

Lucas frowned. 'It's a thought.'

'Do it. That would benefit Abigail financially. Dot says she has to be very careful with her money — she was going to find out what sort of computer she should buy.'

'Tell her not to go to Cheetham's in Medderby, then. They'll sell her something too fancy for her needs and as expensive as they can make it.'

'I'll do that. I'm going back to the big house tomorrow to repair her hall table. Nice little table it is, too.'

'I hope she's paying you.'

Sam gave him a very firm look. 'Lucas lad, I know you've had a hard time of it in the past year, but you're too young to turn so bitter.'

'I'm thirty-eight. That's not young. Though it feels too young to be a damned invalid!'

The old man gave one of his gentle laughs. 'It seems young to me. Janie and I are about to turn eighty, over double your years. And to answer your question, of course I'm not letting Abigail pay me. She's lending us her books, isn't she? She did that before I offered to mend the table, too. So we're both helping one another. As neighbours should.'

'The Beadles aren't famous for helping others.'

'Stop saying things like that. It was the old witch who treated you badly. Well, she didn't help anyone but herself, that one didn't. Them as are Beadles born have helped lots of folk over the years; my grandad told me about them helping *his* father. You're too young to have known old Mr Beadle, the grandfather of Miss Abigail. Lovely fellow he was. And her father was all right too, till he married the old witch. His first wife was a much nicer woman. Pity she died so young.'

He glanced at his watch. 'Well, I must get off home now. Janie will be watching out for me. Pop in for a cup of tea sometime, but not till you're in a better mood. I don't want you bringing a miserable face to visit my Janie.'

Lucas smiled. 'You don't let anyone make your beloved unhappy. You're a real hero, you are, the way you look after her.'

Sam could feel himself flushing. 'Get on with you! It's a pleasure to look after her. She may be in a wheelchair, but my Janie is still good company. The very best. There's nothing wrong with her brain.'

★   ★   ★

Lucas stood and watched the old man drive away. He'd been in a foul mood all right, and Sam hadn't hesitated to call him on it.

The old chap was as near to a grandfather as Lucas ever had. The devoted way Sam cared for his disabled wife was a lesson to anyone about what made a really good person. They didn't give Olympic medals for such quiet devotion, but if they did Sam would be heading for gold.

Lucas sighed as he walked along the street. He'd better buy some groceries and cheer himself up by

120

visiting the local bookshop. You could buy books online, but you couldn't easily browse their contents or find other books you'd never have thought of, on topics that were unconnected with what you usually read. It was only a small bookshop but it carried a very varied stock and he visited it every week or two, usually buying at least two books.

What was he going to do with his life now, though? He'd really enjoyed designing and running the first Introduction to Computers course and the participants had given him some ideas for doing some other worthwhile training for non-computer folk, who were half-afraid of touching a computer when they started.

As he drew near Ashgrove House on his way back home, he stopped to let a car pull out of the drive and studied its driver in shock. Abigail Beadle. He'd seen her a couple of times in the distance but something was different about her today. Her hairstyle. That was it.

He let out a short bark of bitter laughter. He reckoned it'd take stronger magic than a new hairstyle to make a modern Beadle be as kind to people as Sam was. But then he was prejudiced against the family, after what the old witch had done to him and his mother, kicking them out of their house for no good reason other than to separate him from her precious stepdaughter.

And had Abigail tried to stop it? No, she hadn't! She hadn't protested or done anything. What's more, for all that she was supposed to be their friend, she hadn't so much as phoned them to say goodbye, let alone answered his letter suggesting the two of them meet.

His mother had faded away in that tiny council flat

after having a large garden. And he hadn't made his money in time to buy her something better. When they'd tried to find houses with gardens to rent near the village where their friends were still living, every application had been knocked back, even though his parents had been renting in the area for over twenty years, all their married life in fact, and never once been late with the rent.

It had given him great pleasure to buy his old home at a knockdown price when the old witch was struggling to pay the inheritance tax after her husband had died. He shouldn't have done it because going back to live there had stirred up a lot of feelings he'd thought long gone. Only, nowhere else except this particular village felt like home.

He kicked a stone out of his way, watching it clatter against the perimeter wall of the big house. He'd come down with ME so suddenly. No one seemed to understand why it struck some people like that. There wasn't just one cause and therefore no single cure, which was why it was called a 'syndrome'.

He'd been so weak in the early days that he could hardly crawl out of bed, let alone run his business, and had slept about eighteen hours a day whether he wanted to or not, falling asleep sitting bolt upright more than once when he tried mind over matter. He'd had no choice but to sell his business to a company he thought of as 'the sharks' when they came sniffing round.

It wasn't till he'd threatened to close down the business completely rather than sell that the sharks had given him a decent price and an ongoing share of the royalties on what were mostly his own programs and apps. For that he'd had to agree not to contact his former employees, and as they were also his friends he'd been very lonely. But at least they still had jobs and knew why he wasn't around — and he'd had money coming in to see him through this illness and help build a new life.

He was just about right again now, since sorting out a surprising number of food and chemical intolerances. He had money set aside and had even begun working on a new software program. It still needed a lot of fiddling around with but it looked promising — and fun. It'd take a few more months' work to finalise it and work out all the glitches.

The main problem now was that he wasn't a loner by nature. If he didn't have the classes, he'd have to find something else to do that brought him into contact with people. Something worthwhile.

Damn the bean counters and their cutbacks! Closing libraries could only save them peanuts, but the human cost would be huge, especially to oldies and youngsters.

To his surprise, he really enjoyed chatting to the older people of the village and surrounding area. He enjoyed their company, the tales they told of times past, their different and often refreshing views on the modern world.

After the first course he'd helped a couple of them set up their brand-new machines, sharing their delight in buying and using computers. What the hell was he going to do with himself now?

In the meantime, he'd go for a walk. Gentle exercise was important to build up his strength, he'd been told, so he left the car behind whenever he could.

★ ★ ★

As Lucas continued on his way, he passed the local storage units, half a dozen small places, all let out already and noted down who to contact to rent one. It'd be impossible to hold classes there, but he did need a proper workshop, with a good Internet connection and a suitable power supply, not to mention somewhere to store the computers.

Was Sam right? Could he hire a room at Ashgrove House to hold classes in? Did he want to even try?

He came to a sudden halt as he bumped into someone and felt two hands pushing against his chest. He opened his mouth to apologise and shut it again when he saw Dot Eakins scowling at him.

'You never did watch where you were going when you were thinking about something, Lucas Chadwick.'

'Nice to see you too, Dot.' He tried to move on but she grabbed hold of his sleeve.

'Now that I've caught you, I want the answers to some questions.'

'Could we do this another time, please? I need to sort something out in my head.'

'No, we can't. You've been avoiding me ever since you came back to live in the village, so now is probably my only chance.' Her grip tightened and she shook him slightly. 'I want to know why you didn't get in touch with Abigail before you took off into the wide blue yonder the first time. I'd have sworn you two were in love.'

'I did try. I wrote her a letter.'

She frowned. 'Well, if you did, it never arrived.'

'I guessed that later but at the time, when she didn't try to get back to me, I felt I knew where I stood. She was lined up with the other side.'

'I doubt you knew anything with accuracy. Young men don't know which way is up half the time, especially when their hormones and pride are both involved.'

What did you say in response to something like that? He knew what he'd like to say, but unfortunately he'd been brought up to be polite to older ladies.

'What about after her father died? You didn't even write to offer your condolences, Lucas, and I know you were still in touch with other people in the village.'

'I did write. I knew how much she loved him and I had a lot of respect for him myself.' He'd spent hours on his letter, trying to get it just right. 'She didn't reply to that one, either, and I sent it registered post. I got a message to say it had been delivered.'

Dot frowned at him. '*She* didn't receive it. There were a lot of condolences letters, but nothing from you.'

'How do you know that?'

'She told me she hadn't heard from you and cried on my shoulder. She's always come to me when she's upset about something.'

He opened his mouth then shut it again, unsure whether to believe her or not. As she continued to wait for an answer, he muttered, 'All water under the bridge now, Dot. It's several years since Abigail's father died and we've both got on with our lives.'

'It might be years, but from the way you were staring towards her just now when she drove out — yes, I was looking out of the window — you're still attracted. You haven't married and neither has she.' She let go of his sleeve and threw her hands in the air. 'Nearly twenty wasted years! That has to end before it's too late.'

125

'Too late for what?'

'Too late for her to have a child.'

That was so blunt it took his breath away. Dot was right about one thing, though. He'd told himself many times to move on and find someone else to marry, because he too had wanted to have children, but he hadn't been able to fancy anyone else in the necessary way.

Dot's expression softened and so did her voice. 'Some people fall in love only once and it's for life. I think you're both that sort of person. You really ought to try your luck again.'

'As if I'd set myself up for another fall.'

'Life's full of falls, lad. What does the song say? Something about picking yourself up. You can do a lot still, not just sit around moping. And now, I'd better get back. I've got a lot to do.'

He shrugged and was about to move away when he again caught sight of Ashgrove House, standing at the end of its tree-lined drive, looking as elegant as ever. It had lots of rooms, some big ones too. Was Sam's suggestion worth following up?

He swung round to face Dot. 'What's Abigail going to do with the house now?'

'Nothing she can do. She'll probably have to sell it to pay the taxes. That's upsetting her big time, as you can imagine.'

He looked at her thoughtfully, then moved on briskly before he said anything stupid. He was sometimes tempted to act impulsively but had learned the hard way never to act on his initial idea. You didn't win business contracts by being careless and you could never completely trust rivals. He could trust his own brain, though, as long as he gave it time to work through a problem properly. He walked slowly home, frowning and thinking hard.

He loved living in the village again, didn't want to go anywhere else, didn't need to financially, either. But he did want to do something useful, something that would help people.

And there might just be a way.

It was far too soon to think beyond that. He'd have to see Abigail first. Dare he risk that?

★　★　★

'Hey, Lucas! Wait!'

When he turned round, irritated at the thought of another encounter that would delay him, he saw Harry Blair hurrying towards him and his heart sank. This was a meeting he'd rather have avoided. In the past he and his old rival from school had had a couple of minor punch-ups and they'd been stiffly polite the few times they'd seen one another since leaving school.

He nodded, vowing to be no more than speedily polite. He wanted to get home and think the situation and its possibilities through very carefully indeed.

'Just the man I've been trying to catch up with,' Harry said cheerfully. 'My mother wants to go on your next computer course. My auntie Cathy went to your first one and she's lit up by it, says you explained it so clearly even she understood what to do — and she's been afraid of computers for years.'

'Ah, well. The council is closing down the library, so I'm afraid they've cancelled the course.'

Harry's smile vanished and the scowl he had worn for most of his youth replaced it. But this time at least

127

the anger wasn't directed at Lucas.

'You've been doing some real good here, and so has the library. Why the hell are they closing it down?'

'To save money, why else?'

'What they'll be saving is nothing compared to what they're happy to spend on other amenities, like that stupidly elaborate skateboard park. Well, that settles it. I'm definitely going to stand for council next time. I'm not having them wasting my rates money.'

'Good. If that's part of your platform I'll vote for you.'

Harry continued to scowl at him. 'Surely there's somewhere else you could hold a course?'

'Not sure. Working on that. I'll let you know if I succeed. I also need to get hold of some computers if I'm going to do this regularly, you see. They've offered me the ones in the library quite cheaply.'

'Well, let me know if you sort it out. I don't mind paying extra for Mum to get a place. It'll make a good Christmas present for her.'

'OK.' Lucas turned and walked off, hoping no one else would stop him.

He dumped his shopping at home, grabbed a quick snack then went out again and began another circuit of the village. Cold air kept the head clear and he'd always walked his way into ideas. Half a mile further on, he admitted to himself that Dot might have a point about how he felt about Abigail.

If so, following up on Sam's suggestion could prove to be more important than anything he'd done in his whole life.

9

When Dot came to work the following day and said they had a sale on at the dress shop in the village, Abigail stood still, then gave in to temptation. 'Just what I need. Will you come with me this afternoon to choose some clothes? I haven't bought any jeans since I was a teenager and I'm frightened of getting something that's unflattering for a woman my age.'

'My pleasure. It's about time you dressed decently.'

They spent a happy hour in the shop, buying jeans and T-shirts and sweaters at nicely reduced prices. Abigail didn't dare stay longer there or she might have spent far too much.

'You're sure you don't want anything else?' Dot whispered.

'I can't afford anything else.'

'OK. Pay for it and we'll take them home and you can change what you're wearing straight away. I don't want to see you dressing like an old scarecrow ever again.'

'I definitely won't, Dot.'

As she waited to turn right into the drive afterwards, a man who looked very angry stopped to let the car pass. She waved him on and he took two steps then stopped dead in the middle of the entrance, gaping at them, his mouth falling open in shock. She got a good look at him then and recognised who he was. 'Why's he staring at me like that?' she whispered to Dot.

'You look like a new woman.'

'I don't look *that* different.'

129

'You do, love. You look ten years younger, for a start.' And far prettier, but no use telling Abigail that. She'd not believe it. The man suddenly seemed to realise he was blocking their way and moved onto the pavement. As Abigail turned slowly into the drive, he stayed where he was, still watching them as intently as she was staring at him.

Then the moment was past and she watched in her rear-view mirror as he walked away at such a brisk pace he was almost running.

'Lucas looks very different, doesn't he? A lot older and thinner. And he looks a bit weary.'

'Not surprising, Abigail love. He had that horrible ME really badly, poor chap. I heard he couldn't work and lost the company he'd started. It had been doing quite well, too.'

'You never mentioned that before.'

'Your stepmother forbade me to tell you any details, threatened to dismiss me if I did. I knew she'd do it, too. It was one of her no-cross boundaries.'

'Her spite was her prime motivator in later life, wasn't it?'

'Yes. Ironically, after your father died, it was Lucas who bought the cottage his family used to live in. He was the only one offering enough to pay off the death duties, so she had to accept.'

'I wonder why he did that?'

'Who knows? He's moved back there now.' She hesitated then added, 'And you had enough on your plate since your stepmother's last illness began. I wasn't going to give you something else to worry about.'

'Why would I worry about him?'

'We both know why.'

Abigail didn't even try to respond to that. She

couldn't seem to get her head round Lucas being so ill. He'd always been vibrant and energetic, very different from her quieter nature. And yet they'd got on well. Now, he looked bone weary and much older.

Dot got out at the kitchen door and waited for Abigail to switch off the motor and join her. As they went in together she said slyly, 'You had quite a thing about Lucas when you were a teenager, sneaking out to meet him.'

'Until he went away to university and we quarrelled about me not going too, as we'd planned. But I couldn't go with him, for Dad's sake.'

'That was just after your stepmother took over management of the estate, wasn't it?'

'Yes, but I asked Dad whether he'd ordered them to be turned out of their house and he said they'd gone of their own accord. He'd never have lied to me.'

'He wouldn't, no, but he'd just been diagnosed with that horrible Parkinson's, hadn't he, and she'd taken over some of the business stuff? Maybe he didn't know the truth.'

'I did wonder later whether she'd turned them out, but that wouldn't have prevented Lucas from contacting me, surely?'

'Unless someone paid him to keep quiet and he did, for his parents' sake. Not to mention Edwina intercepting his letters to you.'

'Did she do that?'

'I have no proof but he told me she must have done. Who else could it have been here?'

There was dead silence then Abigail shrugged. 'Well, it's all academic. Nearly two decades have passed since then. I'm sorry he's been so ill, though.' She didn't speak again till she'd put the kettle on, then asked hesitantly, 'Even my stepmother wouldn't have gone to those lengths, surely, Dot?'

'She would, you know. She always had to get her own way, whatever it took.'

'You didn't like her, did you?'

'No. It was you and your father I stayed for. You most of all. Even so, I'd have walked out on her like that' — Dot snapped her fingers — 'if she'd treated me badly, and she knew it. So she was always careful not to push me too far because she'd have found it hard to get anyone else to come and work for her. People knew what she was like.'

'I can guess now why she went to such lengths to get rid of Lucas. Back then, I was too worried about Dad to think straight about anything.'

'As you say, though, water under the bridge now. If you let yourself get upset about old quarrels and nasty tricks, you'll never be able to focus on enjoying the rest of your life. She's gone and I doubt she'll be resting in peace.'

'Yes, but he should have —'

'Let it go and move on now, love. You each should have trusted the other and done something about the situation, and neither of you did.' She looked at the clock. 'About time you got ready for your date with Philip, don't you think? And I need to be off home.'

'Can't miss your soapie night, can you? What is that Meela Berring character up to now?'

'Stop trying to change the subject.' She cast a sly glance at her companion as she added, 'Make an effort with Philip. He'd be a very suitable husband for you.'

She paused but when there was no response to this, said lightly, 'I hope you're hungry. They do a really nice meal at the Golden Rose.'

'I'm not sure I feel like going out tonight. Even with Mr Suitable.'

Dot set her hands on her hips, which she only did when utterly determined about something. 'You're going if I have to tie you up and frogmarch you to the pub myself.' Her voice softened and became coaxing. 'Aw, come on! You'll enjoy it, I know you will. He's a really nice guy.'

'I couldn't cancel at the last minute anyway. It'd be so rude.' Abigail crossed the room to stare in the mirror that had been put up many years before so that servants could check their appearance before going into the front part of the house to serve the family. 'But if my change of hairstyle is going to make people stare like Lucas did, I'll start to wish I'd never had it done.'

'No, you won't. No woman minds looking her best.'

Abigail touched the strands at one side, ruffled them, smiling at her reflection in the mirror as they fell into place again, not rigidly or neatly but looking natural. 'I suppose not. I love the way I look now but I don't enjoy being stared at.'

'You always were too shy for your own good. And too stubborn as well at times. They'll only stare for a day or two. You've wasted a lot of years. Don't waste any more.'

'I was happy to look after Dad. He and I had always been close.'

'I know you were, love. But *she* should have been looking after him. She was his wife.'

'She didn't like touching people, let alone caring for them physically. But I do think she loved him in her own way.'

Dot banged down some beakers on the surface.

'Well, she only loved herself after he died. You should have left.'

'If I had, there'd have been no one to look after Ashgrove. And then *she* fell ill, too. She really was ill, so what was I to do?'

'Let her hire a nurse. She could have afforded it.'

'She always said there wasn't enough money for extra help for Dad till it was crucial, so I assumed there wouldn't be for herself either.'

'How convenient for her to get your services free! Now, forget her and concentrate on getting ready. I do wish I could stay to help.'

'Get off with you. Your soapie awaits.'

* * *

At six o'clock precisely someone rang the front doorbell. Abigail peeped out of the window and saw Philip standing there under the outside light. He looked distinguished, but rather solemn. She took a final glance in the mirror then went out to join him, leaving the hall light on to come back to and locking the door carefully behind her.

He smiled at her. 'You look lovely.'

'Oh. Well, thank you.'

'I hope you don't mind but I've not brought my car. I thought we could walk. It's only a couple of hundred yards along the high street and it's a fine evening, even if it is cold.'

'I'll enjoy a walk. I rarely go out in the evenings.'

'What's the menu like at the Golden Rose?'

'I don't know. I've never been there for a meal.'

He stopped walking to stare at her. 'Never! But it's just down the road and you said you used to go there

134

with your father.'

'I mean, I've not been since it changed its name and went upmarket a few years ago. And I got annoyed about them changing its name. It had been called the Golden Hind for hundreds of years, you know.'

'Why ever did they change it, then?'

'Who knows? Something to do with marketing, I should think. Everything's about marketing these days, isn't it? Dot and her friends still call it the Golden Hind.'

As they went into the hotel, he said, 'I booked a table in the conservatory. It looks out on a floodlit garden. Very pretty it is. Is that all right?'

'That'll be lovely.'

After they'd been seated and had ordered drinks, he looked at her ruefully. 'I'd better confess. This is the first time I've dated anyone since I was courting my wife.' His expression turned sad. 'She died three years ago and it's taken me a while to feel as if I'm single again. So I'm nervous and I should probably be wearing L plates.'

She smiled, suddenly feeling better than if he'd been overconfident about everything. 'This is the first time I've been out on a date for years, too, because Edwina didn't like me leaving her alone in the house after dark.'

'From what people have let fall, she sounds to have been, um, rather difficult. I didn't have anything to do with her because she died soon after I arrived in the village. It was Gerard who did her wills. She apparently kept changing them.'

'She was *very* difficult about everything.'

'Why did you stay, then?'

'You're the second person to ask me that today.

Mainly to look after the house. She'd have let it fall apart.'

'You love Ashgrove, don't you? I could see why. It's a very pretty place.'

'Yes. It's part of me and I'm part of it. It's been —' She suddenly saw Lucas come into the hotel with another guy of his own age, laughing over something. He didn't see her, but the sight of him made her feel awkward and forget what she'd been going to say.

She realised Philip was waiting patiently for her to continue and apologised quickly. 'Sorry. I just saw someone I used to know and it surprised me.'

'Who?'

'I don't think you'll know him. Lucas Chadwick. The man in the corner, laughing.'

'I've met him once. I've been going through Gerard's recent appointments. He'd seen Mr Chadwick a couple of times.'

She didn't think Lucas had seen her and she took care not to glance in that direction.

The evening passed pleasantly, the food was excellent, but something was missing between them. Even with her limited experience, she knew that.

Philip walked her home and stopped outside the front door. 'I hope you don't mind me being honest, if rather blunt. I enjoyed your company greatly but the spark isn't there between us, is it?'

She was relieved she wouldn't have to turn down a request for another date. 'No. I'm sorry.'

'Don't be. It works two ways. It'd be nice to stay friends, though, if that's OK with you?'

'Yes, I'd like that.'

When she went inside the house her footsteps seemed to echo across the tiled hall. For the first time ever she felt nervous of being on her own there, which surprised her. Perhaps it was the contrast between the bright lights and bonhomie at the pub that made her feel like that.

Then a faint light shimmered in one corner and Roderick appeared. 'I thought I'd hang around and welcome you home. There was someone prowling round the garden an hour ago, but I showed him an image of a ghost carrying its own head in one hand and he ran away yelping like a puppy. He fell over twice.'

She couldn't help laughing at the scene he'd painted. And feeling relieved to have someone keeping an eye on the place.

'Seriously, though. You need better security here. Those locks were old even in my time, but we had servants then to keep an eye on things when we were out so it didn't matter.'

In spite of his reassurances, she did a tour of the ground floor and could tell that no one had been inside. She slipped the rarely used chain locks into their hooks on the inside of the front and kitchen doors, and made sure the bolts were firmly in place on the French windows in the library.

Roderick drifted along beside her as she moved about and it was comforting to have him there.

'Thank you,' she said when she'd finished.

'My pleasure, many-greats-granddaughter. I checked upstairs, by the way, and all is peaceful.' He faded slowly, one hand raised in farewell.

It took her a long time to get to sleep, not because of security worries, but because of how the evening had panned out. For all his attempts to reassure her, she was still worrying that she'd not reacted to Philip as most women would. He was good looking by anyone's standards, so why hadn't she been attracted even a little? Who knew how such feelings were switched on? She was no expert on sex appeal. But Philip hadn't reacted to her, either. Was there something wrong with her? There must be; she'd had so few men wanting to date her. Unless her stepmother had driven others away.

Oh, who knew? That was all in the past now.

10

The following morning, James Porfrey knocked on the front door just before ten o'clock and waited for Abigail to answer it. He was looking forward to continuing to assess her family's wonderfully diverse collection of books.

When she opened the door, he stared at her in surprise, hardly recognising her. He didn't know her well enough to comment on the new hairstyle, but it was definitely an improvement. As were the casual jeans and top. 'I hope you don't mind me being a bit early.'

'Not at all. Come through to the library.'

They went to stand just inside the library and he saw her immediately start to relax. No wonder. It was a beautiful room, with high ceilings, walls of bookshelves and even one of those ladders that could be attached to rails for reaching the higher shelves. He'd certainly be using that. In previous valuations he'd found some dusty treasures languishing unloved on high shelves.

'It feels as though people have been happy in this room,' he said.

'I certainly have.'

'Do you want to stay with me, Abigail, or will you trust me to work on my own this time?'

'I've got a lot to do, James, and I know you better now, so I'll leave you to it. Ring that bell if you need anything. I'll bring you something to drink in an hour or so. Tea or coffee?'

'Coffee, please. White, no sugar.'

'Duly noted. Oh, and any of the scruffy old books that aren't worth even giving away . . . can you pile them in that corner, please? I'll be taking them down to the cellar till I work out how to dispose of them.'

'Are you going to leave the shelves empty?'

'No. I'm going to fill them with my own books. I know used paperbacks aren't nearly as attractive, but they'll feel like old friends. I only keep ones I might read again, but the numbers have still mounted up over the years.'

'I do that, too. Now, let's get down to business. Once I've finished, I'll make you an offer for some or part of this collection and I can take away the ones you don't want if you like.'

'We'll see what you find. You may not wish to bother.'

She wasn't very optimistic, was she? Well, that might mean his assessment would come as a pleasant surprise. He watched her walk out. She reminded him of a butterfly which had just hatched from its chrysalis, but didn't have the confidence to go out into the world. She was much more attractive than he'd realised before and he could feel a stirring of interest in her as a woman. He suppressed it hastily. He was here on business and anyway, he was older than her. Later, after their business was completed, well, who knew what might happen once they knew one another a little better?

He frowned. No, better not. She was in a difficult situation. He looked round, feeling as if he was settling in emotionally as well as physically. He always preferred to be left alone when valuing books. He opened his laptop and set it on a table. Walking round the room, he took out a volume here and there to sample the books, making a plan of action as he began to get some idea of the range of subjects covered.

A book slipped off a shelf and landed at his feet. He bent to pick it up and gasped in delight. It was another valuable one and in perfect condition for its age. Why had it fallen off the shelf, though? He was sure he hadn't touched it or nudged any of the books nearby. Well, he'd been a good metre away, hadn't he? He went across to his computer to check that he'd remembered the value correctly. Yes, he'd been right. A copy had been sold last year and had fetched even more than the valuable book he'd discovered last time. He hoped there would be other treasures here, for Abigail's sake as well as his own.

Humming, he started work again, jerking in shock as another book rocked to and fro on a shelf near his head. He caught it just in time. It too was valuable, though worth a bit less than the other one that had fallen.

He frowned. You'd think the place was haunted and the ghosts wanted to make sure he didn't miss anything special. He tried to laugh at the idea, but couldn't, because strange things happened occasionally in very old houses and it always made him feel somewhat uneasy. No bad things had ever happened to him, though. Well, not so far. Oh, he was being silly! It was just sheer chance that a badly balanced book should start to fall when someone started rummaging about on nearby shelves.

* * *

Just as Abigail was going to make James's coffee, there was a knock on the kitchen door. When she went to

141

answer it, she found two elderly ladies from the village looking nervous. She knew them slightly.

'Is it true?' the younger one asked.

The older sister dug her in the side. 'That's not a polite way to start.' She turned back to Abigail. 'Good morning, Miss Beadle. May we have a word with you, please?'

'Of course, Miss Courtenay. Would you like to come in?'

'Thank you.' They stood just inside the door, the younger one slightly behind her taller sister.

'I'm Jennifer and this is my sister, Penelope. We own the stationer's and miscellaneous goods shop at the other end of High Street.'

'I know who you are. I've bought things in your shop occasionally.'

'Yes. We never forget a customer.'

She'd already guessed the reason for their visit, but waited nonetheless.

'We heard that you have a large collection of paperbacks and that you're allowing people to borrow them now that the library has closed,' the shorter sister blurted out suddenly, as if she couldn't wait any longer.

'Yes, I am. Those and any other books from the library here once it's been reorganised. For the moment, just the paperbacks.'

'That's so kind of you. Would we . . . um, qualify?'

'Of course. I'd be happy to let you borrow my books.'

They both sagged in relief and exchanged quick half-smiles.

'Would today be too soon to start? Only, we've just taken our books back to the library for the final

142

time — so sad — and our niece is keeping an eye on the shop.'

'You're welcome to borrow books any time, if you find any which appeal to you, that is. Come and see what we've got. We're telling people only a couple of books each for the time being.'

'That makes four for us,' Penelope said happily. 'Oh, thank goodness! The television programmes are so awful at this time of year. Repeats of repeats. Or brand new ones with lots of violence and no older people to be seen, only younger ones with strange hairstyles and weird clothes. I get so angry at the film-makers having so little insight into real life.'

Her sister dug an elbow into her ribs and Penelope said, 'Oops. Sorry. Didn't mean to sound off at you. I just get so angry.'

She introduced them to James and explained why they were there, then gave each a page in the note-book and told them to go ahead and search. Penelope loved romances, it turned out, while Jennifer enjoyed cosy mysteries most of all, but they would both read anything, as long as it wasn't too violent or gruesome.

She left them to go through the paperbacks and went to put the kettle on for James's coffee. She was surprised at how quickly they chose some books and one of them came to find her.

'Sorry to disturb you, but we have to get back to the shop,' Penelope said.

Abigail wrote down the titles they were taking and saw them out. While she finally made the coffee for James, she smiled to think how happy she'd made the two visitors — and herself — with this small loan. She'd thought she would continue to be lonely after her stepmother died, because she knew she was rather shy with strangers. But she hadn't talked to so many people for years and they'd all been what Dot called 'dear worts', pleasant and easy to chat to.

She loved the way Dot made up different ways of using words and they always sounded so real and vivid they seemed to stick in your mind. She'd looked up 'wort' in the dictionary and found it came from 'wyrt', the old English word for plant, and was now used in beer making. Dot said Abigail was also a 'dear wort' because she was the best thing that had come from the Beadle family tree and that made her a type of plant, so never mind the beer. As far as Abigail was concerned, Dot was the best person she knew for kindness and sheer niceness but she didn't have a superlative for that.

Edwina would have had a fit at what was happening now with the books, but Abigail was enjoying helping others and was feeling more connected to the ones who lived in the village than she had for years. People talked about the magic of Christmas but the magic of her amateur library was much better as far as she was concerned. Since her father's death, Christmas had been a time she dreaded, but maybe this year, it would be quietly pleasant.

★ ★ ★

When Abigail took the mug of coffee into the library, James looked up. 'My goodness, is it refreshments time already?'

As he accepted the mug, he beamed at her, clasping both hands round its warmth because the library was distinctly chilly in spite of her switching on a rather elderly electric bar heater.

144

'I think you're going to be pleasantly surprised with my estimates. You have quite a few hidden treasures here.'

'Really?'

'Really, truly.' He eyed her, head on one side. He'd met similar situations to this before. 'Is it the thought of the inheritance taxes that's worrying you?'

'Yes. There's nothing big left to sell, you see.'

'I suppose the valuers will rate the house quite highly, it's such a beautiful place. Pity.'

'That's what I'm expecting. And if the books are valuable, I suppose I'll have to pay nearly half of the money they bring in tax as well.' She blinked away the tears which would well up every time she thought of leaving the only home she'd ever known. She should be used to that prospect by now because Edwina had frequently laughed at her for one day having to face 'the real world' and get a job, making jibes like: 'You'd better look after me, Abigail. You'll be out on your ear after I die.'

To Abigail's relief, James didn't pursue it but said instead, 'I'll need another few hours to do the job properly. Will that be all right? I'll nip out to buy some lunch and I need to visit the post office. It looks like rain so I'll go in my car.'

She was relieved that he needed to go somewhere, because she felt guilty at not offering him a sandwich. Only, she was running low on fresh food and needed to get to the shops herself, so was going to make do with cheese on toast today, using up the last two slices of bread. The trouble was, she didn't trust the ancient freezer so didn't like to keep too much food in it in case it broke down.

'That's fine by me. I'll leave you to it.'

145

When the front door knocker went at quarter to one, Abigail hurried across the hall to answer it. As she stared at the person standing there, she froze, not knowing what to say.

Lucas looked at her with that solemn expression she remembered so well. 'I think you and I have a few things to clear up. Well, we do if Dot is telling the truth, and she isn't known to be a liar.'

A sudden sprinkling of raindrops followed by an absolute downpour made her hold the door open. 'Come in quickly or you'll be soaked.'

He stood next to her in the hall as she shut the front door. The space seemed darker than usual and it reminded her of how often they'd had to meet after dark in those long-ago days when hope of love and marriage had still been alive in her. She shook off those memories. 'Shall we go into the kitchen? It's warmer there. You can hang your jacket on the hall-stand.'

'Thank you.' He did as she'd suggested.

James came out of the library just then, nodding to Lucas as if he knew him. 'I'll nip into the village now.'

'Take one of the umbrellas from the hallstand if you like,' she told him.

'Thank you. I will.'

'Don't bother knocking, just come straight in when you get back.'

She led the way towards the kitchen and Lucas followed more slowly, staring into the rooms they passed as he walked across the black and white tiles. It felt strange to have him here after all these years. He'd delivered their orders from the butcher regularly as a part-time job but that had brought him only as far as the kitchen door. She had never dared invite him into the main house because Edwina would have thrown a fit.

Lucas stopped suddenly. 'Does Porfrey being here mean you're selling your books?'

'Yes. Needs must.'

'Ah. Well, I've only heard good things about him. He'll not try to cheat you.'

'He seems very pleasant.'

She slowed down, giving Lucas time to look round because that gave her a chance to take a good look at him. They'd both been so young the last time she'd spoken to him properly and naturally the years had left their mark. He seemed to have grown taller, with an air of quiet authority. And was that really grey in the hair at his temples? Yes, it was. Well, she had a few grey hairs herself.

She was glad Dot wasn't in the kitchen to give her knowing glances, and tried to act as if Lucas was a normal visitor to the house. 'Do take a seat. Would you like a cup of coffee?'

He looked faintly surprised at that offer. 'I'd love one, if you don't mind. There's a really cold wind blowing today.'

She'd made the coffee, added sugar and handed it over before she thought of asking him how he took it. He'd been watching what she did.

'You remembered how I like it.'

'Yes.'

He took a sip. 'That's just right.'

As silence fell she tried desperately to think of something innocuous to say, but he got in first and it wasn't mere chit-chat.

'I came because of something Dot said. She told me you'd never received my letters.'

'No. I never heard from you again after you and your family moved away.'

'I wrote twice, once when your stepmother was having us thrown out of our house. I wanted to meet you and ask what was going on.'

'*Thrown out?* But my father assured me your family had left voluntarily. He'd not have lied to me.'

'My parents were paid not to say that we'd been given notice to quit. And since we were short of money in those days, they couldn't afford to turn down the bribe. That made it rather difficult for me.'

'Your mother must have been very upset. I remember how she loved her garden and how pretty it was. Where did you go?'

'We found a flat in Medderby. She could never settle there, though, and missed her garden dreadfully. It was even worse for her after Dad died the following year.'

'I heard. I was so sorry. I sent you and your mother a condolences card.'

He choked slightly on a mouthful of coffee. 'We didn't receive it.'

She could guess why. It must have been removed from the outgoing post. It sickened her that Edwina hadn't even been able to allow her to offer them that simple courtesy.

Lucas set his coffee mug down, fiddling with the handle. 'I wrote after your father died for a similar reason, offering my condolences. I sent that one by registered post and I know it was delivered. I didn't know whether you were the one who'd signed for it, though.'

'I wasn't. I never saw it.' She couldn't prevent tears welling in her eyes. It'd have meant a lot to her then. She fumbled for a tissue and couldn't find one so wiped the tears away on the tea towel.

His voice took on a sharper edge. 'Why on earth did you stay on with that woman after your dad died?'

'A lot of people have asked me that. I stayed for the house, of course. Someone had to look after it, though I couldn't afford to give it the attention it really needed. *She* would only pay for the barest minimum maintenance, enough to keep a waterproof roof over her head, she always said, and heating in the rooms she used. She usually added that I could fiddle for money after she'd gone because there would be none left by then.' She wanted to ask Lucas why he'd never married but of course she couldn't. It'd give her feelings away. 'Well, at least we can meet without animosity now that we know the truth.'

'Mmm. If you really mean that, there's a favour I want to ask you.'

Hope flared for a moment, then she realised she was being utterly stupid. 'Yes? Do go ahead.'

'Can I rent a room here for a few days, one of the bigger ones I saw off the hall? I need somewhere to run my computer workshop, you see. The librarian has cancelled it and there isn't time to find anywhere to run the one I've already organised. From the interest it's generated I could probably put on two or three more, another for beginners and a couple for continuing skills development.'

It was the last thing she'd expected to hear. 'But the library gave two weeks' notice that it was closing and yours is due to start in a couple of days, so there would still be time for your workshop to run there, surely?'

'They cancelled it even though the places were fully booked, and you're right, there would have been time to fit it in before the closure date. I'd still like to run it because I know people have made all sorts of arrangements so that they can attend. Many of them can't get to workshops elsewhere because they're carers to family members or they have other commitments. Sam Braxton suggested I ask you whether I could run one here.'

She didn't even hesitate. 'Yes, of course you can.'

He looked surprised. 'You don't mind?'

'Why should I? Which room would you like to use?'

'I don't know. I've never seen the family's rooms properly, only the kitchen and the outside areas.'

She felt guilty all over again about how he'd been treated. 'Come and look round now and work out which would be best.'

She led the way, hoping her face looked calmer than she felt. When she stole another glance at him, he was frowning at her, but she had no idea why. She took him into the drawing room, the formal dining room and what had once been the estate office, but when they went into the library, he said almost immediately, 'Here.'

'Are you sure?'

'Yes. I like how it feels and there are three tables to set the computers on.'

'There aren't many electric points, though. Well, there aren't in any of the rooms, come to think of it. The house really needs rewiring, I'm afraid. How will you manage?'

'I can remedy that temporarily as long as you refrain from using a lot of electricity in other parts of the house while I'm actually running the workshop.

150

Computers aren't very power hungry compared to things like heaters.'

She nodded. 'We can be careful.'

'How much do you want to charge?'

'I haven't the faintest idea.'

He named a sum that amazed her, it seemed so generous.

'Are you sure? That sounds a lot of money.'

A smile suddenly lit up his face, his old smile, full of genuine amusement and warmth.

'Why are you smiling? I suppose I said something stupid.' Her stepmother had often accused her of that.

'Of course you didn't. You're an intelligent woman, but you haven't changed in some ways. You're not commercially minded and you're incurably honest. You should be bargaining with me, getting the most money you can.'

She could only shrug. He was right. She knew more about the minor house maintenance tasks, local history and antiques than she did about the commercial aspects of modern life.

'It's all right, Abbie. I'd never cheat you. I'm offering to pay what I think the facility is truly worth.'

'That's all right, then. I accept.'

'Do you think Dot would cater morning and afternoon tea for us? I'd pay for her time and cover the expenses, of course.'

'I'm sure she would.'

'And do you mind Janie Braxton attending in her wheelchair?'

'Good heavens, no, not at all. Actually, there's wheelchair access via the kitchen now because Dad needed it towards the end. And the downstairs cloakroom is wheelchair accessible, too.'

'I'm sorry he got Parky's. An active man like him must have found that so hard to cope with.'

'He was frustrated at times, but didn't take out his feelings on his carers. We had to bring someone else in to help him towards the end. I couldn't do all he needed.'

'He was always fair and kind. That's why I wondered if he knew we'd been turned out for no reason. But by the time I figured that it wasn't likely he knew, he was quite ill, so I didn't do anything that might upset him. Well, my parents were both dead by then, so it was water under the bridge.'

'Thank you for even thinking that. People still say nice things about him.'

There was silence, with what felt like the same sort of understanding flowing between them as it had done in the old days. She was afraid of betraying how Lucas was affecting her, so said hastily, 'Right then. It's agreed. You go ahead and plan to hold your workshop here.'

He beamed at her. 'That's great. The first step will be for me to buy the computers.'

'Wow, that'll cost a lot for one workshop.'

'The library is offering theirs for sale cheaply and I'll use them for other workshops. There's just one other thing — you said you'd wanted to attend but your name wasn't on the list of people who'd signed up.'

'I didn't get it done in time and when I tried the workshop was fully booked. I was a bit distracted by arranging the funeral, you see.'

'Would you still like to come?'

'I'd love to. I'm in desperate need of brushing up my skills. If it's all right with you?'

'Of course it is.'

'That'd be wonderful. I shall look forward to it.'

'I'll go and get the computers sorted out, then.'

She saw him to the front door, leaning against it after she'd closed it, because her legs felt wobbly. After a few moments she pulled herself together, annoyed at her own weakness where Lucas was concerned.

She went back into the library but couldn't think why she'd come in, so sank down on a chair, closing her eyes. He was still as attractive as ever. And he *had* tried to contact her all those years ago. Oh, if only . . .

If only what? She didn't dare pursue that thought.

11

'He's very good-looking,' a voice said.

Abigail jerked upright and saw Georgiana standing nearby, looking as beautiful as ever.

'And you're still attracted to him.'

She didn't attempt to deny it. 'How can you tell?'

Georgiana smiled. 'I watched you with him years ago. As far as I can see, nothing's changed about how you feel.'

'Oh dear! I hope he couldn't tell that.'

'He isn't sure about your feelings because he's too busy trying to hide his own to see you as clearly as we do.'

'All that is just, you know, echoes of the past, how things used to be between us. We've both moved on.'

A chuckle to her other side heralded the appearance of Juliana. 'You could easily move back into a relationship again, though, and so could he. There's no law against it. Why don't you give him a bit of encouragement? See how it works out. It wouldn't take much effort to start your relationship moving. He's still attracted. Take my word for it.'

'Do you really think so?'

'Yes, definitely. And he's been as lonely as you since he moved back here. I'm sure it wouldn't take much signalling from you to restart it. One small step at a time is all it needs.'

Abigail could feel herself blushing. 'I couldn't.'

'Why not?'

'I don't know how to encourage men. I've not had

much experience. I'd probably make things worse.'

Her two companions exchanged incredulous glances. She turned to leave and get on with her day.

'Wait!'

Georgiana drifted round to bar the way out of the library and Abigail stayed where she was, not game to try to walk through her ancestor, even if she was only a phantom.

'How about we drop you a hint or two when we see a possibility? We could whisper suggestions in your ear.'

Abigail's cheeks felt even hotter. 'I'd only mess up whatever you said to do. I'm incredibly stupid about such things.'

'You're not stupid, just rather timid and lacking practice.'

She shrugged. It amounted to the same thing in the end.

'You could at least have a go. Isn't Lucas even worth a try?'

Abigail couldn't help remembering her recent vow to be more proactive about life. Was she going to fall at the first hurdle? 'Um, well, I suppose I could try. If I think of anything, that is.'

'Good girl. And don't worry. You're not on your own in this. We'll whisper hints if we see even half a chance. Promise you'll do what we suggest.'

'Um —'

'Promise! Beadle's honour.'

'Oh, all right. I promise. Beadle's honour.'

'We know you won't break that particular promise.'

And they were gone as abruptly as they'd arrived.

They couldn't just be figments of her imagination. Apart from the fact that something about them felt so utterly real, her father had seen them too and had told her about them a couple of years before he died. She would have to take great care not to speak to them when anyone else was around, though, or people would think she'd gone mad.

It was a while before she moved, then she muttered, 'I *will* try,' squared her shoulders and gave a nod to emphasise that. She was still sure she'd make things worse not better, but yes, one thing her family ghosts had said had hit home: Lucas was definitely worth taking a risk for. Oh, he was! And besides, she never broke her word.

At least she and Lucas were talking to one another again. That was surely a good sign, wasn't it? In fits and starts, not like their old easy flow of thoughts and ideas, but they were communicating at least. And his smile was as warm as ever. He had the loveliest smile. There was no one quite like him.

Then she heard James return so got on with her day. She started in the old wine store, where Edwina had stacked all the old figurines and ornaments. It had been done carelessly, with them lying on top of one another and no padding. She didn't think her stepmother had realised how valuable they were and she hadn't enlightened her. Fortunately, none of them had been broken.

She suddenly took out of hiding an ornament that she'd particularly loved. It had been removed from her bedroom one day and she knew who'd done it. Edwina had just shrugged her shoulders and said it didn't match modern décor.

After finding it, Abigail had hidden it behind a pile of dusters, wrapped in one of them. She knew her stepmother wouldn't have bothered to check such places as she gradually worked her destructive progress through the house, rearranging, changing, shoving things in the attic. Making it all look so very different.

There were always large boxes in the kitchen, saved by the frugal Dot. Abigail piled the ugly ornaments she'd removed from the main rooms into a large cardboard box, then began taking out the elegant ones and carefully washing them. Once she'd finished restoring the ones that had stood in the drawing room to their rightful places, she stepped back, smiling. She'd surely be able to keep some of her favourites if she had to leave. No, *when* she had to leave. She mustn't fool herself. If there was no money, she'd not be able to pay the taxes.

She shook her head vigorously and concentrated on making her home beautiful again. She wasn't going to think about unpleasant possibilities till she had to.

★   ★   ★

Just before four o'clock, James came to find Abigail. She was in the drawing room and was making a start on putting the smaller pieces of furniture where they had previously stood, some of them clearly for centuries before Edwina had them moved.

Philip had told her that it would take a while to sort out the details of the inheritance tax rules, so she should have a few months here before she had to sell Ashgrove House. She intended to spend those months with her home looking its best. She'd build up memories and take photos. After all, she could please herself from now on how she lived. She saw James stop in front of the last of the horrible ornaments, a group

157

of improbable dogs and other animals with huge eyes and garish colours.

'Where on earth did those ghastly things come from?'

'My stepmother.'

He didn't say anything, didn't need to; his expression showed that he shared her opinion of them. She was standing by the old sofa, which was too awkward and heavy to move on her own, waiting to see what he wanted.

'I hope you're not intending to move that huge sofa on your own.'

'Is there any chance you could help me with it?'

He studied it, head on one side. 'We can give it a go but if it's too heavy, I'm not risking damaging my back — nor will I encourage you to damage yours.'

'We'll just take it slowly and try. If I remember correctly, it's just the awkward shape that makes it difficult to move on your own. It's got old-fashioned castors on the legs.'

He came across to the other end of the sofa, pointing across the room. 'Over there, do you think?'

'Yes. That's where it used to stand before Edwina.'

To their surprise it moved easily and when they'd finished he stood back and looked round, nodding. 'I stopped to look in here earlier on my way out, and I think this room is looking much better now.'

'This is how it used to be. Thank you so much for your help. Now, did you want to see me about something?'

'Yes. I've finished going through your books and came to give you a rough idea of what I think they're worth. Let's sit down on those two big armchairs near the window and discuss things in comfort. I'm happy

158

to answer any questions afterwards.'

The amount James named astonished her and it was a few moments before she could find her voice. 'Are you sure?' she asked huskily.

'Oh yes. What's more, I always try to give a conservative estimate, so they could even be worth more. I know you're worried about money, but by the time you've sold the paintings and the antique furniture as well you should easily have enough to buy yourself a decent house at least, even if you can't keep this one.'

He waited, looking expectant, and she realised he wanted her to tell him to go ahead, so she did.

'Very well. If it's all right with you, I'll come back on Monday with some boxes and start packing.'

'Yes. That'll be fine.'

'Look, there are a few really valuable books. Do you have somewhere safe to keep them till then? I have to go on to a house party this weekend, so I'd rather not take them with me and have to leave them in the car boot. Quite a few of the other books, the ones you don't like the looks of, would make good research books, even if they're not valuable per se, so don't toss them out. I've friends in universities who'd probably be interested in some of them, but would only be able to offer you a modest amount for them.'

'Any money would be welcome.'

'There you are, then. Sorted. I'll see you don't get cheated. Oh, and I've brought you two boxes of old paperbacks that we were going to throw away. They're in the corner of your library. I've got another pile to sort out at the shop and will bring you the ones that don't have any value for us once I've gone through them.'

She beamed at him. 'That's wonderful!'

He seemed a nice man as well as erudite, and very attractive. Most men who were bald tried to hide their hair loss but he didn't seem bothered about it, and anyway he had kind eyes and such a twinkling smile, who cared? 'We have several places that might be safe for the valuable books. It depends on how many there are.'

'Come and look at them.' He led the way back to the library and she was surprised to see several piles of books on one table.

'That many?'

He nodded and told her how much the ones in that pile alone would probably fetch, adding, 'If not more.'

She could only gape at them. 'That's amazing. I doubt anyone's touched them for decades.'

'That'll be why they're in such good condition, considering their age. Do you have a couple of boxes to put them in? Oh good! I only have one with me and it's not even got a lid. I used all the other ones I had in the car yesterday and forgot to get some new ones. Actually, I didn't expect to find so many treasures here. I've thoroughly enjoyed my day.'

She walked with him to the front door, happy at the good news. 'Thank you for coming.'

Then she went to find Dot and ask her where she thought they could safely leave the books.

Dot came to study the piles, shaking her head. 'To think them dull old books are worth all that money. Why, they haven't even got pictures on the covers.'

Abigail chuckled. 'They'd not be valuable if they did have.'

'Well, I'd not have given them a second look.'

'Where do you think we should put them?'

Dot didn't hesitate. 'In the pantry. Who'd look for

books there? I've got some cardboard boxes that had food in and we can lay some packets of food across the top of the books, so even if any burglars came ferreting around they'd not think there was anything worth taking.'

'What a clever idea. Let's do it.'

'Better let me do it. I'm much better at packing than you are. Go and get some fresh air into your lungs while you can. They said on the radio it's going to rain again later. Come back in half an hour or so to help me carry the boxes.'

So Abigail did just that. No one could pack things as neatly as Dot and it'd be lovely to stretch her legs. She'd been busy all day so far. Naturally, she found herself walking across the garden to the ash grove. When she got there, she looked up and giggled at the sight of her horrible old hat, rocking to and fro. Behind it was another rainbow, its colours so luminously beautiful she stayed to feed her soul with its glory.

It was cold and she'd forgotten her gloves, but she didn't care. She'd always loved rainbows. It started to spot with rain before the half-hour was up, so she ran back to the house, filled and restored by the beauty of that place.

She needed to go to the shops soon or there would be nothing for tea.

After she and Dot had lifted up the boxes, her friend gave her a list of cleaning materials to buy as well, handed her the gloves she'd forgotten again, then wrapped a scarf round her neck.

Abigail gave her a sudden hug.

'What's that for?'

'Just for being you.'

'Well, have one back.' And Dot gave her a big hug too.

By that time they were both rather pink because neither was in the habit of showing emotions and they'd done quite a lot of hugging lately. The warmth of that quick embrace stayed with Abigail all the way to the little supermarket in the village.

When she got back, Dot had gone home and the house seemed very quiet. Too quiet.

She put everything away and wished, as she had many times before, that she had someone congenial to chat to. Maybe — No, she was wishing for the moon.

'Don't be silly!' she said aloud. 'He's just being kind to you.'

* * *

Just before nine the following morning, Abigail heard a car stop outside the front of the house, so went into the drawing room to peep out and see who it was. Unfortunately, it wasn't the congenial visitor she'd wished for yesterday evening; it was Cousin Cynthia. What on earth did that horrible woman want now? And why did she always run her car into the edges of flower beds?

Sighing, she waited to open the front door, because she wasn't in a hurry to be harangued. Indeed, she was very tempted to pretend she wasn't at home. But she knew Cynthia would go round the back, see Abigail's old car parked under the open side of the barn and start hammering on the kitchen door. Giving in to the inevitable, Abigail waited till the second knock before she opened the door.

'It took you long enough to answer the door.'

Taking her by surprise, Cynthia pushed past her into the hall and started to take off her coat. Abigail put one hand out to bar access to the coat stand. 'I'm going out shortly, so I'm afraid I can't ask you to stay.'

'You can go out if you want but I'm staying here till I've got satisfaction.'

'What on earth are you talking about?'

'Edwina's will. She assured me there was something in it for me and last night I found her note about it.' She patted her handbag and gave Abigail a challenging look, absolutely radiating triumph.

'Nothing in the will mentioned you, Cynthia. Perhaps she didn't get round to arranging it officially. After all, she was quite ill towards the end, however hard she tried not to give in to it.'

'Not too ill to think straight and make sure I knew what to expect. Anyway, I have an appointment to meet Philip Danvers here at ten o'clock to talk to him about it, so I can't leave yet.'

'You didn't think to ask me whether I'd mind you bringing him here?'

'No. You'd only have said no, and as you'll see, I have the right.'

'Why do you think you have the right?'

'You'll see. I'm not saying anything till he arrives.'

'What do you think he can do?'

'There was definitely another will made. He can help me look for it, that's what, and when we find it, he'll make sure you don't destroy it as the one at their office must have been got rid of.'

'I haven't destroyed anything!'

'Someone has, that's for sure. But I'm certain Edwina will have brought a copy home, so I intend to check the whole house for it, if necessary.'

'Oh no, you won't. In fact, I'm not having you alone in the house at all with that attitude so you will kindly leave at once.'

Cynthia struck a would-be heroic pose, failing miserably to look impressive, bearing more resemblance to a scrawny, bedraggled rat. Abigail suddenly had great trouble keeping her face straight, but her amusement quickly faded because the situation wasn't at all funny.

'I'll come and go as I please, just as I always have done here because I'm Edwina's cousin, as close a relative to the previous owner as there is. And anyway, unless you've changed overnight and found a backbone, you won't dare lay a finger on me. You'd hardly say boo to a goose. How we used to laugh at you.'

Abigail had had enough. 'Edwina's cousin or not, unless you've got a search warrant you're not looking anywhere here. Please leave my house this minute or I'll call the police.'

Her visitor immediately sat down on one of the upright chairs at the side of the hall and clutched its wooden arms so tightly her knuckles turned white. 'I'm not going anywhere till I'm good and ready, and if you try to forcibly remove me, I'll sue you for assault. Mr Danvers will make a very credible witness to that.'

The door at the back of the hall opened just then and Lucas strode across to join them.

'Or I can act as a witness that you've refused to leave Miss Beadle's house. I came to set up some of the computers, Abigail, but when I heard this person shouting I thought I'd better check that you were all right.'

He stared at the older woman, surprised that she was glaring at him as if *he* was doing something wrong.

164

'Who is this female, Abbie?

'This is my stepmother's cousin, Cynthia —'

'Miss Polson to strangers like him!' the older woman snapped.

'— who has pushed her way into the house and is refusing to leave. I'm thinking of calling the police, Lucas.'

Cynthia suddenly gasped, her mouth dropping open, then turned to Abigail and asked in a hushed voice, 'Is this who I think it is?'

He swept the older woman a mocking bow. 'Lucas Chadwick at your service, Miss Polson.'

'I might have known *you* would come back here. It can't be her you're after, because Edwina always said she couldn't attract a man to save her life, so you're probably sniffing around after her money *as you did before*. Only my cousin got rid of you, didn't she? Well, this time Abigail is trying to cheat me and I'm meeting my lawyer here. And there won't be anything for you to get your hands on, so you might as well mind your own business and leave me to mind mine.'

Lucas looked at Abigail questioningly.

'Cynthia is convinced my stepmother made another will just before she died, leaving her something substantial, though she hasn't said what, and she thinks I've destroyed it.'

'It's more than something substantial,' Cynthia shouted. 'If you must know, she's left the house to me.'

There was dead silence for a few moments as Abigail tried to take this in. It wasn't possible. Surely even Edwina wouldn't do that to her?

Lucas broke the silence by saying calmly, '*Miss Polson* doesn't know you very well, then, does she,

165

Abbie? If you'd found anything like a later will, you'd have given it to the lawyer. Personally, if what she claims is true, I'd have destroyed it rather than let this beautiful house fall into the hands of anyone who isn't family and who, if she's anything like her precious cousin, would have no idea how to care for historical treasures. Your father would turn in his grave at the thought.'

'Unfortunately my father left it to his second wife.'

'Without any conditions?'

She frowned. 'There were a lot of long words involved. At the time I got the impression it was going to come to me afterwards but I didn't understand the legalities. I was too upset at losing Dad.'

Cynthia sniffed scornfully. 'Well, you're the last of the family, they're such an effete bunch, so it doesn't really matter. Your father couldn't even give Edwina a child. She wanted a proper heir to keep the house safe, but at least she knew I'd look after it properly and get the best price for the pictures and such. She was sure you'd fritter away anything left to you and she couldn't bear the thought of that.'

'Why didn't you speak to Mr Liddlestone after the funeral to say that you believed she'd left you some-thing?'

'Because I couldn't find the letter to prove it and I knew he'd do nothing without proof.'

Lucas couldn't bear the scornful way this old woman was treating Abigail. The little he'd seen of the second Mrs Beadle had shown him a similar attitude towards Abigail — when her father wasn't around. People in the village said the woman had grown twice as nasty when Mr Beadle's Parkinson's got really bad and she had to take over managing everything.

'When the lawyer arrives, you should ask him who he's representing,' he said to Abigail. 'If he's representing her now, you should find yourself another lawyer quick smart.'

She nodded, looking so desperately upset, he had a sudden desire to put his arms round her and comfort her. Oh, hell! What was there about her that so attracted him? Whatever it was, it clearly hadn't gone away. He wondered how she felt about him. Sometimes he thought —

No, he mustn't even think of trying to do anything till he was sure of how she felt. He wasn't going to risk being treated badly again by a Beadle. The way they'd been driven out of their home and away from their village had destroyed his parents.

12

Dot arrived at work soon after Lucas got to Ashgrove House. She parked round the back as usual but since she'd seen Cynthia's car at the front, she didn't go looking for Abigail. She stood listening in the kitchen, hearing angry voices coming from the hall. In the end she couldn't resist eavesdropping.

It wasn't long before what she heard made her so anxious her heart began thumping in her chest and she clapped one hand to her mouth to hold back a whimper of fear. What Cousin Cynthia was claiming was too close to the truth. And to think she'd thought the woman nothing but a nonentity, had even thought her less spiteful towards Abigail than Edwina. All the time the woman must have been worming her way into her cousin's good books and working to steal the house.

Dot stood still, telling herself to stop panicking and think. If Edwina had brought a copy of that final will home, she'd hidden it well, because they'd found no signs of anything like that when they cleared out the old witch's bedroom. Naturally Dot hadn't mentioned it to Abigail, but she'd kept her eyes open. She'd taken note of every item that left that room, every single one.

As she continued to worry, she suddenly realised where Edwina's copy of that will must be. In the safe, of course! It was the only place left. Unfortunately Dot had no way of getting into it to check, let alone dealing with it.

Abigail had mentioned bringing in a locksmith. What if they opened the safe and found the final will? What would they do then? She shuddered. If they accepted the copy as genuine, that would start them looking for the original at the lawyer's rooms and they'd not find it because it had gone up in flames. Would they bring in the police? They might and they'd only have to check who'd been around at the time poor Mr Liddlestone had his stroke to realise that apart from the staff members, who'd usually been there with other people, she was the only person who'd been there alone.

She didn't think she could hold out against being questioned about it, even to protect Abigail. She had never been a skilful liar. If they found out she'd destroyed the will, would she be arrested and sent to prison? As the worries piled up, tears welled in her eyes. She didn't dare go into the hall to join the others in case she betrayed herself, could hardly move a muscle for fear of what might happen next.

Stay calm! she told herself. *Find out what's going on and then . . . Then what? Who knew?* She forced herself to listen carefully to the conversation in the hall.

★ ★ ★

'Go away, Lucas Chadwick,' the new and more aggressive Cynthia snapped suddenly. 'This has nothing to do with you! Why, my cousin Edwina wouldn't even have you and your family living in the village, let alone coming to the house. It cost her a lot of money to get rid of you, but she did it for the family's sake.'

He simply folded his arms and stared at her.

She turned her attack towards Abigail. 'What's this

169

rogue doing here anyway? You know he's never been allowed into the house.'

'That was before. Things have changed. He's welcome here now.'

'One thing won't have changed. He's probably plotting to steal something through you.'

Lucas spoke in a mild, reasonable tone of voice, which contrasted greatly with Cynthia's shrillness. 'I'll ignore that remark this time, Miss Polson, but if you say anything remotely like that again, I'll sue you for slander. You need to see a lawyer if you have some query about the will, not push your way in here and harass Abigail.'

Her mouth fell open in surprise, then she drew herself up to her full height, still barely reaching his shoulder. 'The lawyer who drew up the will had a stroke and there is only his junior partner left, who wasn't involved in drawing up the will. However, he *is* a lawyer, so is likely to be honest. I've arranged for him to come here today as a matter of urgency because I'm sure my cousin would have brought a copy of the will home with her and I don't want Abigail to have a chance to destroy it.'

She jabbed a finger at him. 'I'm glad I did that now I see you're lurking around the place again. If necessary I intend to tell Mr Danvers to apply to the police for a warrant to search the house or do whatever is necessary to prevent you two from cheating me.'

'Rubbish. Abigail would never cheat anyone. In the meantime, I heard her ask you to leave and I think you should do that. Let me open the front door for you.'

Cynthia glared at him and as he took a step towards her, she shrieked and called out, 'Don't touch me, you brute!'

The front door was still half open and Philip was standing outside. He'd been about to use the door knocker when he realised someone was arguing and he'd quickly heard enough to make him hesitate to interrupt.

He let his hand drop from the door knocker when he heard his own name because he'd suddenly recognised the woman's voice. Miss Polson had been so offensive on the phone that his secretary had beckoned to him and turned on the speaker. After listening to her he'd told his secretary to let him deal with this woman in future. He wasn't having his employees harassed like that. Philip wasn't looking forward to dealing with Miss Polson and it was with the greatest reluctance that he'd agreed to meet the woman here. He was only doing it for his client's sake.

He pushed the door a little further open and peered inside, seeing a scrawny woman with fury written all over her face treating Lucas Chadwick as if he was physically threatening her. Only, Lucas was several paces away from where she was standing. She was just about incoherently hysterical.

He sighed. He'd have to join them but as far as he was concerned, it'd be to protect his client Abigail Beadle, not do the bidding of this ranting, irrational female. He heard Lucas say scornfully, 'As if I would attack anyone, especially a small woman like you. Please leave.'

Lucas gestured towards the front door, but though it wasn't a threatening action, Miss Polson shrieked again.

'Don't come near me, you brute!'

Lucas didn't move or raise his voice, and Philip had to admire his self-control.

'For goodness' sake, woman, I'm nowhere near you. Miss Beadle has asked you several times to leave her house. Are you going to do that or should she phone the police for help in removing you?'

There was dead silence for a moment, then Cynthia took one short step forward. 'I'm only going outside to wait for the family lawyer because I'm afraid of you getting violent. I have every right to be here as *she* will find out.'

Philip abandoned his faint hope of not getting involved and rapped on the door, pushing it fully open without waiting for anyone to answer because he didn't want this trouble to escalate.

'Oh, Mr Danvers, I'm so relieved to see you. I've been terrified for my safety.'

When the owner of the shrill voice rushed across to him he stepped back hastily, one hand outstretched to hold her off if necessary. 'Please calm down, Miss Polson.'

'Calm down? They've attacked me! Arrest them.'

'No one's touched her, Mr Danvers,' Abigail said quietly.

Philip nipped Miss Polson's lie in the bud straight away. 'I could see that for myself. The door was open and I'm afraid I've been eavesdropping on the conversation, Miss Beadle, checking what was going on.'

'What a relief!'

'Why are you talking to her?' Cynthia demanded. 'I'm the one who asked you to come here.'

'Could we perhaps sit down somewhere and discuss this calmly?'

'She told me to get out! This is my own cousin's

172

house!' the elderly woman said, still with a penetrating edge to her voice.

'It's not her house now she's dead, is it, nor has it ever been your home, from what I understand? And actually, we need to get one thing straight from the start. I'm Miss Beadle's lawyer, not yours, and I'm only here because you said she was involved.'

He looked at Abigail, raising one eyebrow and jerking his head slightly in the direction of the nearest door, hoping she'd help him to sort this out peacefully.

She gave the slightest of nods. 'Do come into the drawing room and sit down, Mr Danvers.' She threw a disapproving glance at Cynthia. 'And I suppose you had better join us. But you're not staying long. And I wish it made plain from the start that there is no way I'd knowingly cheat anyone.'

She led the way into the nearby room and out of courtesy the two men stood back to let the older woman go first. Instead she stopped dead, blocking the doorway as she stared round. 'She's changed the room! Already! She's probably sold off some of the family silver, too. You'll need to make lists of the valuable items before you leave here today, Mr Danvers.'

He was amazed. Whatever would she claim next? 'If you cannot refrain from making ridiculous accusations, Miss Polson, and wasting all our time, I shall have to ask you to leave my client's house immediately.'

'Well, I shan't go.' She looked round smugly and pulled an envelope out of her handbag. 'In fact, she's the one who will have to leave. This house is mine now, as you'll see when you read this.'

There was dead silence in the room as she thrust it

173

into Philip's hand. 'Read it. Go on! It's a letter from my cousin Edwina.'

He scanned the letter quickly, frowning. Edwina said she was leaving the house to her dearest Cousin Cynthia and she trusted her not to waste this inheritance and to keep her extravagant stepdaughter away from it. Without a word he passed it to Abigail, stretching out one hand to stop Cynthia grabbing it back.

She read it, gasping in shock and holding it out for Lucas to see before she passed it back to the lawyer. Philip read it again, just to be sure, it was so shocking.

Cynthia snatched it out of his hand, clasping it to her meagre bosom melodramatically and looking round in triumph. 'So you see, this house has been left to me.'

All of them were looking at Philip now, waiting for him to say something. The trouble was, the letter was dated a month later than the will he'd dealt with. If the letter was genuine and what Miss Polson was claiming was true, then the will he'd seen might have been superseded. He needed to check and if it had, do something to implement the change. He was, after all, a lawyer, and he hoped an honest one.

'I haven't seen any sign of another will at our rooms, Miss Polson,' he said eventually.

'Obviously. I've thought it through carefully. Anyone working with Mr Liddlestone is likely to be honest, so I believe you didn't know about it. But who can say what *she* will do or has done to keep the house — especially with *him* urging her on.' She jabbed one finger towards Lucas. 'She must have found a way to steal it or she sent her maid to do it. Dot works as a cleaner both here and at your practice.'

'Please refrain from making any accusations, Miss

Polson,' Philip said hastily.

She breathed deeply, then continued, 'But there will still be Edwina's copy of the real will, and we need to find it. I know where it'll be so I've asked someone else to join us here today: a locksmith.'

He looked at her in puzzlement. 'How can you be so sure?'

'I know her ways. The most likely place for the will is in the safe. She put everything she valued in there and kept the combination to open it a secret. Abigail is claiming she can't open it, and that part of her story I do believe, so as I said, I've made arrangements to have it opened.'

There was another dead silence as the other three gaped at her.

*　*　*

Dot, who had crept out of the kitchen to eavesdrop from the hall once the others were sitting in the drawing room, couldn't hold back a thin whine of terror. That woman was a fiend in human form!

Dot was going to be outed as the one who'd destroyed the new will, she just knew it. And she could think of no way of stopping this happening because she had done it, had committed a crime. It had been to prevent an injustice, not to benefit herself, but the law wouldn't take that into account. People were right when they said the law could be an ass. She'd read about cases that proved that in the newspapers more than once. Who knew what that Cynthia would say or do next?

Dot stayed where she was, listening intently. She had to find out and be prepared.

'I'm afraid I can't allow that, Miss Polson,' Philip said. 'If we need to bring in a locksmith, it'll be one chosen by my client and myself, who will be an impartial witness to the contents.'

'*What?*' It was another of those irritating near shrieks. 'That'll give these two time to break into the safe and hide the evidence. There's no way I'm allowing that to happen.'

'There's no way you can force your locksmith on us,' Philip said firmly.

Lucas nodded in approval. He'd already met Philip Danvers and thought him a decent chap, but he was glad to see the lawyer wasn't afraid to stand up for his client. Philip saw Abigail staring at Cynthia as if she'd suddenly grown two heads. He was just as shocked and surprised.

Abigail broke the uncomfortable silence. 'I think Miss Polson had better leave this house now, don't you, Mr Danvers?'

'Yes, I do. And this matter is serious, must be dealt with by the legal system, not by someone pushing her way into the house. Let me escort you to the front door now, Miss Polson. You may leave this matter in my hands.'

He stood up and moved across to where Cynthia was still standing, taking hold of her arm before she could prevent it and turning to Lucas. 'Could you please come out with us so that I have a witness who can testify that I've committed no act of violence against this woman.'

'Happy to.'

Cynthia stared from one implacable man to the

other, shook off Philip's hand and glared across at Abigail. 'You haven't heard the last of this, believe me.'

As they got to the front door a van drew up, with a logo on the side showing a lock and key.

'Do you know this firm?' Philip asked Abigail, who had followed them. 'Is it someone local?'

It was Lucas who answered, pointing. 'No, it isn't. Look at the signage on the van. They're based on the far side of Medderby. Why is Miss Polson trying to bring someone in from there when we have a perfectly good locksmith in the village?'

'Do you wish to tell him to leave or shall I?' Philip asked Abigail.

But Cynthia had already gone across to the van to speak to its driver, and was soon shouting at him, saying she had no intention of paying a bill when he hadn't done anything. When he drove away she got into her shabby old car and simply sat there.

'She'll go in a minute. Come back inside,' Philip said softly.

They found Abigail waiting for them in the hall.

'I've never seen Cynthia so upset about anything,' she said. 'I didn't know she had it in her. Look, I'll just go and check that Dot's all right, if you don't mind. She will be upset about this, too.'

When she'd gone, Lucas moved closer to Philip. 'Her stepmother was far worse than this woman, would you believe? You should have heard how she talked down to my parents when she threw them out of their house. And when they protested she shrieked and yelled, threatening them. I've never forgotten that day. Abigail must have had a terrible time.'

Philip couldn't hide a slight smile.

'What the hell's amusing you?'

He kept his voice low, even though Abigail had gone to the kitchen. 'I gather you and she were childhood sweethearts. You still sound rather fond of her, Lucas.'

'I used to be fond of her in the way you mean, but that was years ago.'

Philip saw the way Lucas glanced towards the kitchen and that made him remember how he'd felt about his late wife. Sometimes love didn't fade. He wasn't over Kathy, as his date with Abigail had proved. He might never be. And it seemed clear to him that Lucas wasn't over his client, either, so he spoke out.

'If you ask me, Lucas, it's time someone gave Abigail some steady support. She's been fighting battles on her own for too long.'

Lucas stiffened and cast him a suspicious glance. 'She's not been on her own. She's had Dot to support her. She's been working here since the days of the first Mrs Beadle, Abigail's mother. In fact, it's well known in the village that Dot has been more of a mother to Abigail than an employee. I wouldn't care to stand in her path if anyone was trying to hurt her lass.'

'I know, but will her support be enough? Will she have enough educated knowledge of how to set about this? You've run a business for years, and not a Mickey Mouse operation, either, from what you told me. Your savoir faire about dealing with the law would be invaluable given the circumstances — as well as the fact that your expression betrays you. It's obvious you still care for Abigail. Unfortunately I have to remain impartial but you don't.'

He watched Lucas look at him and open his mouth as if to protest then shut it again and stare into the distance.

178

Satisfied he'd made his point, Philip took out his phone. 'I'll just call my secretary and tell her I'll be here for longer than I expected. I'll join you in a minute or two.'

Lucas went inside the house and to his surprise saw Dot sitting on a chair in the hall with a tray abandoned on the table nearby. She was looking upset and being comforted by Abigail, but kept insisting she was all right, just a slight dizzy turn. Only, Dot's face was white and to him she looked worried, not dizzy. What else was going wrong here, for heaven's sake? Hadn't Abigail enough on her plate?

He moved forward to join them.

★ ★ ★

The three invisible spectators had watched the encounter with some amusement, not revealing their presence to Abigail. But as Cynthia went from bad to worse, their smiles vanished.

'What's got into that female?' Georgiana muttered. 'She's often been here in the past few years, and used to be rather quiet, not spiteful like this.'

Roderick frowned. 'I think there's something else behind all this, something that's driving her to take desperate measures. Don't you wish sometimes that we could read living people's minds and stop them doing stupid things?'

'I've wished it many a time,' Georgiana agreed.

They followed the group into the drawing room and their smiles faded completely as they continued to watch and listen.

'They should never have abolished putting obnoxious people in the stocks,' Georgiana said abruptly. 'I would personally like to help a few rotting missiles to find a target on Cynthia's face at the moment.'

'Shall I speed her on her way?' Roderick asked. 'I could rock the car and make a few ghostly noises till she drove off.'

'I know it's tempting but better not,' Juliana said.

'Spoilsport.'

★ ★ ★

When Lucas came back into the house and said Philip was just making a phone call, Abigail asked Dot to make them all a pot of tea and watched her go off to the kitchen.

She was about to speak to Lucas when she noticed the three ghostly figures to one side of the room. What were they doing here? They had never appeared when she was with other people before, except for Dot.

She stopped dead and frowned at them, then looked hastily away.

Only, that made her realise that Lucas was looking at her strangely and then glancing towards the mirror over the fireplace. Surely he couldn't see them too?

She looked through the window at where Cynthia was still sitting in the car. If Edwina's cousin was proved correct, what would happen to the family ghosts?

And to herself. She still hadn't got her head round the idea of leaving Ashgrove House in a few months. If she had to leave straight away and with nothing, how would she cope mentally, let alone financially?

It was all going to be very difficult. To put it mildly.

13

In the kitchen, Dot put on the kettle then glanced furtively towards the hall before getting out the cooking port. It had been bought to soak the mixed dried fruit to put into the Christmas pudding. Now, she wasn't even sure there would be a pudding, or a real Christmas.

She wasn't much of a drinker, but then she didn't feel to be much of a criminal, either, even now. You did what seemed right at the time. Now she was feeling desperate, so she unscrewed the top of the bottle and took a good, big swig, hoping it would help her to calm down. She was likely to be in big trouble if anyone found out what she'd done. Only, if she hadn't done it, Cynthia would be mistress here already and her dear girl would be out on the street. Or in Dot's spare bedroom.

Life sometimes gave you very hard choices about the right path to take. Could it be possible that they'd not find out what she'd done? She shook her head. She doubted it, not if there was a copy of the final, horribly unfair will in the safe. That thought made her shiver and take another big swig before she put the port away in the cupboard again. She didn't know what she was going to do about this, but clearly she had to do something.

Only what?

Taking a deep breath, she finished preparing the tea, set the teapot on the trolley under its cosy and wheeled it into the drawing room. Only Lucas and

Abigail were there and they told her the lawyer was making a quick phone call and would be joining them in a minute, speaking like a couple of close friends now.

Once she realised that she left as quickly as she could, this time smiling. Maybe one good thing would come out of this mess.

★ ★ ★

Outside the house, Philip finished his phone call while keeping an eye on Miss Polson. She still hadn't started the motor and had her head on her hands, which were resting on the steering wheel. She looked genuinely upset.

After a few seconds she raised her head and opened the car window to call, 'I'm relying on you to deal honestly with this, Mr Danvers. Don't let her cheat me out of what's mine.'

He could see the sheen of tears on her cheeks, so he inclined his head and watched her start the car and drive off. Of course he would deal honestly with the situation. But he was getting rather concerned as to why Cynthia was so very sure she had a right to be here. It had surprised him to see her weeping. She hadn't seen the will itself, only received the letter from Edwina. Had there really been another will made? Surely not?

But he'd have to find out for certain.

When Miss Polson's car had moved out of the drive and turned right, going away from the village, he went back inside to join Abigail, who poured him a cup of tea. He took a sip and set it down. 'Look, I need to ask you formally, Miss Beadle: is there any truth in

182

Miss Polson's claim that you're trying to conceal the existence of another will?'

She shook her head immediately. 'None at all. I've only ever seen the one you showed me and I hadn't seen that beforehand.'

'So you haven't destroyed anything?'

'No, of course not. I wouldn't.'

He didn't think she would, either. She had such an honest face. He took another sip, staring into space for a few moments and thinking this through. 'Well, I've seen no sign of one at work, either, but Miss Polson is being very tenacious about this and seems genuinely upset. I think *she* believes what she's claiming. Was that note she showed us in your stepmother's handwriting?'

Abigail swallowed hard but couldn't lie to him. 'Yes, it was.'

'You're sure of that?'

'Definitely. Her handwriting was very distinctive. She always used black ink and created spiky, ugly words as if her nature spilled out into her writing.'

'Hmm. Well, I must tell you that it's my duty to look into this claim. I do wish Gerard were not incapacitated. If anyone can know the truth for certain, it's he.'

'Is he no better?'

'His wife says he's improving each day, but she's adamant that she doesn't want him disturbed.'

'I'm glad he's getting better.'

'Hmm. I might phone Mrs Liddlestone later and tell her what's happened here today. Perhaps if I explain that it's a matter of urgency and I only need a brief word with her husband, she'll allow me to speak to him.'

'I hope so. I trust him absolutely. If he says there is another will, I'll just have to — cope.'

He could sense the despair behind her words. 'Do you have any money of your own? Just in case?'

'Only a few hundred pounds. After my father died, my stepmother doled out a small amount each week for my personal expenses because I said I'd have to get a job and leave if she didn't pay me. It wasn't much and I found it hard to save anything.'

That would account for how badly she usually dressed, he thought. She had worn smarter clothes to meet him at the pub but Dot had told him in confidence later that Abigail had been so short they'd had to search the attic for suitable clothing.

'If she is the heir, you can probably put in a claim that you're a dependent relative and ask for a share of the estate.'

'Would I be entitled to that?'

'Possibly. Unfortunately, it can take years to resolve such matters legally and one can never be quite certain of the outcome, especially with adult claimants.'

'And in the meantime, what do Cynthia and I do? Could I continue to live here? Would she wait to move in?'

'I doubt it.'

'The trouble is, I've been looking after the fabric of the house and she wouldn't know how to do that. Edwina kept a very firm hand on the finances and management after my father died, but I was the one who dealt with practical daily matters.'

'It's hard to say what would be allowed.'

She shivered, despair on her face. 'Bad enough to lose the house for inheritance taxes, but to lose it to Cynthia Polson would be . . . utterly devastating.'

He patted her arm. 'If there is such a will, I'd be happy to represent you in a claim for a share. But we're putting the cart before the horse. First I need to check what Cynthia Polson said.'

'We're back to the safe again.'

He stood up. 'I'd better get back to work and start a big search for any later will there. I've made arrangements for the locksmith to come here.'

★ ★ ★

Lucas offered to help Abigail to collect the tea things ready to take into the kitchen but she said, 'You and I had better eat a piece of cake or Dot will be offended. She makes it specially for me. And I think I can squeeze out two more cups of tea.'

'Well, if you don't mind and you'll join me.'

When they were seated again he said, 'I'm not only sorry about this claim. I'm rather surprised, though, that your father left everything to your stepmother instead of just a life interest or whatever it's called.'

'Edwina was very good at getting her own way. She could nag for England, as the saying goes.'

'She was certainly ruthless in the way she dealt with my family.'

'Yes. And the older she got, the more she seemed to glory in being unkind to people. Except for Dot. She couldn't easily have found anyone else to take care of the housework, you see, so she avoided Dot as much as possible and they mostly communicated through me.'

She shook her head. 'I should have expected Edwina to try something like this, getting at me even after her death. It's par for the course with her. I'm so sorry she drove you and your family away.'

185

He shrugged. 'I'm most sorry that she destroyed our letters and separated us.' He stared at her and added softly, 'Very sorry.'

'Me, too.'

'Well, we can't change the past but we can be friends again now. Can I still run the computer course here?'

'Of course you can. I don't think even Cynthia would stop you if she knew you were offering good money for the hire of the rooms.'

'Thank you. So with your agreement, I'll come back later and set up the rest of the computers? Then I'd really like to test them all, so can I stay as late as necessary?'

'Yes.'

'I'd welcome your help with that if you have time. Apart from speeding up what I need to do, it'll give you a preliminary taste of using a modern computer.'

'I'd like that.'

'It's rare to meet someone of our age who isn't computer literate.'

'My stepmother threatened to smash one up if I brought it into the house and she never threatened what she wasn't prepared to carry out. I found that out after my father died. I had nowhere to hide one, even in a house as big as this, because you still need to be connected to electricity, if only to recharge a laptop. I know she searched my room regularly and prowled round the whole place.'

He was startled. 'Could you not stop her?'

'No. Besides, I had other more important worries than getting online. A house this old needs so much maintenance and I learned to do the smaller jobs myself.'

186

'You clearly love your home very much.'

'I do. I feel as if it's as much a part of me as my own body.'

'I envy you that. I've never really settled anywhere since we left the village, and after my parents died I spent more time at the office than in my flat. Maybe that's why I fell ill.'

Another silence fell, but this one was far more comfortable. She was the one who broke it.

'I'm looking forward to your class.'

'Even now, with all your other worries?'

'More than ever. I'm going to need to be able to use today's computers to have a chance to get a job.'

'It isn't all that hard or all that different and you're an intelligent woman, so I expect you'll easily pick things up. I use the word 'fiddly' in my classes, because that's what it feels like when you first start using a computer and it'll probably be just basic details that you'll need to know because computers aren't very good at guessing.'

He finished his last bite of cake, drained his cup of tea and stood up. 'Thanks for that. I'd better get going. I'll be back in an hour or so with the other computers.'

When he'd gone, she cleared up and went to find Dot, who seemed unusually glum. 'Something's wrong, Dot. I can tell.'

'Well, you have enough on your plate so I'll sort out my own problems, love. Would you mind if I left early today?'

'Not at all. You aren't due in tomorrow so I hope you get your problems fixed.'

'If you need me, I can change my arrangements for tomorrow.'

187

'No need. I can manage on my own.' She'd have to learn to do that, wouldn't she? Manage on her own. And she doubted Cynthia would continue to employ Dot, even if her friend was willing to work for her.

As she waved goodbye and locked up the back door, Abigail tried to focus on the one positive to her current situation. Lucas was holding his course here and she'd be on it. She'd looked in the papers occasionally over the years when Edwina did something worse than usual, searching for jobs, and hadn't felt optimistic about getting one. But each time she left the papers open at the Jobs Vacant page, her stepmother seemed to realise she'd gone too far and reined in her horns for a while.

Oh dear, Abigail thought, as she tried to make a list. The practicalities of the changes that would be needed if Cynthia was right seemed to be piling up into a mountain. If she lost her home she'd have to not only move out but go on social security till she found something. And find a cheap room to live in, though she was sure Dot would let her stay in her spare bedroom temporarily.

And what about the ornaments and furniture she'd grown up with and loved? Would she lose every single thing? She blew her nose hard and tried to smile at the inevitable thought — everything except for several bags of old paperbacks. They were hers, surely? Only she'd have nowhere to put them.

She wasn't going to sit and weep. Lucas was coming back soon and she wasn't going to greet him with red eyes, looking like a pitiful wreck of a creature, even though she felt bad. It seemed a long time till she heard his van pull up outside but at least by then she'd calmed down.

Lucas gave Abigail a few furtive glances as he began to bring the computers into the house. She looked so desperately sad. Was it any wonder? At this stage he could think of no practical way to help her except distract her a little from her worries.

He set her to unpacking the keyboards and placing one in front of each monitor, then went to check the old-fashioned electrical master board in the hall cupboard to sort out a way of connecting and providing an electricity supply. The house was woefully short of power points.

'All right if I improve a couple of things permanently in your electrical systems?' he asked when he came back from his van with a box of equipment and tools.

'Fine by me as long as you know what you're doing and it's legal.'

'I trained first as an electrician. I knew I could probably use it as a career path into some aspect of computing later on and they paid electrical apprentices a wage, while those attending university courses had to pay for the privilege, so it was a no-brainer. I abandoned university, was determined not to be a burden on my parents in any way.'

When he had brought in the final computer, he showed her what to do to set one up, which wasn't much different to what she'd already learned then let her try it out.

'You pick things up quickly.'

'Perhaps I should train as an electrician if they pay for you to do it.'

He knew she was trying to make light of things but

189

her voice came out wobbly.

'Are you going to have financial difficulties if Cynthia's claim is true?'

'Yes. I don't have much money. There is some jewellery I inherited from my mother but I don't want to sell that and it's not very valuable anyway.'

'Then let's hope the claim isn't proved valid and you can keep your home.'

'I'd probably lose it to the inheritance tax after a few months or so, but that wouldn't feel as bad and I'd get something out of the residue of the estate.'

She changed the subject by asking a question and he guessed she was learning as much as she could. By the time he left, she was more at ease with a computer.

He hesitated at the door. 'Will you be all right on your own tonight, Abbie?'

'Yes. I'm used to being here.'

'I shan't be able to come tomorrow, I'm afraid. I have a meeting in London. I'll be back on Sunday to check that everything's working properly, if you don't mind.'

'Come any time. You're paying for the privilege after all.' Her voice grew softer. 'I didn't mean that to sound as if you'd not be welcome otherwise. You would be.'

'Thank you.'

When he'd gone, she sighed and walked round, checking that everything was locked up. The house seemed even emptier than usual tonight. And since there was no one there to see it, she didn't hold back the tears.

14

The following day seemed very quiet and threatened to drag on, so Abigail filled the time by cleaning two of the bedrooms that hadn't been used for a while. She'd do all the rooms thoroughly if she had time. She wanted her home to look as good as it could when someone else took over.

The only interruption to the silence was a phone call from Philip saying Mrs Liddlestone had agreed to him phoning Gerard on Monday as long as her husband continued to make steady progress.

'That's good news — isn't it?' Abigail asked.

'I hope so. I wish she'd let me phone him tomorrow, but she was adamant. And she stressed that the call was to be no longer than five minutes or she'd cut us off. She's a real dragon where Gerard is concerned, isn't she?'

'I don't know. I haven't had a lot to do with him in the past few years, let alone his wife. My stepmother took over everything, both social and to do with business after my father died — and just left the cleaning and shopping to me.'

'I'll do my best for you, Abigail, and I'm sure Gerard will too.'

'Thank you, Philip.'

What a pity she didn't fancy him, or he her. But it had only ever been Lucas for her and she was still attracted to him. She could admit it to herself and face it now.

He was keeping his distance, though in a kind,

polite way, so had clearly moved on. When he was fully recovered, he'd probably leave the village once and for all. She might have to do that too if Cynthia took over her home. Or, even worse, if she sold it to developers and they found a way to get round the Grade 2 heritage listing that protected the fabric of the building from being altered without permission. Abigail didn't think she could bear to watch it being demolished.

* * *

On the Sunday morning, Dot turned up looking a lot better and insisting on helping out. Her determinedly cheerful smile lightened the atmosphere considerably.

'We'll get through it love, somehow,' Dot told her. 'And you know there's always a bed for you at my house.'

'You've taken in a few strays over the years, haven't you, Dot? Talk about leaving a good trace behind you in the world.'

Dot blushed furiously. 'Get on with you. I just do my bit to help people when I can. And we'll surely have got things sorted out by Christmas, so I'm telling you now, we're going to make it a very special one. You've earned that, if anyone has. Your father and mother would be very proud of you.'

It was Abigail's turn to blush.

They worked together as harmoniously as always, with Dot telling her about the new steps she'd learned at her Saturday night dancing class and had practised at the casual dance afterwards.

'You should come with me, love. She isn't around to stop you now.'

'I only ever dance with you these days.'

'I won't nag you now but I warn you, I will get you out meeting people later. I'm not letting you sit at home and mope, whatever happens. And just for the record, you're a good dancer. I like having a twirl with you.'

They smiled at the memory of their last foray.

'Let's put some music on and I'll show you the steps I learned yesterday,' Dot said suddenly, half an hour later as they finished one job. 'All work and no play isn't good for anyone.'

Abigail shook her head, but somehow Dot chivvied her into coming downstairs, putting on a record and learning the new steps. After that they did some nifty quick-stepping round the house.

★ ★ ★

When Lucas arrived, he went to the kitchen door. He knocked but no one answered, and as he could hear music playing inside he wondered if it was too loud for a mere door knock to register.

Inside the kitchen he paused for a moment with the music beating loudly in his ears and making him wag his head in time to it. There was no one here, so he went into the hall, where he found the doors of all the rooms open. When Dot appeared in the doorway of the drawing room and started to lead her partner into the hall, he grinned at her and mimed a few dance steps in time to the music.

'Try it with Abigail!' she called and before Abigail could stop her, Dot had waltzed across to him, spinning the younger woman round into Lucas's arms.

Abigail stiffened but a whisper in her ear said,

'*Dance with him, you fool!*'

She'd promised to do as the resident ghosts suggested, and anyway, she wanted to, so she moved into Lucas's arms and began following his lead.

He gave her one of his old, devastating smiles. 'I still enjoy dancing.'

'So do I.'

She let him swoosh her off round the hall then into the dining room, round the big dining table and then back into the hall and on through the drawing room. It felt wonderful. Their steps still seemed to match as perfectly as they had back in the day.

The music stopped for a moment then started up again. It was provided by a suite of dance records she'd used with her father. Old-fashioned vinyl, people called it, only it was in fashion again as a collectible. It'd be rude not to say something. She found it difficult to speak normally while she was so close to him, but she managed. 'Um, I'm enjoying this.'

'I am too. I don't get much opportunity to dance these days. I was too ill to do much physical activity for a while and by the time I started to feel better, I'd lost touch with people.'

'Are you tired? Should we stop now?'

'No. Definitely not. I'm enjoying it enormously. And I'm just about better now. This makes me feel like my old self.'

'Me too.'

They did another circuit of the house, not speaking, but close together physically and emotionally without needing words to make bridges. She was sorry when the record ended but almost immediately another tune began and she guessed Dot had changed the record quickly. This time it was a tango, one of her favourites.

194

He struck a masterful pose. 'Are you up for it?'

'Oh, yes.' She raised one hand and spread the other out to the side in a graceful gesture she'd practised in front of the mirror when she was a teenager. She knew Dot was interfering, pushing them at one another, but she was glad. It was wonderful, just absolutely wonderful.

'This is the most cheerful I've seen you look since I got back,' he said abruptly.

'It's the most enjoyable thing I've done for weeks.'

After a while, she spoke her thoughts aloud. 'We always did dance well together, didn't we, Lucas? Remember the after-school dancing classes?'

'I've never forgotten them. '

Someone hammered on the front door just then and they stopped.

'Oh, damn!' he muttered. 'Do you have to answer it?'

The knocking was repeated.

'I suppose I'd better,' she said reluctantly.

'Pity.'

For a moment they stared at one another, then she moved out of his arms and towards the front door. Her legs felt wooden and reluctant to move but she didn't let them stop her. When she opened it, Philip was standing there with a man dressed in overalls behind him.

'I phoned a short time ago and Dot said I could bring Mac round straight away. This is Mac, by the way, our locksmith. He's busy all week but has agreed to have a quick look at the safe today to find out if he can open it, since the matter is rather urgent.'

Dot came in from the kitchen. 'I thought you two might as well enjoy your dance till they arrived.'

'Yes. I see.' Abigail turned back to the stranger and waited for instructions.

'No use risking damaging the contents by forcing your way in if you can fiddle it open. With some of them you can't but Mr Danvers says this is an old one,' Mac said with a strong Scottish accent.

'Can you show us where the safe is?' Philip asked her.

'Shouldn't we bring Cynthia in on this?'

'Not yet. So far we only have her word for it that your stepmother made her the heir.'

Lucas began to move away, but Philip said, 'I wonder if you'd come and act as an impartial witness for us?'

He hesitated, then shrugged. 'If you don't mind, Abbie?'

'No. I don't mind.'

But as she led the way to the estate office, she felt as if an icy wind was suddenly blowing through the whole house. How would she keep calm if they found another will and Cynthia was proved right? She'd find a way to control her feelings, she supposed. She'd had enough practice at that. But it'd tear her apart if she had to leave Ashgrove House straight away.

★ ★ ★

In the room used as the estate office, Abigail opened the cupboard door that hid the safe and gestured towards it.

Mac rolled his eyes. 'A child would find that safe within a minute of coming in here. And if you don't mind me saying so, you need to upgrade your general security as well, Miss Beadle, judging by the locks on

196

that front door.' He turned to stare at the safe. 'This is even older than I'd expected. Not many people still using this sort these days.'

After that he ignored the people standing nearby watching and started examining the safe, muttering to himself. Dot could hardly breathe for fear of what might be found.

He turned his head abruptly, still kneeling. 'The easiest way with this type is finding the combination. Do you have any idea what it might be? People who use such old technology can be very naïve about choosing combinations so it's worth a try.'

'I'm afraid I have no idea. My stepmother was very secretive.'

'Let's try the most obvious ones before we think about breaking into it. What's her birth date? You'd be surprised how often people use that.'

She told him.

He tried that but to no avail.

'Who installed this safe? Your grandfather, I should think, from its age. What was his birth date?'

Lucky she had a good memory, she thought.

He tried the first numbers, listening intently, but shook his head. 'Your father's birth date?'

Abigail told him the date; Mac tried it but it failed. 'Any significant dates you can think of?'

'How about Edwina's marriage date?' Philip suggested.

Mac tried it and to Dot's dismay the lock clicked after the first four numbers had been entered.

He opened the door with a triumphant, 'Ta-da!'

She held her breath, clutching Abigail's arm as he lifted out the safe's contents, item by item, piling them nearby. The third item was a large envelope. Her heart sank and she could feel her dear girl stiffen.

'This might be what we're looking for.' Philip took the envelope and fished out the contents with the others watching closely, not making a sound.

'Yes, it's a will.' He checked the end and added, 'I'm afraid it's dated after the one I read out to you, Abigail.'

As Philip glanced quickly at the contents of the envelope, only pride kept Abigail's head up and (she hoped) her expression calm. She was very glad of Dot's hand on her arm. The will was very short, only two pages, and when Philip looked up, she knew it was bad news before he spoke.

'I'm afraid Miss Polson was right. This will does leave everything to her. And it's duly signed and witnessed.'

He offered it to Abigail and she read it. She didn't know what to say and when Dot peered at it, she let out a sad little mew and reached out to Abigail again. But there was no comfort anyone could offer.

'I'll consult Gerard tomorrow. Ask him what he wants to do about this.' Philip frowned in puzzlement. 'He must have known about it, because he's on it as a formal witness.'

Abigail looked at him numbly. 'I'd be grateful if you'd tell Cynthia and ask her to give me a couple of days to get used to the idea before she moves in.'

'I'm not telling her anything until after I've spoken to Gerard. I don't understand how he could . . .'

He wanted to see whether his partner could think of any way to mitigate the bequest's consequences. Gerard had hinted once before the funeral at there being complications to the will. What complications? This was a simple, straightforward document. What a terrible thing for the second Mrs Beadle to have done. It sickened Philip sometimes how people could treat others, because the law couldn't always put things right again.

'What's in the other envelope?' Lucas pointed to a bulging padded envelope of the sort generally used for parcels.

Philip peered into it. 'Good heavens! It's money. Quite a lot of money, too. Why did she not keep it in the bank?'

There was silence, then Lucas said, 'Perhaps so that there would be no record of it. I wonder if Cynthia knows about this?'

'I'd better keep it till I've spoken to Gerard, Abigail.'

'Do what you think best, Philip.' Abigail took a step backwards. 'Is that all?'

'All I can do here for now, yes. Don't say anything to Cynthia yet.'

'I need time to get used to it, so I'll leave you to deal with telling her. Dot will show you out when you're ready to leave.'

Then she fled to her bedroom, locking the door on the world and cuddling her pillow close, for lack of another human being to care for her. She didn't cry. This hurt far too much for tears. She could only sit by the window, holding the pillow and trying to survive a tidal wave of anguish as she stared out at the leafless ash grove beyond the gardens.

She felt lost, couldn't even try to work out what to do next. Did you just walk out and hand over the keys as you passed the new owner?

15

Mac had already driven away by the time Dot escorted the other two men to the door. 'I'll stay here tonight. Abigail always did hold her griefs to herself so I doubt I'll see much of her, but I'll feel better if I'm here.'

'Good idea.' Philip got into his car.

Lucas lingered on the doorstep till after the lawyer had driven away. 'If there's anything I can do, Dot, you only have to phone me. You're right. I do still care about her.' He got out a pen and scribbled on a business card then pressed it into her hand. 'This is my private number.'

She slipped it into her pocket. 'I don't think anyone can help my girl now, Lucas.'

'There's something else to sort out before I leave you: I'm supposed to be running the first day of that computer course here tomorrow.'

'Oh, yes. I'd forgotten about that.'

'Shall I cancel it?'

She didn't hesitate because it'd give her an excuse for spending the next day here. 'No. But if you could pay my girl directly for the room hire, it'd help. She's going to be very short of money from now on, you see. After all, she hasn't handed over the house yet, has she? Nothing's been proved. So it'll be payable to her.'

'I'll pay her tomorrow morning in cash.'

When he'd gone, Dot washed up the dirty cups and plates. Then she sat down and couldn't hold the

200

tears back any longer. It just wasn't *fair*! She sat and sobbed quietly at the kitchen table. She didn't care now whether the police came after her or not. All she cared for was her girl. But all the caring in the world didn't point her towards any way to help.

★ ★ ★

Upstairs, Abigail sat by the window for a while longer but eventually thirst drove her downstairs. She wasn't surprised to find Dot sitting at the kitchen table with a tear-stained face. She hugged her dear friend and wished she too could cry out her pain but it had gathered in a hard, heavy knot in her chest and was weighing her down.

She patted Dot's shoulder as she passed, then got a glass of water and drained it. 'I'm going out for some fresh air. I'll be in the ash grove if anyone needs me.'

'I'll stay here tonight, love.'

'Thank you, but I'd rather be alone.' As Dot gave her a sharp look, she added firmly, 'You know I would.'

'Even with something as bad as this?'

'Yes.'

'Well, all right, love. But I'll stay here till you come back from your walk, in case your lawyer phones. He might find something that helps you keep the house.'

Abigail shrugged and gave her a sad smile. She didn't dare count on that because another let-down would tear her apart. As she walked outside, she grabbed an old shawl from the hooks near the back door. It had been her grandmother's and the colours had faded, but she liked to wear it.

She walked more slowly than usual today, feeling numb and listless. She'd sort of grown used to the idea of losing the house to the tax man, bad as that was, but to lose it even earlier because of Edwina's spite seemed worse by far. It felt as if her stepmother had won a major battle, won the whole war between them, in fact. She couldn't bear the idea of sharing the house with Cynthia, not even for a day. *If* that woman did offer to let her stay, which she didn't think would happen.

Well, she wouldn't have to worry about that. Dot would give her a bed and help her look for a job. She didn't even have to check to be sure of that. But she wouldn't stay with her any longer than necessary, because it was a small house and anyway, Dot did have a tendency to try to take over your life if she thought you needed help.

She wasn't going to let anyone take over her life again. That was as far as her thinking took her. She sat on a fallen log, finding comfort in the thought that her father had sat here before her and then with her. They'd often enjoyed the peaceful spot together. For some reason, Edwina had never even attempted to come to this part of the grounds. She looked up at the stupid hat, riding alone on the bare branches. It'd still be here when she had gone.

In the end she started to feel cold and made her way reluctantly back to the house. Even her favourite refuge hadn't helped her work anything else out this time. She didn't think she would ever get over leaving Ashgrove House. She'd just have to struggle on through life with a vital part of her missing.

* * *

When she got back Dot insisted on making her a cup of cocoa, so Abigail let her, knowing her friend would

202

feel better for doing something.

It was a relief when Dot left, persuaded eventually that there was nothing further she could do. She stopped in the doorway. 'You'll come to stay with me? Afterwards.'

'I've taken that for granted.'

'Good.'

Abigail locked the back door then walked slowly round the house, checking once again that all the outer doors were locked. As she tested the French windows in the library and moved away from them, she heard a whisper of something behind her and turned to see all three ghosts standing in a row near the huge, old-fashioned fireplace, solemnly staring at her.

'I'm afraid I've lost your home,' she told them.

'*You* didn't lose it, that horrible woman planned to steal it,' Roderick said, a much harsher tone in his voice than she'd ever heard before.

'We're not sure what'll happen now, but we feel that something will,' Georgiana offered. 'We can't tell the future, but sometimes we get feelings about whether things are going to turn out well or badly for our descendants. And we can still talk to you. That augurs well.'

'It's kind of you to try to comfort me, but I'd rather you didn't. I shall just have to endure what happens.'

'It's a Beadle trait, being stoic in adversity.' Juliana frowned, head on one side. 'But I really do think something will happen to help you.'

Abigail held up one hand. 'Thank you, but I'd rather stay realistic about my future. Now, I'd prefer to be alone if you don't mind.'

'We'll leave you but if you need us, you only have to call out our names,' Georgiana said quietly. 'We've comforted descendants before. It's one of the reasons for returning.'

They faded slowly and after a while Abigail went up to bed. No use shelving any more books now. She'd be losing the library as well as everything else. That made her feel even sadder. It had felt good to help people.

As she was getting undressed she suddenly remembered that she hadn't eaten an evening meal, but couldn't be bothered to go down and get anything. She didn't feel at all hungry.

She'd managed to make one more decision: to attend the computer class tomorrow. It would be a start in updating her skills, at least.

After lying awake for a while she felt herself getting drowsy out of sheer exhaustion and was glad when sleep made her troubles fade.

16

At the appointed hour on the Monday morning, Philip phoned Gerard. Mrs Liddlestone answered and for a moment he worried that he wouldn't be able to speak to her husband after all. He sighed in relief when he heard her confirm that he could.

'I'll remind you, Philip, that I said five minutes only. I meant that. Five — minutes.'

'Yes. I'll remember.'

There was a slight clatter and Gerard came on the phone, his voice only slightly slurred. 'Philip, how nice to speak to you.'

'Are you OK for a brief chat?'

'Yes, of course I am. I only had a minor stroke, fortunately. Renée tells me there's a slight problem at work.'

'Something I need your advice about, since it's one of your cases. Actually, it's rather urgent or I wouldn't disturb you.'

'Disturb away, then.'

Philip explained quickly about the wills.

'Oh, damn. I remember now. That's the one case I'd been concerned about. When I first started to recover, I couldn't remember exactly what I'd been doing before the stroke hit me except that I'd been looking at the Beadle wills. Some of the details were still a bit hazy, but things are gradually coming clear to me. When Edwina died so suddenly, I knew that her last will was going to cause problems for Abigail.'

'The will I found at our office left everything to

Abigail.'

'Made when?'

'Three months ago.'

'Ah. There's another will, made a couple of weeks before she died.'

'I know that now, but it wasn't among our Beadle family records.'

'It should have been.'

'It wasn't, truly.'

'How did you find out about it, then?'

'Cynthia told us and showed us a letter she'd received from Edwina. When I said there was no such will, she suggested we look in the safe at Ashgrove House because apparently Edwina kept all her important papers in it. Only we couldn't open it, so I brought in the local locksmith. He got the safe open and I found a copy of the later will there. I need to verify, preferably with you, that it's genuine before I do anything, so I haven't told Cynthia yet. She makes such a fuss.'

Gerard sighed. 'Unfortunately Edwina did make another will just before she died. I shouldn't have let her do that, but I thought she'd soon change it again.'

'Oh dear. I think I should show you the copy before I proceed, so that you can verify that it's the final one you drew up. I'm treading carefully because it'll mean Abigail loses the house.'

'It's a good job you are treading carefully.'

'What do you mean?'

'It's too difficult to explain on the phone. Look, I'll have to come into work and take you through the necessary paperwork. There's another important document stored somewhere else.'

Mrs Liddlestone came abruptly on the line, proving

206

she'd been eavesdropping. 'I let you two go on for longer than five minutes, because of how important this sounded, but you are not going into your rooms tomorrow, Gerard Liddlestone.'

'My dear, I shall have to.'

The connection was cut off abruptly and though Philip rang back, his call wasn't answered. He felt extremely frustrated and was inclined to get in his car and drive over to see the senior partner in person so that they could finish the discussion. What had Gerard meant by another important document? As a lawyer you weren't supposed to take sides but if there was any chance of Abigail retaining ownership of that house legally, Philip would seize it with both hands.

However, when he thought about it, he calmed down gradually and in the end he decided to leave it till tomorrow or the day after to contact Gerard. The main thing was that his partner had said there was some other factor that needed to be taken into consideration, so he wouldn't do anything till he found out what that was. Gerard would surely persuade his wife to let them get together about this? There was no one who knew as much about the Beadle family as he did.

Philip didn't want to leave the question of this inheritance hanging uncertainly over Abigail for too long. The poor woman was looking ravaged and upset, and no wonder. Should he phone her and tell her . . . Tell her what? He had nothing definite to tell her and wouldn't have until Gerard gave him the necessary information.

He'd told the two women he'd get in touch when he had further news and that would have to do.

★ ★ ★

In a very small attic flat in Medderby, Cynthia was fretting about her future. What would happen about the safe now? She didn't trust Abigail to deal with this honestly because she'd be losing everything. Edwina had laughed about that, but Cynthia felt a bit guilty.

Could she trust Mr Danvers to obey a lawful will? After all, he'd made it plain that he was working for Abigail, not herself. When he did get that safe opened, would he even allow her to be present? She felt uncertain what to do to guard her interests, whether to wait for him to get back to her or to hire a lawyer of her own to defend her rights. Only lawyers were expensive and she had very little money.

In the end she phoned Philip, wanting further reassurance that he would involve her. But the secretary said he was busy and would get back to her when he was free.

There was nothing else she could think of to do. She checked her food stores and wondered whether to go out and buy some more food from the little local supermarket, but decided she could make do with what she had. With a bit of luck, in a few days at the latest surely, she'd be moving into Ashgrove House and that would be such a relief.

Oh no! You had to get probate on the will first, didn't you? How long would she have to wait to take possession?

She was eager to get out of this horrible little flat, had hated living in it for years but it cost her nothing. It had been offered to her by a distant relative in return for keeping an eye on the tenants of the other four flats in the building and dealing with any breakdowns or repairs. She had done that, though there had been one or two difficult tenants who had made everyone else's life a misery. There was a rather unpleasant young man living here at the moment, upsetting all the other tenants because he was so noisy and messy. She was desperate to get out before that looming trouble with him came to a head.

Since the relative didn't pay her a wage, she had found it very hard to manage on the tiny annuity that was all her parents had left her. *She* hadn't found a rich husband like her cousin Edwina had.

After that husband died, it had been a godsend to Cynthia when Edwina started asking her to run occasional errands and pressing the odd five-pound note on her for doing it. She'd also been invited over for meals at Ashgrove House from time to time.

So far she'd managed to avoid going on social security, which would have been so humiliating. But there was no Edwina to turn to now and unfortunately the last handout of cash had been a while ago. She needed to sort out that will and move to the big house as quickly as possible. She'd have to wait till tomorrow to contact Mr Danvers but she intended to press him for a speedy resolution. There was nothing she could do about Abigail losing her home. It had been Edwina's decision to cut her out of the will. Besides, Cynthia had spent years sucking up to Edwina, depending on her handouts, and it had been hard to take sometimes. She felt she'd *earned* her inheritance.

Abigail had been a captive of Edwina's too after her father died, so to speak, only she hadn't always behaved tactfully and had upset her stepmother once too often, so it was her own fault she'd come out of it with nothing.

Oh, stop feeling guilty, you fool, Cynthia told herself. *You have to look after yourself in this life, because no one else will.*

210

17

Given the other things that were happening to her, Abigail was surprised at how excited she felt when she woke up on the Monday morning and remembered that the computer class was starting today. Being able to do something to help her future made her feel a bit better. She'd had years of practice at pushing her worries to the back of her mind and managed to do that now — more or less.

She got up immediately and dressed in one of the two new pairs of jeans and simple tops she'd bought at the shop in the village, studying herself in the mirror before she added a heavy sweater for warmth. This old house was not a cosy place in which to live and work in winter, but you got used to it.

She thought she looked quite good, especially with her new hairstyle. Was that why Edwina had stopped her from wearing such clothes? Had she been deliberately keeping her stepdaughter looking frumpy? Oh, what did that matter now? Done was done, as Dot would say.

Lucas arrived early and looked at her in a way that showed approval of her appearance but didn't comment. He made sure all the computers were set up and working, then switched them off again because the first lesson would be how to start a computer and what to expect to see on the screen. She was surprised that he was taking such trouble about a simple action. It was only pressing a button, for heaven's sake. Only he said sometimes older people weren't used to anything about computers, so it was best to start at the absolute beginning.

'They don't all have grandchildren to keep them up to date. Fortunately, I haven't met anyone yet who can't learn what to do and not to be afraid of computers if someone will only take the trouble to be patient with them.'

By that time Dot had arrived and was setting up the big tea urn, which Lucas had produced.

'Much more efficient,' she said, putting it on the side table in the hall, together with mugs, instant tea and coffee, milk and biscuits.

She stared round when she'd finished. 'Eh, this hall is as big as my whole ground floor. I'm used to being here now, but I still remember how awed I was when I first came here and sometimes it hits me all over again. Big rooms are my idea of luxury.' She nudged the younger woman. 'It's good for practising our dancing in too, isn't it?' Then she remembered Abigail's new situation and her smile faded.

She returned to the kitchen, trailing a sigh behind her. Would they ever dance here again? Dot wasn't her usual ebullient self today, Abigail thought. Something was definitely on her mind. Well, her friend would no doubt deal with whatever it was, as usual. In the meantime, Abigail must concentrate on today's course.

Once people started arriving, she took on the task of letting them in, directing Sam to escort his wife, Janie, in her wheelchair round to the kitchen entrance. Dot opened it for them and showed them the way through the house to the library, pointing out the separate cloakroom with wheelchair access. She chatted happily as the two women went off together to the back of the house.

Abigail watched them, seeing her friend's smile return. Dear Dot. She loved helping others. Every single person who'd booked on the course turned up on time and soon they were in the thick of it, learning the rudiments properly, as Lucas emphasised.

In the middle of the day's class, a couple of people she knew by sight turned up wanting to borrow some books, so Abigail saw to their needs quickly, noted down what books they'd taken and re-joined the group. She wasn't going to turn anyone away from the amateur library while she could still help them.

By the end of the morning all traces of tension had vanished from the participants' faces and they were enjoying playing solitaire, then some other games that made them practise using a mouse and dragging items across the screen. Lucas had given Abigail some more advanced programs to work through. Sam beamed round as they broke for lunch, most having brought sandwiches. 'I didn't expect to have fun today! I'm really looking forward to the afternoon's programme.'

There were nods and murmurs of agreement from all sides.

During the break, another couple of people who had just found out about the makeshift library came to borrow books. Abigail felt fairly certain that Cynthia wouldn't even consider keeping up this service, even if she gave her the books.

Janie grew tired and Dot noticed that as she was refilling the tea urn. In her usual capable way she found a spare sofa in the small rear breakfast room where the other woman could get out of her wheelchair and lie down for an hour.

Abigail was just about to join the others when there was a knock on the front door. She hurried to answer it, thinking someone else must be wanting to borrow a book. But it was James.

'Have I come at an inconvenient time? Only I was nearby and I thought I'd collect the more valuable books.'

'Oh. Yes. Do come in.'

Abigail wished he'd come later, because she didn't want to miss any of the course.

★ ★ ★

When Dot went into the hall to finish clearing up the tea and coffee things after the break, she saw that the book man was there.

Abigail beamed at her. 'Dot, Mr Porfrey has come to collect the books we hid. Can you get them out for him and then do whatever else he needs so that I can go back to the class?'

'Yes, of course. In fact, why don't you let me deal with the books you're selling from now on, love? You've got this course to see to as well as who knows how many other things.'

'Oh, would you? Is that all right, James?'

'Fine by me.'

She hurried to re-join the others.

Dot led the way into the kitchen and showed him where they'd hidden the books. He went to bring his car round the back and she stood thinking.

When he came back, she studied his face and decided to risk it. 'Can you please give any money you make from the books to me? Things are in a bit of a mess financially, and I'll keep it all safe for Abigail

214

till the will is settled. She's going to need as much money as she can get.'

He looked at her and she guessed he understood why she said that. Well, she couldn't be the only person trying not to let their family pay more inheritance tax than necessary.

'Up to you what you do with the money. As long as Abigail is OK with that.'

Abigail rushed into the kitchen then and said, 'I need a cloth. Someone's spilled a cup of coffee.'

'I'll get you one. I've asked Mr Porfrey to give me the money the books bring, and I'll look after it all for you. Is that OK?'

'Yes. Of course it is. Isn't that what we agreed?' She grabbed the cloth and rushed out again.

'She doesn't want to miss any of the course,' Dot explained. 'She's loving learning about the more modern computers.'

James winked at her. 'That's fine by me then. Up to you two what you do with the money. I just sell books.'

Dot watched him take the boxes out to his car. One thing sorted. She was, she thought ruefully, about to do something else a bit dodgy. Well, too bad. Someone had to protect that lass.

★ ★ ★

Abigail had wondered how Lucas would keep people's interest, but he'd structured the shorter afternoon session very cleverly.

He taught the participants to use a program he'd written, which they could work their way through at their own speed, learning some of the fiddly little tasks involved in using computers. That allowed him to give extra help to those who were still timid about trying anything new on their own while letting the faster learners get ahead.

It all went so well that people exclaimed in surprise when he announced that it was time to stop for the day. 'Tomorrow we'll learn how to update the security program, a few basic safety rules and then we'll move on to using the Internet. I've set up a temporary connection here and you can go online for a while on your own in the afternoon, choosing what to look at.'

Abigail had been keeping an eye on Lucas, but he didn't look to be too tired by his day's work. On the contrary, he seemed visibly energised by the excellent response to his teaching methods.

A couple of participants walked off together, chattering away. They'd come separately so she hoped friendships would also be made from the course. Older people could get so lonely as they lost friends and relatives, not to mention their joints growing stiffer and that impinging on their general mobility. Even Edwina hadn't been immune to it. She sighed. It wasn't only older people who got lonely.

After the participants had all gone, Lucas went round checking that every computer was properly switched off, then stretched his arms and waggled his shoulders, smiling across the room at Abigail. 'You did well today, made good progress on your own.'

'You taught us well. Um, would you like a glass of wine before you go?'

'Are you sure?'

He wasn't only asking about the wine, she guessed. But she was quite sure she wanted to spend more time with him, so even if she was guessing wrongly that he wanted that too, she had decided to give it a try. Her reply was firm. 'Yes. Very sure.'

He nodded and from his expression was giving her an answer to the unspoken question as well. 'Good. I'd really enjoy that.'

★ ★ ★

The phone rang in Philip's office just after ten o'clock the next morning. When he picked it up, he found he was speaking to Gerard's wife.

'We're coming in to see you *briefly* later this morning and we'll not be staying long. I'm only allowing it because my husband hasn't been able to settle since you phoned.'

Her tone sounded accusing, so Philip tossed back, 'That's because you cut us off in the middle of an important discussion. I haven't been able to settle either.'

'I care more about my husband's welfare than any legal case,' she snapped back.

There were some faint noises, then Gerard took over. 'I've promised not to stay long but could you please email me a copy of the will you found in the safe at Ashgrove. I want to check that it's the genuine article before we start out. It's no use coming if it isn't.'

'I'll do that straight away.'

He smiled as he put the phone down. Gerard must be getting better if he was putting his foot down about being kept at home. And his voice didn't sound quite as slurred. He did hope that was so. His partner was a truly decent human being.

He received a return email from Gerard a few minutes after he'd sent the copy of the will.

Pity, Philip thought. He told his secretary to cancel his eleven o'clock appointment. Seeing Gerard was much more important at the moment.

Poor Abigail.

* * *

Before the Liddlestones arrived, Philip heard the sound of the outer door opening followed by a shrill voice he recognised with a sinking heart. He wasn't letting that annoying woman berate his secretary again, not that Miss Cawdell wouldn't give as good as she got in icily polite tones. She was nobody's fool.

He marched out into the reception area and took over. 'Good morning, Miss Polson. I'm afraid I have no slots to spare this morning. If you wish to make an appointment for a more suitable time, I'm sure my secretary can book you in tomorrow or the day after.'

'I need to see you now.'

'I'm sorry. It's just not possible and anyway, nothing else has been sorted out so we've nothing to discuss.'

He didn't like concealing the fact that they'd found a copy of the later will, but then he didn't like her trying to push him around either. He went back into his office, astonished to hear her footsteps behind him and her voice saying, 'Now just a minute!'

'I really am busy!' He shut the door firmly in her face and locked it, amazed to see the handle turn then hear her arguing with his secretary. Thank goodness there were no clients in the waiting area.

When he heard a car pull up outside in their private car park at the rear, he looked out of the window and saw Gerard's big silver Mercedes. He groaned aloud. He definitely didn't want Cynthia upsetting his partner at this delicate stage of recovery.

Since the two women were still to be heard arguing in the reception area, he left his office through the side door that led to the storerooms, restroom and kitchen. He ran down the back stairs and out to the car park, waving to Gerard to get back into the vehicle and slipping into the back of it, explaining breathlessly, 'I'm having trouble with Miss Polson, who's refusing to leave the premises. Could you please drive us round the block, Mrs Liddlestone, and I'll phone my secretary, who will let us know when it's safe to come back?'

'Only under protest. This stress isn't good for my husband, you know.'

Gerard let out one of his rich, deep chuckles. 'On the contrary, I'm finding it very amusing. Here we are all hiding from one small woman.'

'One small but extremely shrill woman,' Philip said ruefully. He studied Gerard. 'You're looking well, far better than I'd expected.'

'I'm feeling better than I have for a while, actually. I don't need Renée to tell me not to come back to work, though. I don't want to risk another stroke, thank you very much. I'm sorry that will leave you in the lurch, but I still have the contact details for a couple of the other people I shortlisted and interviewed for the job you got.'

'That might be useful.'

'The woman sounded very efficient and was pleasant to deal with it. It's only been a few weeks, so it might be worth finding out whether she's still free. But if you prefer to look for someone else, that's your

choice from now on.'

'I'll get Miss Cawdell to look into it and find out whether either of them is still interested. You don't need to worry about the practice, Gerard. I'm managing just fine and your clients are being very understanding about the situation. I love the quieter pace of life here.'

'The long-term business arrangements we agreed when you became my junior partner can remain as we discussed and be brought forward. I'm glad you've settled in so well.'

'I like living in this village. It's large enough to have the basic shops and services I need, and yet not so big there's a lot of traffic and parking problems. I even enjoy that we do a variety of legal work, rather than specialising in one sort of service.'

Gerard turned his head to smile at the younger man. 'That's good to hear.'

'I'm honoured that you trust me to take charge after such a short time, Gerard. Which just leaves Mrs Beadle's will for us to sort out today.'

'Damn the woman!'

At that moment the secretary phoned to give them the all-clear, so they parked in the deliveries area and went in by the rear door, to make sure of not being intercepted. Gerard went to sit behind the desk in his office for what he insisted would be the final time. 'You might as well take this room over, Philip. I shan't be coming back for more than brief visits. You can get Miss Cawdell to pack my personal possessions and send them to my home.'

He glanced round a little sadly then became brisk again. 'Now, if you'll get me the Beadle family box from the records section, I'll see if I can find what I need.'

As he went through the top few documents, Gerard began to frown and checked them for a second time. 'It's not there.'

'What isn't?'

'The agreement made when Stephen Beadle married Edwina Polson. It's not a nuptial agreement, though. I insisted on writing a business agreement instead, since Edwina was going to work with him on managing the estate. Not that there was a lot of it to manage by then, but still, she insisted on being fully involved. She always did like to keep her eye on her own benefits.'

'I didn't know there was any sort of official agreement between them.'

'It was only brief, but it stipulated that if Edwina survived her husband she would be in charge of managing the house and estate, but these were to be passed on to his daughter unconditionally after she died. Edwina signed it but when she was making that final will, she didn't mention it, so I didn't remind her. I think she was failing a little mentally by then and becoming a trifle erratic.'

Philip was surprised at that and must have shown it because Gerard said, 'Towards the end she kept changing the details of her damned will every few weeks, so I thought it wasn't worth her making a scene, and having her ranting and raging at me, when she'd probably be changing it again shortly. I was wrong, very wrong, but I have to admit that I wasn't feeling all that well myself for the few weeks before I had the stroke.'

'Where did you put this agreement?'

'In this box, attached to the end of Stephen's will.'

'Wouldn't it have been easier to give the woman a

life tenancy of the house?'

'Yes. But she was the one who insisted on a proper business agreement and at first Stephen was so taken by her, he'd have agreed to anything. She wasn't always as bad-tempered as she became after his death.'

Philip frowned and tapped the box. 'I certainly didn't see any sign of an extra piece of paper in here when I found the penultimate will and showed it to Abigail, or when we looked for the final will either.'

'The agreement was still there when we drew up that final will. Edwina didn't come into the office again after she'd signed the will, so she couldn't have taken it. Only, I don't think anyone else could have removed it. You'd better check with Miss Cawdell whether anyone else had been into the records room.'

Philip flipped through the papers in the box again, then shook his head in bafflement. 'That makes two things missing: our copy of the final will and the agreement.'

'That's very strange.'

'Someone must have removed them, Gerard, because I certainly didn't. I have to ask it: has Abigail been here on her own at all?'

'No. Definitely not. And she wouldn't have taken anything if she had. She's a very honest, straightforward young woman.'

'That's what I thought but it doesn't hurt to verify such details.'

'Dot used to grumble to me sometimes that Edwina took advantage of Abigail's kind nature.' He stopped, waving his forefinger to and fro as he realised something else. 'Actually, Dot is the only other person I know of who's handled this box. I asked her to put it away for me the last time I was here. I was feeling so ill I didn't even wait to see her do it. I just wanted to get home and lie down.'

Philip was startled. 'Surely she wouldn't have taken the will?'

'I doubt it. I've always considered her totally honest.'

Mrs Liddlestone cleared her throat to get their attention. 'You're overlooking one thing.'

'What?'

'You know how devoted Dot is to Abigail. If she was tempted to read the will as she was putting it away, she'd have been extremely upset about Abigail not being left the house. She could have taken the will then.'

'That doesn't explain what happened to the agreement.'

'You'd better ask her.'

Gerard rubbed his forehead and Philip could see that he was tiring rapidly, so he tried to sound confident. 'Well, I can take over from here. I can always get back to you again if I need clarification about something.'

'You'll — deal with Dot gently, won't you?'

'Of course. Now, you'd better go home and rest.'

'You'll let me know everything that happens as soon as it happens?'

'Naturally.'

Gerard's wife scowled at Philip as he saw them out of the building. She let her husband go first towards the car and lingered to whisper, 'No more pestering him! Look how tired even this short visit has made him.'

'I'll do my best to sort it all out without needing to upset him, I promise you, Mrs Liddlestone.'

18

That afternoon Philip closed the office early, then drove along the high street to Ashgrove House. If he remembered correctly, this would be the second day of the computer course and Dot was doing the catering. At a guess it'd be ending about now.

He wanted to speak to her today if possible.

When Abigail answered the door, she felt instantly anxious when she saw who it was. 'Come in, Philip.' She led the way into the drawing room where Lucas was sitting with a half empty wine glass on a small table in front of him, looking comfortably at home.

She had been enjoying their after-class drinks session, but at the sight of Philip's serious expression, Lucas put his wine down. 'Do you want me to leave you two alone?'

She shook her head. 'I'd rather you stayed.' She turned back to watch Philip anxiously and the minute he'd sat down, she asked, 'Is there some news?' If so, it was going to be bad news, she was sure.

'Not yet. Look, is Dot still around? I need to check something with her and I'm happy to have you two present.'

'Oh dear! You've just missed her, I'm afraid. She left for home as soon as she'd cleared up the tea things but that was nearly an hour ago now. She was going to pick up a friend once she'd changed into some smarter clothes, then they were going out to another friend's to play cards.' Abigail glanced at her watch. 'I doubt you'll catch her at home. I'll phone her and see if she's still there, shall I? It might save you a wasted journey.'

She did that and the three of them waited in silence for someone at the other end to pick up the call, but after a while she shook her head and put the handset down. 'There's no answer and she always answers straight away if she can. She switches off her phone when she visits friends.'

'Do you know where the friend lives?'

'I'm afraid not. I don't even know which friend it is. She's friends with half the village.'

'Oh, hell.' He thumped one clenched fist into the other.

'Am I allowed to know what's going on?' she asked. 'Maybe I could help?'

'I don't think so. And if you don't mind, I'd rather not say anything till I catch up with Dot. There are still a few things to check in connection with that later will.'

There was silence and when Lucas slipped his hand in hers, she felt comforted by his presence and gave his a squeeze.

'Could you let me have her home address, please, Abigail? It'll save me going back to the office and searching for it in employee records. I told Miss Cawdell she could leave early, so she'll not be there to help me. I'm still learning the various office systems.'

'Yes, of course.' She told him and he scribbled it in a little notebook.

'Why don't you join us for a glass of wine, Philip?'

'Thanks, but not today. I still have some work to do.'

★ ★ ★

225

Philip couldn't resist driving home via Dot's house, just in case, but there was no sign of her car and no answer to his knock.

It was fully dark when he got home and he was surprised to see that the neighbours had put some Christmas lights up on the outsides of their house, quite a lot of lights. They certainly hadn't skimped.

The lights took him by surprise, twinkling away cheerfully on most nearby houses and he suddenly remembered a neighbourhood group sending him a note explaining how the people in the street usually got together to deal with Christmas. Oh hell, he'd forgotten about that. He'd better put up some token decorations to show willing — if he could find the ones he and his wife had used years ago, that was. He hadn't celebrated Christmas properly since she died. It simply didn't feel real to him without her there the first year and by the time the next Christmas came round, his children were both at university and getting on with their own lives, which included holiday jobs in hotels, so he hadn't bothered with decorating anything.

He should make a bit of an effort this year, didn't want to start off with new neighbours thinking him Mr Grumpy. Perhaps he'd even buy some proper decorations for the outside of his house, just a few.

His son and daughter had made arrangements to spend part of the festive season with their university friends and were now coming to his new home, so he'd definitely need to do more this time. He dismissed Christmas planning from his mind. Before he did anything about that, he needed to sort out the confusion about the will. That was occupying centre stage in his thoughts at the moment. He hated the idea of something so unfair happening to such a nice woman. Abigail and her problems continued to occupy his thoughts all evening and he was only half-aware of the TV talking to itself in the background. He kept coming back to that business agreement. What could have happened to it?

Could Dot really have taken the will? She didn't seem like the type to steal anything but who else could it have been? He couldn't see her taking the agreement because that was something in Abigail's favour.

* * *

As Abigail walked out of the room to escort the lawyer to the front door, Lucas wondered whether he too should leave. But he still had half a glass of wine and anyway, he was enjoying her company. This seemed promising for their future interactions. He relaxed at that thought. All his old feelings for her were starting to fire up again. He was more cautious these days, wanted to get to know her properly as an older person before he dived into a relationship. Though actually she didn't seem to have changed much.

He should invite her out for a meal at the pub. Yes, he'd do that. Hell, how long had it been since he felt this hopeful about the future? The illness had side-swiped him after a life as a fit, active person and he'd got very depressed for a time. It was clear from what she said that they'd both been lonely. Most significant of all, neither of them had found a permanent life partner in nearly two decades. Maybe they needed each other to feel emotionally whole. Perhaps there really was only one woman for him, as he'd joked in his youth. Was that possible? He'd dated other women over the years, of course he had, but none of them had become permanent, or even been around for more than a few months.

He stared idly across at the huge mirror above the fireplace, opposite to where he was sitting, admiring its ornate, gilded frame, then he stiffened in shock as he saw in it a reflection of three people in what looked like fancy dress. He swung round to ask them who the hell they were and was even more shocked to see that there was no one in the room with him.

Only, when he turned back to gaze at the mirror, the three of them were still there. His voice came out croaky with shock. 'Am I going crazy?'

'No, you're not, Lucas Chadwick,' the older of the two women said quietly. 'It's just that now you've started to see Abigail more clearly and have fallen in love with her all over again, we're letting you see us too.'

'I don't understand. Is someone playing a trick on me?'

'Definitely not. We're some of the Beadle family ghosts. Only the owner of the house can see us most of the time — but sometimes we appear to other people.'

He didn't believe in ghosts, so he prowled round the edges of the room, blinking his eyes, checking. Someone must be playing a trick. Only he didn't find anything suspicious and they didn't disappear nor did their reflections change even though he walked through the spot where they seemed to be standing.

He came to a halt, muttering, 'I don't believe this.'

The man in the mirror, who seemed to be wearing a sort of Mr Darcy costume, grinned at him. 'Don't you believe your own eyes, Lucas?'

He turned round quickly but again saw nothing behind him so continued to stare at them in the mirror where they were all too clearly reflected. He couldn't deny that he was seeing something, but what?

Then Abigail came back into the room and stopped dead, only she wasn't looking at him, but behind him. 'Oh.'

Lucas's voice came out as a near whisper. 'Can you see them too?'

'Yes.'

'I don't understand.'

'They're my family ghosts but I thought only the owner of the house could see them.'

'And quite often the owner's husband or wife as well, if they truly love their spouse,' the younger female said. 'Your mother used to see us too, Abigail.'

'She could?'

'Oh, yes. She loved your father very much, you see, so we grew fond of her. After she died, she came back sometimes to watch him. Whereas we've never let Edwina see us.'

'She definitely didn't marry my father purely for love.'

Lucas moved across to grab her hand, glad of its solid warmth. She gave it a squeeze and gave him one of her beautiful, warm smiles.

'I think that's enough for his first time, don't you?' The older woman turned to her companions and they nodded. She turned back to point one forefinger at Abigail. 'Look after him, my dear. He's worth it. What do they call men like him in your times? Oh yes, keepers. Very apt for this one. You should definitely keep him.'

Then they faded slowly away.

229

Abigail didn't know what to say, but Lucas kept hold of her hand and surprised her by saying, 'They think we love one another.'

'Yes.'

He moved closer. 'Does that mean yes, you do love me or are you only referring to what they think?'

What her ghosts had said gave her the confidence to say it aloud. 'It means I love you. I don't think I've ever stopped loving you, Lucas. Or grieving that we'd been separated.'

He took her in his arms, looking at her with utter seriousness. 'I feel the same way about you that I did before, only I've been afraid to give in to my feelings; it hurt so much to lose you last time.'

'Misunderstandings.'

'No,' he corrected, 'nasty tricks played by an evil woman.'

'Why did you never come back to see me and sort it all out in person?'

'She threatened my parents' safety if I came anywhere near you.'

She was shocked. 'Edwina did that?'

'Yes. And later on your father became ill and he needed you more than I did. Also, I had a business by then and it went through a crisis or two.'

'I couldn't have left Dad anyway. He needed me to protect him against Edwina half the time because she didn't cope well with illness. Since then I've stayed to look after the house.'

'I remember how much you loved it.'

'It's always been there for me, somehow, a comfort in troubled times and a family responsibility we Beadles take very seriously.'

He raised her hand to his lips and kissed it and for

a moment she couldn't speak as warmth ran through her, then she said sadly, 'Edwina's gone now but I'm going to lose the house one way or another.'

'Inheritance taxes?'

'I thought it'd be that but Edwina's willed it to someone else. Even if she hadn't, I'd still lose it to the taxes.'

'I'm so sorry about that. I think inheritance taxes are iniquitous.'

'Me too. But it's good to have you around again.' She was determined not to be a total misery. 'The family ghosts seem determined to reignite our relationship. So does Dot! They've all been giving me advice about how to deal with you.'

'Are you going to follow that advice?'

'Some of it, yes. Why do you think I invited you to stay for a drink? They keep telling me to kiss you.'

'What a great idea!' He pulled her close and kissed her properly.

When the kiss ended, she felt breathless, young, more like the old Abigail than she had for years, so she kissed her fingertips and pressed them on his cheek, something they'd done when they were young, to seal a kiss, they'd said. She caught her breath as she pulled her fingers away. It was amazing how sensual that simple gesture could feel.

'Just to make sure it's absolutely clear, Abigail, I would very much like us to get together again. Permanently if all goes well. And I shan't need nudging by anyone now that I know you feel the same way.'

She kept hold of his hand. 'Good. But can we take things slowly? I'm feeling a little overwhelmed by the inheritance question as well as by the possibilities with you. My life seems to have been turned upside down and inside out.'

'I don't want to go too slowly.'

She didn't protest when he kissed her again. In fact, she kissed him right back. She wasn't a stupid heroine in a book to leave all the initiative to her man; she was a mature woman who had wasted far too much of her life without him. Besides, she'd always enjoyed kissing him.

And she still did. Very much.

This was the second ray of brightness in what was still, in many ways, the most terrible time of her whole life.

19

Foiled in the end by Miss Cawdell's icy politeness, Cynthia left the lawyer's office feeling aggrieved. Mr Danvers was brushing her off, not taking her claim seriously, not even offering her an appointment later today. What was he up to?

Had he got the safe open? If he hadn't, why couldn't he just see her for a few moments? It'd be only polite to explain that he was still waiting for the locksmith — though she was still angry that he hadn't used *her* locksmith.

She frowned. He might even have made an appointment to get it done sneakily, for all she knew! She had a right to be kept informed about all the details of what was going on. When she got her inheritance, as she surely must if her clever cousin Edwina had arranged things, she would find another lawyer to handle her affairs, one who didn't leave her in the dark.

She paused as it occurred to her that there was another lawyer in Medderby. She'd passed their rooms many a time. It was just before you got into the town. She had a very good mind to go there straight away and see if she could get help from someone at that practice.

And why not? She had no money to pay them with until she got probate on her inheritance, and that could take some time, she knew. But surely a lawyer who saw the justice of her claim would wait for payment? Yes, of course they would.

When she arrived, she scowled at the garish Christmas decorations framing the entrance to the office, which seemed to house several lawyers, according to a brass plate to one side. Christmas already, and it'd probably be as bleak and boring as it had been last year. And for most of the years before that. She had to do something if her life wasn't to continue in the same dreary way, just had to. Edwina had been telling her for years that you only got what you wanted by pushing for it.

'Here goes,' Cynthia muttered, taking a deep breath and marching in.

At first the young woman at reception didn't want to let her see either of the lawyers currently there, so Cynthia continued to put Edwina's instructions into operation. She argued and talked down the woman barring her way. It didn't come as easily to her as it had to her cousin, it never had, but she was feeling utterly desperate and the young woman's rather scornful attitude stiffened her spine.

In the end she was shown into an office where a sharp-faced young woman was sitting behind a desk.

'I'm Janet Smalley. Please take a seat.'

'I'm Cynthia Polson.'

'I can only spare you a few minutes.'

She explained her situation quickly and the young woman began to pay attention.

'If you can wait half an hour, till after my next appointment, I'll have no more people coming to see me today. I can come with you to see Mr Danvers. Your cousin would definitely have received a copy of that will and I doubt Danvers would destroy it if he found it. He is a lawyer, after all, and I've never heard anything bad about him. Once I see exactly how it's worded I'll have a better idea of whether to proceed.'

Cynthia felt almost sick with relief and was glad to have the next half hour in which to pull herself together in a small private waiting room, especially when the receptionist brought her a cup of tea and two biscuits. She heard the woman trying to get through to Mr Danvers on the phone and then, after Ms Smalley had shown out her client, telling the lawyer that she'd not succeeded.

Ms Smalley came to see Cynthia. 'Even the answering machine at his rooms isn't switched on, apparently, but as it's almost on my way home, we can give it a go tonight, if you like, and if not we can go there tomorrow.'

'I'd appreciate that.'

When they got to Mr Liddlestone's rooms, however, that horrible Miss Cawdell said Mr Danvers had left for the day and she wasn't sure where he'd gone.

'I need to see him ASAP,' her new lawyer said firmly. 'Kindly get a message to him. If he can come in early tomorrow morning, I can easily pop in for a quick chat on my way to work.'

Miss Cawdell scowled at them both. 'I'll see what I can do. If necessary I'll get back to you with an alternative time to meet. Kindly give me your personal contact number.'

Outside, Ms Smalley looked at her watch. 'I have your phone number, Miss Polson, so I'll get back to you after I've spoken to Mr Danvers tomorrow.' Then she walked smartly away, not even waiting for an answer, which left Cynthia feeling almost as dissatisfied as she had before.

* * *

235

The following morning, Philip drove to Ashgrove House before he went into the office, determined to see Dot before he decided what to do. He'd told Miss Cawdell to make an appointment for this Ms Smalley to see him later in the day. He had a vague memory of meeting her at some kind of social function for lawyers in the Medderby area, but couldn't be sure.

Anyway, if she was representing Cynthia, it'd be better to make some progress with the investigation into the will before he spoke to her formally.

At Ashgrove House he saw through the window that Abigail was sitting in the kitchen with Dot, chatting over a cup of tea. When he knocked on the back door, Dot turned and saw him peering in at the window. She froze, looking suddenly terrified. Which wasn't like her. He saw Abigail stare at her friend, could tell she too was surprised by this reaction, then she came to unlock the door and let him in.

'I need to speak to Dot urgently.'

'You'd better come in, then.'

Dot hadn't moved from her place at the kitchen table.

He sat down opposite her and said gently but firmly, 'It's about time we had a discussion about what happened to the final will, don't you think?'

Dot burst into tears and it took a while for her to calm down.

Abigail poured him a cup of tea while they were waiting. 'Tell me what you need to discuss. Surely that will concerns me rather than Dot.'

'Not this time. You can listen to what we say but it's Dot I need to talk to and the fact that she's so upset makes me think I've come to the right person.'

After Dot had blown her nose and looked at him

236

with apprehension in every line of her body, he asked quietly, 'What happened to the final will, Dot?'

She stared at him for a moment, then said in a tight voice, 'I found it in the office and was so upset I took it home to read again and think about it, then Cynthia Polson came here to the house. She was so rude to my lass, I got angry and . . .' She fell silent, twisting her handkerchief into a knot.

'And what?' he prompted.

'I tore the will up and burned it.'

'And the piece of paper that was underneath it in the Beadle records box?'

'Piece of paper?'

'Mr Liddlestone said there was a special agreement in the box as well. It's important that we find it. That's far more important than the will.'

'Oh. Well.' She frowned then said slowly, 'Now I come to think about it, there was a piece of paper on the floor. I thought it must have fallen out when I was pulling the will out. I'd trodden on it and crumpled it, so I picked it up and shoved it into the box again.'

'As long as you didn't destroy it.'

'No. It didn't look important. It was only the will I was bothered about. I've never touched your papers before, never.' She mopped away some more tears.

'And I want your solemn promise that you'll never touch them again if we allow you to continue working for us.'

'I promise.' She shuddered. 'I've been so upset about what I did. Believe me, I could never do something like that again.'

'Good.' Philip turned back to Abigail. 'I'll go back to the office straight away and hunt for it.'

Abigail went to the door with him and Dot stayed where she was, staring down at her sodden handkerchief. 'Will you let me know when you find it, Philip?'

'Once I get this little problem sorted out, you'll be the first to know.'

What sort of answer was that? she wondered, looking at Dot reproachfully. She didn't know what to say about all this but when her dear friend showed every sign of bursting into tears all over again, she had to comfort her.

Afterwards, they got on with their day's work, but Abigail felt as if the load of worry had turned into an even heavier lump and it was pressing down on her chest.

When Lucas arrived to run the final day of his computer course, she had to pull herself together and help him get things ready. She might have had years of experience at hiding her emotions, but he knew her better than anyone ever had, except her father and Dot, and the way he looked at her said he wasn't fully convinced everything was all right.

She hoped Dot would manage to do the catering properly today, and she hoped she and Lucas would continue to make progress in their relationship. Beyond that she didn't have much hope about anything because she'd spent the past few days feeling alternately depressed, then happy, then back down in the dumps again. It was a good thing she had the workshop to distract her.

But however nice the group of participants was and however well organised the final day's lessons were, it was going to be hard to get through the day.

238

When they were alone in the library getting the computers ready, Lucas said, 'Are you going to be all right?'

Abigail gave him a wan smile. 'Yes, of course.'

'Anything I can help with?'

'Not really. Trouble with the will is ongoing. I'm not sure exactly what's happening at the moment, so I can only wait for Philip to find out about it all. You and I should just get on with our day. The course is going well, at least.'

'All right. But after the course ends, I want you to tell me exactly what you know so far. We'll not be hiding anything from one another from now on, if I have my way. Misunderstandings stole our years away once and I don't intend to let them do it again. Besides, I may be able to help you.'

'It's a help just to have you around.' She summoned up a smile and a nod, then saw he was waiting for some real response, so she kissed him quickly on the cheek, clinging to him for a few moments, then going back to work.

She hoped there would be nothing that needed hiding, but she'd have to protect Dot. She'd never seen her dear friend so upset.

★ ★ ★

When Philip arrived at work he found Ms Smalley waiting for him, tapping one foot and scowling at him.

'A later appointment didn't suit me,' she said.

He looked at Miss Cawdell.

'I cancelled your first appointment since Ms

239

Smalley was so insistent on seeing you,' she said.

She was a good judge of character so he turned back to study his visitor. He'd rarely seen a more determined expression on a woman's face. 'Please come into my office.' Once there, he gestured to a chair.

'I think you're prevaricating, Mr Danvers.'

'No. I need to do something important before I can discuss anything.'

'Something to do with the will?'

He hesitated, then shrugged. 'Yes. There's another document I have to find before I can discuss anything — with you or anyone else.'

'Perhaps I can help you? I don't intend to leave until I'm satisfied I know all the facts, but I don't cheat or try to trick people, not about anything.'

He stared at her, then gave in to fate, or call it what you liked. 'Oh, very well. I'll call in my secretary then you and she can act as witnesses, but only on condition that you promise not to touch anything.'

'I promise — as long as you don't try to destroy anything.'

'I would never destroy documents.'

She studied him then nodded, as if he'd passed some sort of test. 'No, I don't think you would.'

When they were all three in the records room, he explained the situation, then asked both women to stand where they could see what he was doing. 'And remember, you've promised not to touch anything, Ms Smalley.'

He took the documents out of the Beadle records box one by one, showing the two women the title pages, then when the box was empty, he sighed and put all the documents carefully back. To give Ms Smalley her due, she didn't try to interrupt his concentration, but she did watch extremely carefully. He'd bet nothing escaped her sharp gaze.

'What exactly were you looking for, Mr Danvers?'

'I was looking for an agreement, and Dot said a piece of paper had fallen out and she shoved it back hastily. Only there's no sign of it. I can't understand that. Mr Liddlestone had seen it there recently. Dot was, um, putting a document away for him in the Beadles' record box.' He saw Ms Smalley's scornful expression. 'Yes, I know. Some things here are very old-fashioned. Anyway, it was after she'd put the box on the shelf again that she found the piece of paper. She didn't look at it, just stuffed it back in the box.'

'How reliable is this Dot?' Ms Smalley asked.

'She's been employed here and at Ashgrove House for many years and we've always found her very reliable. I'm quite sure she wasn't lying.'

Miss Cawdell nodded. 'Dot is a very honest person. I too have dealt with her for many years.'

As he stared down at the box, wondering what could have happened to the agreement, Ms Smalley took a step forward.

'It's all right. I'm not going to touch anything. I just thought of something.' She stared up at the shelf.

'To help your client?'

'She's only just become my client and I care much more about the truth than about her. You clearly believed you'd find that piece of paper and you believed Dot when she said she'd stuffed it back in the box, so I have a suggestion to make.'

'Go on . . .'

★ ★ ★

The final day of the computer course crawled by and it took all Abigail's willpower to keep concentrating. Then at last it was over. She sagged back in her seat and watched people saying farewell, exchanging phone numbers, looking energised and happy.

That was something positive, at least, and it was good that she'd helped make it possible.

When they'd all gone Dot came to stand in the doorway of the library. 'Do you two mind if I go home now? It's been hard to keep going today. I've cleared everything up in the kitchen and hall, and I'm exhausted.'

Lucas reached into his pocket and fished out an envelope. 'Here's your pay.'

'Thank you.' She stuffed it in her pocket, not even looking at it.

Abigail gave her a final hug in the kitchen and Dot clung to her for longer than usual, whispering, 'I'm sorry.'

'Shh. It's over and done with.' She went back to re-join Lucas.

'Now are you going to tell me the details of what's going on?' he asked gently. 'Not if it's too private, but I can't comfort you, let alone help you, if I don't know what we're up against.'

He'd said 'we' and it was beginning to feel as if they were starting to become a real team. He walked across with her to sit on the sofa, pulling her close. 'Tell me. I want to help.'

She went through what she knew and waited as he sat quietly for a few moments. He seemed to be checking it all through mentally.

'It must be hard to face losing Ashgrove House. I've never seen a family as attached to their home as

242

you Beadles.'

'It's part of us, somehow,' she said simply.

'Even the ghosts?'

'I didn't see them until I thought I'd inherited.'

He frowned.

'What's the matter?'

'Well, if only the owner can see them, how come you're still able to see them if you're not the owner? That doesn't make sense, Abigail.'

'I never thought of it that way. You're right. That is strange.' A little shiver of hope ran through her but she didn't dare let it grow any larger.

'Do you want to call up your ghosts and ask them about it?'

'No. I want to sit here quietly with you and gather my strength. I don't think we'd better have a drink tonight, though, because apart from me wanting to keep a clear head, I may have to grab a few things in a hurry and drive somewhere. I've got an emergency bag packed.'

'Why would you need to leave so abruptly?'

'Because I couldn't bear to stay here with some-one else in charge, just couldn't face it. When Edwina died I vowed I'd never let anyone boss me about in that unreasonable way again, even for the sake of the house. I'm moving out if Cynthia is allowed to move in.'

'You can always come and stay at my place.'

'I don't think we're at that stage in our relationship yet.'

'We don't need to share a bed. I have a spare bed-room and am quite capable of keeping my desire for you under control.'

'Thanks, but Dot has already offered me a room in

243

her house for as long as I need one.'

'All right. Your choice. Hmm. You do need some comfort, though. Do you still love hot chocolate?'

'Yes.' It pleased her every time he remembered details like that.

'Let's go and make some. I'll start loading the van with computers if you'll do it. I don't want to leave them here if Cynthia is going to be in charge.'

'Do you have room for them all in your house?'

'It's the same house I used to live in as a kid. Rather small. There's room to dump them but not to live with them. I bought the house from your stepmother a few years ago.'

'She never told me.'

'She needed the money to pay the inheritance tax after your father died.'

'I wondered how she managed it. She left a packet of banknotes in the safe, a lot of money, no one knows why. Philip took it away.'

'Perhaps it'll provide you with a nest egg.'

'I'm not relying on anything. Go on. Will you have to store the computers in your house?'

'No. I've just leased a unit on the industrial estate. I'm going to set it up as a working space. There's nothing in it yet so I can leave the computers there till they're next needed.'

'You don't seem short of money.'

'I'm not. I've worked hard and saved hard too.' He wasn't ready to tell her the details yet.

'I'm glad for you.'

After they'd finished their drinks, he said reluctantly. 'Well, I'd better make a start. It's dark now. Good thing the units are floodlit.'

'Let me help you. I need something to keep busy

244

with. I'll go mad just sitting around waiting to hear something.'

He put his arm round her shoulders and gave her a quick hug. 'Fine by me. I'll come back and wait with you afterwards, if you like.'

'Thank you. I'd really welcome your company.'

They walked across the hall to the library hand in hand and it felt so right.

★ ★ ★

When Philip arrived at Ashgrove House, there was clearly no one there even though Abigail's old car was parked in its usual place round the back. He got out of his vehicle and waited for Ms Smalley to park hers and join him.

'Looks to me as though they've gone out.'

'But they've left lights on, quite a lot of lights, so I'd guess they're expecting to come back quite soon.' She shivered. 'It's a pretty house, isn't it?'

'Very pretty. Let me buy you a drink while we're waiting. It's too cold to hang around.'

'I live quite near here, only a couple of minutes' drive away. We could have a quick coffee at my place then come back in half an hour or so.'

'I think we'd be better having our meetings in public places till this is sorted out, Janet. But I'd be happy to take you up on the coffee another time.'

'You would?'

'Yes. I mean that. I don't play silly games.'

She studied him. 'You're not married, then? You look married.'

'Not now.'

'Divorced?'

'No, widowed.'

'Oh, sorry. And I think you're right. We should find somewhere to have a public coffee. It's a bit of a ticklish situation. We don't want to be accused of collusion. Follow me. We can grab a quick coffee at that little pub nearby.'

She didn't wait for him to agree, but got back into the car. He smiled. A decisive woman, Ms Smalley, but he rather liked that.

★ ★ ★

Dot went home, had another little cry at how she'd messed things up, then gave herself a telling-off for being so weak. 'Get over it!' she told her reflection in the mirror. But the reflection's lips wobbled and a tear ran down its cheek. She dashed the moisture away, angry at her weakness, then went up to the spare bedroom and made up the bed, getting it ready for Abigail to stay. Sadly, that seemed to be the most likely thing that would happen, if not tonight then quite soon.

After going back downstairs, she wondered how to pass the time. She was desperate enough to contemplate clearing out her fridge, but couldn't face it.

When the doorbell rang, she hurried to answer it, delighted to see an old friend who called in for coffee occasionally. She didn't tell Lois about her problems and when taxed with not paying attention, admitted that there was something on her mind. 'Sorry. It'll get it sorted out in a day or two, I expect.'

The trouble was, she couldn't settle into a nice chat, as they usually did, and had to ask Lois to repeat something. In the end her friend gave her a hug and left her alone. Being on her own didn't feel good either, though.

Dot was just about to start on the dratted fridge when her phone rang.

20

Philip drove back to Ashgrove House after they'd finished their coffees and saw a van parked in front of
the house, and Lucas carrying a big box out towards
it. He'd expected the workshop equipment to have
been taken away by now. Clearly not.

He pulled up nearby and by the time he'd got out
of the car, Janet Smalley had parked next to him once
again.

Abigail was standing near the front door watching
them. She looked so anxious Philip felt to be hurt-
ing for her, but he didn't think it right to say or do
anything until Janet had phoned her client and asked
Cynthia to join them. And perhaps Dot should come
too. She was deeply involved in this affair, after all.

'All right if my colleague and I come in, Abigail?
We need to talk to you. But first we'd like to phone
Cynthia and Dot and ask them to join us here, if you
don't mind. What we have to say concerns you all.'
He waited.

Abigail shrugged. 'OK. Whatever you think best.'
She took a step back and waited just inside the front
door, out of the cold wind.

Lucas, who'd paused to watch and listen, put his
box in the van then closed its rear doors and joined
her in the hall, one arm protectively round her shoulders.

Dot picked up the phone straight away and said
she'd come over at once. Philip put his phone in his
pocket and waited for Janet to finish her call. He intro-

duced her to Abigail and Lucas as Cynthia's lawyer, which made his client look even more worried.

'You both look so solemn. Is something else wrong?' she blurted out.

'Nothing to worry about. Dot says she'll be here shortly.' He looked at the other lawyer questioningly.

'Cynthia is coming straight over too. We should wait to go through what's happened until she arrives.'

'Let's sit in the drawing room, then.' Abigail turned and led the way. Lucas stayed beside her, Philip noticed as he closed the front door. They looked very much together. Strange how quickly that seemed to have happened.

'Please sit down. Let me switch the heater on.' She moved across to do that, shivering. 'Sorry it's so cold in here. I don't usually heat the whole house. It's too expensive.'

Janet stopped in the doorway to look back at the hall. 'What beautiful panelling. I bet it's original. Late eighteenth century?'

'Yes, it is.'

When they were all seated Philip asked, 'Do you know how long it usually takes Cynthia to get here?'

'About ten minutes.'

'I know Dot isn't directly involved but she's very much a part of all this, don't you think?'

'Oh, yes. Besides, she's more like an auntie to me than an employee. I don't know what I'd have done without her help and support over the past few years.'

Philip saw her exchange worried glances with Lucas and was tempted to hint that there wasn't any need to worry. But no, he'd agreed with Janet how to do this and would stick to their bargain. It was hard to keep people waiting, though, when they were so desperate for resolution of a crucial problem.

'Would you like a cup of coffee?' Abigail offered as the silence lengthened.

Ms Smalley answered. 'Thanks, but no. We've just had one. May I switch the lights on again in the hall and look at the portraits there? Those two on the rear wall looked to be eighteenth century as well. Tell me no if you don't want me to, but I'm a bit of a history buff and I love old paintings. They're windows into our past, don't you think?'

'Oh yes, I love that sort of thing too. I'm as near a curator as this house has had for the past couple of decades, so I know the details of most of its contents. My father began training me when he fell ill. Please feel free to wander round the hall and do ask if you'd like to know more about anything in particular.'

Dot was the first to arrive, coming in via the kitchen, stopping to stare suspiciously at the woman in the hall then hesitating again in the doorway of the drawing room.

Abigail gestured. 'Oh good, you're here. Come and sit near me, Dot.'

Ms Smalley re-joined them and went across the spacious room to sit down.

When Dot was sitting next to Abigail, she looked across at Philip. 'Did you find it, Mr Danvers?'

'We'll tell you everything once Cynthia arrives, if you don't mind.'

She sighed and continued to sit bolt upright, hands tightly clasped, looking worried.

It was a relief to them all when shortly afterwards there was the sound of a car stopping outside. Abigail got up and peered out of the window. 'It's Cynthia. I'll let her in.'

'Let me do that, if you don't mind,' Ms Smalley said. 'She's my client — for the moment, anyway.'

What did that mean? Abigail wondered as the front door opened and closed again, followed by a murmur of voices. When the two women came to join them, Cynthia was frowning, clearly as puzzled by all this as the others.

Philip stood up. 'Right. Let's make a start. Thank you for your patience.' When everyone turned towards him, he said, 'We found the copy of the final will in the safe as you suggested, Miss Polson.'

Cynthia sat up straighter, her face brightening.

'We had to find another document before we could do anything about the will. Mr Liddlestone was well enough to tell me about an agreement made by your cousin Edwina and Stephen Beadle on their marriage and it was crucial. It wasn't in the Beadle records box as it should have been, but thanks to a suggestion by Ms Smalley, we searched the nearby boxes for it as well and she saw us retrieve it. It proved to be a good guess. The agreement had been, er, accidentally misplaced and was in the record box next to that of the Beadles.'

'You mean I put it in the wrong box?' Dot exclaimed. 'That's not like me. You can tell how upset I was feeling.'

'Did you do that on purpose?' Ms Smalley asked.

'No, of course not. I didn't even know what the paper was. I was in a hurry to go home and it didn't occur to me that it was connected to the will.'

Philip pulled out a transparent plastic envelope containing a single sheet of paper. 'Is this it?'

She studied it. 'Looks like it. It was creased like that when I picked it up. I must have trodden on it.'

'Well, it is the document Mr Liddlestone told me about, as he's confirmed. This is a business agreement made between Stephen Beadle and his second wife, Edwina Maud Polson, before their marriage as to how they would manage the estate. It isn't a prenuptial agreement but a business agreement, duly signed and witnessed.'

He saw Cynthia's smile fade as he said that and she began to look anxious. He hadn't been looking forward to dashing her hopes, much as he disliked the woman, and was worried about how she'd take the news. He wasn't surprised when she didn't wait for him to go on.

Her voice was shrill. 'What does that *mean*, Mr Danvers? Surely a business agreement doesn't affect a later will.'

'I'm afraid this one does, Miss Polson. The paper is rather crumpled but there's no doubt it's genuine. Not only has Mr Liddlestone confirmed that it's the one he drew up and witnessed, but your lawyer has also examined it and spoken to him.'

He looked at Ms Smalley for confirmation and she nodded. Cynthia opened her mouth to speak, but he raised his voice and carried on. 'The agreement is very straightforward, so I'll summarise it then you can look at it yourselves if you wish to check what I've said. In brief, it was agreed that the two of them would work together as a business partnership after their marriage. If he died first, she would continue to manage the estate until her death and act as its owner, unless she wished to resign from the task. After that everything was to go to Abigail.'

Ms Smalley added quietly, 'The agreement specified that no later will could revoke the arrangement

252

for the house to be passed to Mr Beadle's daughter by his first marriage.'

Cynthia jumped to her feet, yelling, 'I don't believe it! Edwina said everything would come to me. She promised.'

'We don't know what she was thinking when her final will was drawn up. It was shortly before her death and perhaps she was getting a little confused.'

'No, no! It can't be true.' Tears began to run down Cynthia's face.

'I'm afraid Mr Liddlestone is partly at fault for the confusion, Miss Polson, and he wishes me to apologise unreservedly to you on his behalf. He told me that Edwina Beadle grew rather eccentric in the two years before she died and rewrote her will several times, changing the details, usually after taking offence at someone's behaviour. When she changed it that final time, leaving everything to her cousin, he knew it wasn't valid, but he expected her to change the will again within a few weeks.'

Cynthia was rocking to and fro now, tears running down her face. He might not like her, but that didn't mean Philip did not feel very sorry for her.

'Since Mr Liddlestone was feeling rather unwell himself at the time, he allowed her to sign it, which he now acknowledges he should not have done. Shortly afterwards, as you know, she had a massive heart attack and died two weeks later without properly regaining consciousness. Mr Liddlestone intended to clear the matter up, but he had a stroke and was rushed to hospital. He's still recovering and has decided to retire, so has asked me to sort it all out. He's truly sorry for the confusion and since he's retiring, I feel the matter need go no further legally.'

Cynthia continued to sob and Ms Smalley went to sit next to her client, speaking to her quietly.

She scrubbed her eyes and glared at the lawyer. 'You've lost me my inheritance by your stupid suggestion to look in the other boxes, so I'm not paying you anything. Not one single penny!'

Ms Smalley looked round the room. 'Just for the record, I am in complete agreement with everything Mr Danvers has said about the legal status of that last will.' She turned back to the sobbing woman. 'I shall not be charging you anything for my services, Miss Polson.'

Philip nodded. 'Thank you for your help, Ms Smalley.'

She spread her hands, making a helpless shrugging gesture. 'I don't think I can contribute anything further to this discussion, so I'll take my leave unless you wish me to stay.'

He shook his head.

She glanced across at Cynthia, but the poor woman didn't even look up as she left.

* * *

Abigail couldn't think what to do next. She felt torn between tears and jubilation, not to mention a sense of utter, bone-deep relief at this outcome. It would not only give her breathing time but also leave her with some money and possessions for whatever life she made for herself after she'd sold the house and paid the inheritance tax.

She turned sideways to Dot and saw that her friend was still looking very subdued, then turned the other way to smile at Lucas, who put his arm round her shoulders again and returned her smile. Cynthia stood up abruptly and ran out of the room, still sobbing. They heard the front door bang open.

Abigail sighed. 'I'd better go after her.'

'No, let me do that, love. This mix-up was partly my fault. I'm never going near them record boxes again as long as I live.' Dot hurried outside.

Philip waited a moment or two but Abigail said nothing. 'Unless there's anything else you want to ask this evening, I'll leave you in peace. I don't think you're in a state to discuss any further business at the moment.'

'No. I think what I need most is to sit quietly and take it all in.'

'I'll set about applying for probate as soon as possible. If you phone the office tomorrow, we'll fit you in for an appointment whenever you can make it.'

She had to ask it again. 'There can be no doubt that I'm the heir?'

'No, none at all. I'll be in touch.'

★ ★ ★

Dot followed Cynthia outside and found her sitting in her old car, head resting on her folded arms on the steering wheel. She was still weeping, but in a tired, hopeless way now. Dot had never liked the woman but it upset her to see anyone in such extreme distress, so she went round towards the driving seat and opened the car door then crouched down to speak to her.

It was a moment or two before Cynthia even noticed her, then she said in tones of loathing, 'What are *you* doing here? Come to gloat, have you?'

'What should I be gloating about? I don't like to

see anyone so upset.'

'Then don't watch. Just go away and leave me to it.'

Dot hesitated but she had to ask it. 'Why did you think you had a right to the house? You're not a Beadle.'

'I had a moral right because of all the years I put up with Edwina for. I didn't think she'd really leave me the house, though she teased me that she might. But she was twenty years older than me and I did hope she'd leave me something fairly substantial after she died. She was always hinting that I'd not find her will ungenerous if I kept in her good books.'

Dot frowned. 'We all thought you really cared about her.'

'Well, I didn't. She had enough money to help me properly during all those horrible and sometimes hungry years, but she doled it out and enjoyed watching me do what she wanted. She never cared whether I wanted to do certain things or not. She didn't care about anyone except herself — and maybe her husband until he dared to die on her. She was very angry about that right till the end.'

'So you're not grieving for her?'

'No, I'm upset for myself. I don't know where to turn now. Look at this!' Cynthia fumbled for her handbag, took out her purse and upended its contents into her lap. A few small coins fell out and there were no notes left behind. She picked the coins up and thrust her hand out towards Dot. 'Take a good look at these! They're all I have left until next month, less than a pound. How do I buy food and petrol, let alone paying my utilities bills?'

'I thought you had an annuity from what Edwina Beadle used to say about you.'

'It was a fixed annuity from my grandmother, not nearly enough to live off with modern inflation. Edwina knew that but she only gave me money when I got desperate. If she hadn't done that, I'd have had to apply for social security.' She shuddered visibly as she said that.

'What's wrong with applying for it if you're genuinely in need?'

'My mother would have turned in her grave if I had done. Besides, Edwina used to tell me that social security was another way of begging and would embarrass the family, let alone she'd never speak to me again if I did it. Now, I've got to or I'll starve to death. And I don't even know if they'll give me anything.'

Dot patted her arm. 'Of course they will. That's what they're there for.'

'What do you care? Just leave me alone, will you?' She suddenly shoved Dot away and slammed the car door shut, as Dot fell backwards on the ground.

But when Cynthia tried to start the motor, all she got was a click. She tried again, with the same result, then leaned her head on the steering wheel and wailed like a beaten child.

Dot pulled the car door open again. 'Eh, love, you can't go on like this. Let me help you. For a start off, you're coming home with me tonight and I'll feed you a nice, warm meal.'

Cynthia tried to push her away, but Dot was stronger and suddenly the weeping woman gave in, getting out and stumbling across to Dot's car. She stood next to it as if she didn't know what to do and Dot had to help her into it and even fasten her seatbelt for her, before going back to pull the car key out and lock up the abandoned vehicle.

When they drove off, Cynthia simply leaned against the headrest and closed her eyes. Dot could see occasional tears leaking down her cheeks by the light of street lamps. She felt like weeping with the poor creature. She'd never seen anyone so at the end of her tether and was quite sure Edwina had enjoyed all the years of tormenting this woman.

Well, Dot wasn't going to let this anguish continue. She simply couldn't walk away. No one else was likely to help Cynthia, so she would have to do something. She'd helped other people in trouble, was secretly proud of that. You left a sort of invisible track of actions behind you in the world and people should do positive things as they passed through. These didn't have to be major contributions but if you made the world a better place when you left it, you could be proud of what you'd done with your life.

She wasn't sure how to help Cynthia, but was certain she would find a way. She could try her best, anyway. And for a start, she could help her apply for social security benefits.

'Where are we?' Cynthia asked when the car stopped.

'My house.'

'Why?'

'I'm not leaving you alone. You're too upset to be sensible.'

'What do you care about that? You're on *her* side.'

'Abigail's, you mean?'

'Who else?'

'Of course I am. Ashgrove is her family home.' She held up one hand to stop Cynthia interrupting. 'That doesn't mean I don't feel sorry for you.'

'Oh, everyone feels *sorry* for me. It doesn't put

money in my purse and food in my belly, though, does it?'

'Well, I'm not everyone. And I'm definitely going to *do* something to help you. But not till you've had a good meal and then a sound night's sleep in my spare bedroom.'

Cynthia gaped at her as if she didn't believe what she was hearing.

Dot got out of the car, went round to the passenger side and pulled at the other woman's hand. 'Come on, love. You've nowhere else to go, so you might as well give me a try. I'm not like that Edwina, I promise you. I've never tormented anyone in my life.'

Cynthia came with her, saying nothing and walking slowly, looking weary and hopeless. Dot bullied her into eating some food, sat her down in front of the TV and made her watch a favourite soapie.

'You can go to bed after this,' she said cheerfully. 'I never miss it.'

'But I don't w —'

'Hush. It's going to start. I'll explain what's been going on.'

When it was over, she said, 'Bed now. Cup of cocoa first. And a biscuit if you like. You seem hungry.'

'I hope I'm not eating too much. Only, I didn't have much food left this morning.'

'I'm happy to feed you.'

'I can't understand why you're doing this?'

'Because I like to help people whenever I can and also, I'm an interfering old biddy from way back, so get used to it.'

Cynthia looked at her in shock, then almost managed a smile. Later on she followed her hostess meekly upstairs and took possession of the spare bedroom.

Dot went back down and locked the doors then took the keys out and put them on her bedside table. Sometimes it was good to have old-fashioned locks. She wasn't having that poor creature running away. She was too afraid that Cynthia might do something silly like jumping off a cliff. Not that there were any cliffs round here, but Dot didn't like to say that s– word.

* * *

Abigail didn't go to the door with Philip as she'd usually have done. Instead she stayed on the sofa and leaned back with a long, weary exhalation of relief. She felt almost too tired to move.

'You need to have a good rest then work out what to do next,' Lucas said. 'But it's great that you've still got your home.'

She didn't even open her eyes to look at him as she corrected that. 'Only for a few more months, at best. I'll still have to sell it to pay the inheritance tax.'

He opened his mouth as if to say something, then closed it again and pulled her into his arms. 'Maybe you've got paintings or silver that you can sell.'

She smiled ruefully. 'Either my ancestors were very ugly or they hired mediocre artists because they were cheap. I'm pretty sure none of the paintings is particularly valuable. Look at them! With one or two exceptions they aren't attractive to look at, either, so I doubt they'd make much money, not if those antiques programmes on TV are any guide. It's just that I'm fond of them, warts and all, because the people in them are family.'

'I can understand that. I envy you your visible line

of relationships.'

'Thanks. The best thing about this is I'll be able to save some of the items I love and I'll probably have enough money left to buy a house big enough to keep the things I care about most.'

'I may have a couple of helpful suggestions to make but we'll talk about that after you've had a good night's sleep. You look weary beyond belief.'

'I feel it.' She rubbed her forehead, which was aching.

'No wonder your ghosts still appeared to you.'

'Yes. Clever of you to have picked up on that.'

'I'll finish loading the computers and take them away now if you can bear me to stay a little longer. All right if I come round to see you tomorrow morning? I have some news of my own to share, but it can wait till then.'

'You're not — leaving the village?'

'No, of course not. Nor am I leaving you. I'll never leave you again unless you want me to.'

They stared at one another and she gave a faint smile. 'I don't want you to leave me.'

'Good.'

'You're right about one thing, though, Lucas. I am too tired to think straight or take in new information. But not too tired for a goodnight kiss.'

A gentle, almost chaste kiss, followed by a brief rocking cuddle. Which were both exactly what she needed at the moment. After he'd finished loading the other computers into the van, she watched him drive away. She suddenly realised that Cynthia's car was still there but there was no one in it. Dot's car had gone. Had she taken Cynthia away? She must have.

Shrugging, too tired to care, Abigail shut the front

door on the dark, windy world. She went round checking the locks as usual, feeling as if her ghosts were just a whisper away. But she didn't have the energy to deal with them either, was still not used to their ways and was relieved when they didn't appear of their own accord.

As she went upstairs, she tried to focus on another positive of her current situation. She'd at least be able to spend some time here before she had to move out. That was so much better than losing everything to Cynthia straight away. But there was still the pain of losing Ashgrove House ahead of her. It was going to be so hard to face that.

To her surprise she'd felt a bit sorry for Cynthia this afternoon. As Edwina's cousin, the poor woman had had a difficult time. In fact, during the final two years of her life, Edwina had seemed to delight in spreading discord around her in every way she could find.

Abigail felt nothing but anger towards her now. Indeed, it wouldn't surprise her to find that her stepmother had perfectly well understood the situation legally and had enjoyed bullying Cynthia and promising much, with the prospect of leaving everything in turmoil.

Suddenly so weary she didn't even bother to undress, Abigail kicked off her shoes, crawled into bed and closed her eyes.

21

When Abigail woke the following morning, it was later than usual. The first thing she remembered was that the house really did belong to her now. For the time being, anyway. It was the best outcome she could have expected, given the taxation laws.

She grabbed a hasty shower then put on her jeans, nodding approval of her modern image in the mirror before going downstairs. It seemed strange not to see or hear Dot. Now that the course was over, this was one of her days for working and it was well past her usual arrival time. Perhaps she'd slept in as well.

Abigail got herself a quick breakfast then went into the library to clean up properly, wiping down surfaces, straightening books and thinking about the course. She'd learned so much and enjoyed the company. She was going to buy herself a computer now and get online. Lucas would be able to tell her what sort of computer would be best value for her.

In the middle of stacking some more of the second-hand books on a shelf, she suddenly remembered that Philip wanted to see her. How could she have forgotten that? She glanced at the clock and phoned for an appointment. She needed to sort out with him how best to deal with the legalities of inheriting from now on.

He would be free at ten o'clock, she was told. That didn't give her much time to get ready.

But just as she was about to leave the house, Lucas drove up, so of course she had to let him in and have a quick word. She felt a bit shy, wondering how they would get on now there wasn't the course to run. But when he stood still and opened his arms wide, her shyness vanished and she walked straight into them.

It felt so *right* when he held her.

Then she remembered her appointment and pushed him away.

'I have something for you,' he said.

'Oh?'

'Yes. A computer. It occurred to me that I've got ten of them, so I brought one back for you. How about we set it up?'

'Brilliant! But you must let me pay you for it.'

'No way. Except with regular coffee and snacks, of course.'

'You'll have to make your own snack if you're hungry at the moment, I'm afraid. I have to go and see Philip to work out where we go from here with the house.'

'What time's your appointment?'

She glanced at her wristwatch and let out a squeak of shock. 'In ten minutes. It's very useful living so close to the village centre but I have to set off straight away.'

He looked at her as if he could see the sadness she felt whenever she talked about the house. 'Do you want me to come with you?'

She didn't want him to see her cry, which she probably would do as she discussed getting everything ready to sell with her lawyer. 'I think I can find my way into town on my own. You stay here and set up the computer. I'll come straight back.'

'Well, don't make any irrevocable decisions because what I have to tell you may affect what you do about the house.'

'Tell me about it when I get back.' She was already hurrying towards the door.

'Where do you want the computer putting?' he yelled after her.

'In the library. Anywhere you like.'

Then she was gone.

He wished he'd had time to explain his own situation to her before she left but he could do that after she got back. He guessed she wanted to stand on her own feet with the lawyer. But he didn't intend to let her push him away or refuse the help he could give her, was going to give her, whatever she said. No way. He'd lost her once and didn't intend to lose her again.

★　★　★

Dot woke early as usual and prepared a simple breakfast for her guest. She was, she decided, going to take Cynthia to see the social security people first, however much the poor woman protested.

Where else would you go for help if you were genuinely penniless? This wasn't a country that left people to starve. She rang up as soon as the local office opened and since she knew the woman who answered and wouldn't take no for an answer, she got an emergency appointment for her friend.

Then she went and woke Cynthia, who was wearing an old nightie of Dot's which absolutely drowned her. It betrayed how thin the woman was. You could tell she hadn't been eating properly for a while. She mumbled something and tried to turn over again, but Dot shook her shoulder.

'Come on, sleepyhead! You need to get up and dress

quickly. You've got an appointment in half an hour.'

She opened her eyes and blinked at Dot. 'What? I don't understand.'

'I'll explain while you're eating breakfast.'

She had the porridge in a bowl by the time Cynthia came down and plonked it in front of her, plus some honey and dried fruit to add if she liked.

When Dot explained what she'd arranged, Cynthia said, 'No!' in an anguished voice.

'Yes, yes and double yes. Who do you think is working at social security? Dragons? They're just people like you and me.'

She laid one hand on her companion's arm. 'I have an old age pension and I'm entitled to it, so I don't feel guilty. How old are you?'

'Fifty-two.'

Dot was surprised because Cynthia looked quite a bit older. She quickly revised mentally what they could expect to get. 'You'll tell them you're destitute, explain about your flat and small income and let them work out the benefits you're entitled to. And you will be entitled to support, I'm quite sure. They may ask you to apply for jobs or send you to courses to help you get work. I don't know exactly what they do for people of your age, but we're going to find out.'

When Cynthia began to shake her head, Dot grabbed her hand and gave it a little squeeze. 'You need help, love. You know you do.'

After a silence that went on for too long, Dot felt Cynthia's hand slacken in hers and knew she'd won. She had her guest out of the house within five minutes of her finishing the hastily gobbled breakfast and hurried her into the social security office at a fast trot two minutes before the time of the appointment.

Cynthia grabbed her hand again. 'Stay with me. Please!'

'OK.'

When the interview was nearly over, the officer looked at Cynthia and asked gently, 'Why didn't you come to us sooner?'

To Dot's delight, Cynthia faced the truth. 'Because I let an older relative bully me into thinking it'd be a form of stealing money from the government that would embarrass the family.'

He chuckled. 'We don't get many people thinking that way these days. Mostly they want more than we can give them. Anyway, I'm happy to tell you I'll be approving regular payments from now on, unless your circumstances change — for example if you get a job. In the meantime I'll make sure you get an emergency payment before you leave here today.'

She stared at him as if she couldn't take this in.

'It's your right, Ms Polson, not a favour. We're in the twenty-first century now, you know, not the days of workhouses.'

'Thank you.'

'You'll need to attend some courses on basic job-seeking skills. Is that all right?'

'How much do they cost?'

He rolled his eyes. 'Nothing.'

Her face brightened visibly. 'I might enjoy that. If you don't think I'm too stupid.'

His expression was sympathetic. 'Who's been telling you you're stupid? You answered all my questions today very lucidly.'

Dot expected Cynthia to weep again as they left but she looked more bemused than anything. 'You all right?' she asked once they were walking along the street.

'I didn't — expect to be looked after like that.'

'Well, there you are. Now, let's go to a charity shop and find you some clothes.'

Cynthia stopped walking. 'Charity shop! I don't need anyone's charity, not now. Thanks to you.'

'I've still got things to teach you, though. So don't get so huffy. I buy most of my clothes in those places. People give them garments they no longer want or need, but which are still wearable. Good things too, some of them. The shops sell them cheaply to the public, so I'm supporting a charity I approve of and at the same time buying clothes for myself at bargain prices.'

'Oh. I didn't know.'

By the time they'd visited three charity shops, Cynthia was smiling and was dressed respectably. Dot saw her stroke the new clothes and peer at herself in a shop window as they passed and hoped she'd hidden her smile. Her companion still looked too thin, but Dot intended to feed her up. And get her exercising. And meeting people.

She'd enjoy doing it, too.

She wondered suddenly whether Cynthia could dance. That'd be a good way to meet people and was Dot's favourite way of exercising.

'Have you ever tried ballroom dancing, Cynthia?'

'Oh, yes. I had lessons as a girl. I loved it. But I haven't danced for years so I've probably forgotten how. Why?'

'I go to a dancing club for oldies. It's good exercise.'

She'd try her companion out at Ashgrove first. Abigail wouldn't mind, surely, once she knew the whole story behind Cynthia's behaviour. She'd take Cynthia along with her everywhere for the time being, because she didn't want to risk leaving her on her own. Not yet. And besides, the poor woman had been treated badly, even worse than Abigail in some ways, first by her mother then by Edwina. She deserved a bit of cosseting.

★ ★ ★

When Abigail was shown into Philip's office, she braced herself not to show how much she was dreading moving out of her home, but she relaxed a little as he went through the necessary paperwork, which sounded fairly straightforward.

When he'd finished he leaned back in his chair. 'That's it for now. I'll see if I can expedite the probate and get some estimate of what you might have to pay. Just a ballpark figure to give us a start.'

'I'd rather you didn't speed things up. The longer it's drawn out, the longer I can stay at Ashgrove.'

'On the other hand, you might just squeak through with enough money to pay the inheritance taxes if you sell a few things.'

'I can't see that happening. There's nothing left of real value.'

'Well, you can start with this. It belongs to you now.' He pulled out the envelope of money they'd found in the safe and told her how much was in it.

She gaped at him. 'That much? She must have been saving it for years.'

'Yes. And I gather you have some valuable books, which Dot is going to sell for you.'

She waited for him to say she should declare them, but he didn't. 'I, um, don't want to — well, break the law.'

269

'It's not up to you. You've given them to Dot.'

There was silence and, slowly, she nodded. She couldn't see the books bringing in enough to make a difference to the final result, but they'd keep Dot occupied.

'I'll just say, off the record, that some of us think the inheritance tax isn't fair on people such as yourself, who are property rich and cash poor, and caring for our nation's heritage. Now, let's change the subject. Hasn't Lucas spoken to you yet? He said he was going to do it first thing this morning.'

'About what?'

'Some suggestions he has for helping you with the inheritance problems.'

'I overslept so didn't have time to talk to him.'

'Well, that should be your next task. You need to know what he's offering before you can start your detailed planning. I can't tell you any more; it's his suggestion.'

She walked slowly out of his rooms and back to her car, clutching her shabby old shoulder bag with the packet of money in it very tightly to her chest. Should she declare it in the coming assessment? She wasn't going to think about that yet. Or decide anything.

She wondered what Lucas had to do with her keeping her home. She wasn't going to let him lose all his hard-earned money by helping her out. She was going to be very firm about that. Besides, she doubted it'd be nearly enough. She could imagine how huge a sum might be demanded in inheritance tax if they took into account how much the grounds would bring if rezoned and sold for housing development. Her father had discussed that with her a few times.

★ ★ ★

270

Lucas set up the computer he'd brought for Abigail, then made the mistake of looking in a mirror. And there they were again. All three of them. He stopped dead, not sure whether to greet them or wait for them to speak to him first.

He'd admitted to himself that they were real, whatever 'real' might mean for family ghosts. Were they going to keep popping up out of the blue? It was disconcerting, to say the least.

Roderick gave him another of those roguish grins. 'I'm glad you and our dear Abigail have got together again. You'll make a very suitable husband for a Beadle. Though you'll have to change your name to Beadle, of course.'

Husband? Name changing? That was going a bit fast for Lucas. Admittedly he was thinking of them getting together permanently but he wasn't ready to announce it to the world yet. And why did he have to change his name?

'You are going to marry her, aren't you?' Georgiana asked. 'You're not just expecting a quick fling.'

'Um, yes — I want to marry her eventually — and I'm not the sort to have quick flings, thank you very much.'

'You lost her once. You need to make sure of her this time,' Juliana warned him severely.

'Right. Well, I don't intend to lose her but I'd rather deal with my love life myself, if you don't mind.'

'As long as you're going to have a love life together. Ah, she'll be back in a minute.'

And as suddenly as they'd appeared in the mirror, they faded away.

Lucas disliked such intrusions. How would he make love to her if he felt he was being spied on all

271

the time? Not that he and Abigail had got that far. They'd been too busy coping with the will and allied problems. He wished he knew what she and Philip Danvers were planning. Before he could do anything else, he heard the sound of a car at the rear of the house and put his screwdriver down. He put the kettle on as he passed through the kitchen, then opened the back door.

* * *

Abigail smiled at him and spread her arms out, feeling that two could play at the game of signalling a need for a hug.

'How did it go?' he asked as they walked into the kitchen together after a lingering kiss.

'I'll tell you over a cup of coffee. Isn't Dot here yet?'

'No. And she didn't phone earlier, either.'

'That's not like her. I'd better phone her. I hope she's all right.'

But Dot didn't answer her phone, so Abigail could do nothing else but worry.

'Perhaps she's helping Cynthia?' he suggested.

'Why should she? She can't stand her.'

'Because Cynthia's car is still there. I didn't take to the woman myself, but you had to feel sorry for her yesterday. The more I hear about Edwina, the worse she sounds. I don't know how you survived all those years with her.'

'I looked after Dad for a lot of the time. I think she did care for him in her own way, but she was no good at looking after people so she put up with me being there and didn't push me too far because I looked after him.'

'She was lucky to have you.'

'I stayed for Dad, not her. After he died, I kept away from her as much as I could. There's always something to do in an old house and she never interrupted me when I was working on it. My labour came free, after all.' She looked round and felt the sadness come back. 'I shall miss this place so much.'

'Let's make the coffee then we'll sit down and chat. I need to tell you something about me that will impact on your situation.'

'All right. Philip said I was to listen to you.'

'Well, he's my lawyer too and he knows a few details about my business affairs.'

22

Lucas was finishing making the coffee when someone knocked on the front door.

'Leave it!' Lucas said. 'We need to talk.'

Abigail shook her head. 'I can never do that. I won't be long.'

She found two more older women standing there, looking nervous.

'Is it true?'

'I beg your pardon.'

'About the library. Is it true we can borrow books from you?'

'Oh, um, yes it is.'

They looked so hopeful at that, she held the door open. 'Come in. I'll show you where they are but if you can choose your books quite quickly, I'd be grateful. I'm a bit busy today.'

'Oh, we will.'

When they'd gone, she went back to the kitchen, took a sip of the now lukewarm coffee and looked ruefully at Lucas. 'I've had a steady trail of people wanting to borrow books. Some of them are quite desperate since the library closed. Each time I get furious at these bureaucrats, who don't understand how much good libraries do besides lending people books.'

'And now you're able to help some people. We'll keep a list of names and complain to the Medderby Council.' He held up one hand to stop her speaking. 'In the meantime I'm getting quite desperate to tell you something. Let's go and sit in the drawing room. I know it's cold there but it feels like the right place for this. Finish your coffee quickly.'

When she put her mug down, he took her hand and walked with her to the big, beautiful and extremely chilly room. 'I love this part of the house.'

'So do I.'

'Sit down.' He carefully avoided looking in the mirror in case *they* had come back. 'There's no way to tell you this, except bluntly. I'm quite rich, Abigail. I sold my business when I fell ill, but kept a minority interest in it, and the programs I wrote bring me a regular income still, a very good income.'

She stared at him in shock. 'You're — rich? But you're living in your old home again.'

'I didn't want anyone to know, least of all your step-mother. I was only just starting to feel better — and remember that chronic fatigue syndrome can include a foggy brain, so I wasn't thinking properly about anything. Since I knew that, I didn't push myself.'

He gave a wry smile. 'No amount of money can hurry things up till your body has healed and is functioning properly again. I only moved back here quite recently. I'd rented my old home out till I was ready to start making a new life for myself and was holed up in a simple to maintain flat.'

'Edwina was furious when she found out it was me who'd bought the house. She tried to buy it back to stop me returning, but I wasn't giving in to her bullying again as I did when I was younger and financially helpless.'

He ran one hand through his hair, not quite knowing how best to continue. 'I was going to wait and court you properly, to use an old-fashioned word, but

275

I don't think there's going to be time. So I'll tell you now, I want to marry you, I want that so much. It was always you. I couldn't find anyone else who suited me. I think I must be a one-woman man.'

She gaped at him. 'Are you — proposing to me?'

'Yes, I am. I'm no good at fancy words, but you won't turn me down, will you?'

'I don't know what to say.'

'Say you will, of course?'

'If I do that, it'll sound as if I'm marrying you for your money.'

'No one who knows you would ever think that. And I feel pretty certain that you're starting to care for me again.'

'I never stopped,' she admitted, as she had done before.

'Well, there you are.'

'But I can't take all your money.'

'Why not? I'd have to buy a bigger house for us to live in, anyway. We can live here instead. Don't tell me you wouldn't prefer that, because I'd not believe you.'

'This house will probably be worth a lot more than you've got stashed away, Lucas. And even if it isn't, I don't want to swallow up your nest egg. Ashgrove needs so much doing to it. Dad used to say it absolutely eats up money.'

'That's beginning to sound as if you're going to turn me down.'

'Not exactly.'

He was starting to feel a bit angry. 'What the hell do you mean by that?'

'I mean, I want to wait until the amount of inheritance tax has been worked out. And whatever it is, I won't take all your money.'

'Didn't you hear me say I was rich?'

She held up one hand. 'Yes. But if I think the tax people are asking more than I'm prepared to take from you, I'd rather sell it, much as I love it.'

'But that's crazy!'

'Is it? Beadle sons and daughters have married money over the centuries and, well, I know my family history. Only rarely have such marriages been happy. I won't do that to us. I need to wait and see how much is needed then, if you're still interested and it's not too much — and I shan't blame you if you're not interested — well, then you can propose to me again.'

'You have gone crazy. I love you, dammit. That's why we should get married. Saving the house comes second to that. The money isn't important to me. You are.'

'I love you, too. But I won't take all your money and sink it in this house, much as I love Ashgrove.' She stood up. 'I have to know how I stand first.'

He looked at her stubborn face. He'd seen that expression before. He wasn't giving in to her on this but things might work out better if he took another tack towards his goal, something he'd been considering doing anyway.

He studied her, eyes narrowed. She stared back at him, determination in every line of her body. Well, she was about to find out he could be just as stubborn. There was just under a month to Christmas. He was used to setting difficult deadlines and meeting them. This was going to be the most important deadline of his whole life. He was going to celebrate their engagement at Christmas, whatever it took. Only he wasn't going to warn her, let alone ask about how he was going to achieve that. He was going to arrange it.

They would have a very special Christmas together, whatever it took. He moved towards the door. 'Come and find me when you have enough information to decide what to do. You know where I live.'

Her mouth dropped open and he'd walked out of the house before she could stop him.

He drove straight to see his lawyer. Who happened to be her lawyer. Who was, Lucas felt, on both their sides.

★ ★ ★

Philip agreed to see Lucas for five minutes only between appointments. He listened to a quick outline of the situation then shook his head. 'Sorry, but I don't know her well enough to persuade her to change her mind.'

'Oh, I don't want you even to try to do that. I just want you to keep an eye on her while I'm away and make sure she doesn't do anything rash or irrevocable legally. I'm going up to London to sort out my affairs and find out how much I'm worth at the moment.'

'I beg your pardon?'

'I told you I was quite wealthy when I hired you as my lawyer, but we haven't gone into details. I probably have a good deal more money than either you or Abigail suspect. It clearly matters to her how much more.'

'But won't that change her mind?'

'Not necessarily, so I'm going to use my contacts in London to get a preliminary estimate about the value of Ashgrove House for inheritance tax purposes within a week or two.'

'I doubt anyone can do that.'

278

'If anyone can, it'll be me. If I can't, I'll still find a way.'

'Good luck on that.'

'I don't need luck. I need help from friends. One of them will be able to give us a pretty close estimate of what Ashgrove is worth, believe me.' He smiled rather sadly. 'I fell ill because I became a workaholic. I tried to fall in love during those years. In theory I was ready to marry and have a family, and somehow I never could bring myself to do it. It was always Abigail. None of the other women, pleasant though they were, were suitable for life partners. So I put all I had into my work. Too much.'

He hesitated, then added, 'I realised it was either her or no one, I had someone check up on her from time to time, just from a distance. But her father was nearing the end and depended on her, then I began to feel ill, so the time never seemed right for us to get back together.'

'And now it is?'

'Not exactly. But it never will be perfect, will it? So I'm going to push things through as I used to do when I ran a rather large business and had set my heart on a deal.' He stood up. 'Keep an eye on her while I'm away.' He pulled out a business card. 'This number will reach me any time if you need help reining her in.'

Philip remembered his own feelings for his wife. 'You definitely love her.'

'Yes. Oh, and you're invited to a Christmas party to celebrate our engagement.'

'You're that sure?'

'That determined.'

'Good luck. If I can —' But his client had gone.

Lucas went to see Dot next to get her on side too. No one would be able to keep an eye on his beloved as well as Dot.

Abigail wasn't going to know what had hit her by the time Christmas arrived. This would be the most important deal he ever made.

* * *

Lucas found Dot at home, sharing a late lunch with Cynthia. He looked at her visitor in surprise and then asked, 'Can I see you privately, please, Dot?'

Cynthia stood up. 'I'll go and have a lie-down. It was a tiring morning. I might be asleep when you've finished your talk and if so, please don't wake me.' She looked at Lucas and added, 'This woman is a miracle worker.'

As she went up the stairs, Dot turned to him. 'Before you ask, Cynthia was destitute. That horrible Edwina had been tormenting her for years and giving her barely enough money to keep body and soul together. I'm going to teach Cynthia to enjoy a normal life. It'll probably take a while but there you are. If I decide to do something I stick with it.'

He smiled. Another stubborn person speaking. He could relate to that. 'Good for you.'

'Anyway, now that Abigail has you to look after her, she won't need me as much.'

'She will need you for a while.' He explained his plan and was surprised when Dot suddenly threw her arms round him and hugged him.

'What's that for?'

She mopped some happy tears from her eyes. 'Loving my girl as she deserves. You go ahead. I'll do what you want when it's necessary.'

'What about her?' He looked upwards.

'Cynthia will be all right with a little encouragement. Leave her to me.'

He relaxed visibly. 'It seems we're engaging in plots within plots. They're going to work out all right, though. I'll make sure of that.'

He pulled out another of those special cards. 'Don't give this to anyone else. That number will get through to me anywhere, any time.'

He turned at the door to say, 'And don't put it in the wrong box.'

She threw the tea towel at him, laughing now.

It had better all work to plan. Her lass had had enough troubles to face in recent years. But she rather suspected Abigail had met her match in that lad, thank goodness.

* * *

After Lucas had left, Abigail sat on in the drawing room. Had she done the right thing? She didn't know. Only it seemed so unfair to take all his money and let the house eat it up.

'He might be happy to spend his money on you and your house,' a voice said. 'That's up to him.'

She looked up to see Juliana standing nearby. 'If you don't mind, I'm not in the mood to chat.'

'I know. But we're not sure you're doing the right thing, so we're worried about you.'

'I shan't be sure what the right thing is until I find out how much the inheritance tax will be. I'll get in touch with Philip tomorrow and ask him if he can hurry things along, after all. I think I'll go mad if I have to wait over six months to find out.'

'Good idea. And in the meantime, you should go through the things in the attic. It's needed sorting out for decades, but your ancestors were rather untidy people. There are some things up there which might be worth selling and anyway, if you have to leave here, you can't let our family's possessions fall into the hands of strangers, can you?'

'I was going to spring clean the whole house thoroughly to make it look its best. Who's going to care about an attic full of rubbish?'

'Waste of time. If you're staying, how the house looks won't matter. If you're leaving, you'll want to take the family bits and pieces with you and some of them are up in the attic.'

She grimaced. 'I suppose so.' What she really wanted was to throw herself down on the rug and howl her eyes out every time she thought about leaving. She'd stupidly sent Lucas away and been regretting that ever since. Only it had been the right thing to do, the *decent* thing.

Hadn't it?

She wasn't sure, wasn't sure about anything. Maybe she should phone him tonight and ask him to come back? She shook her head. No, she mustn't take advantage of him. Somehow she had to find the courage to treat him and his hard-earned money fairly. If she didn't, she'd never be able to live with herself. It couldn't be enough to save her house. How rich could he be? Look at how he dressed. Casual clothes from recognisable chain stores. No man who was truly rich would dress like that. Mind you, computer nerds were notorious about dressing casually and not caring about such details as fashion — or at least they were in some of the newspaper articles she'd read or programmes she'd seen on TV.

No. She'd done the right thing and must stick to it, however much it hurt. It'd be wrong to take all his money away from him.

If they did get married eventually, if he stayed around till things were resolved, they'd be marrying purely for love. And they'd be happy. That was what she wanted most of all.

★ ★ ★

Later that afternoon the phone rang and Abigail hesitated, then ran to pick it up, in case it was him. When she found it was Dot, she didn't know whether to be glad or sad.

'Sorry I didn't turn up today, love. Can I come round now and tell you why?'

'Yes, of course.'

Ten minutes later Dot's little red car stopped at the back of the house and she got out. Abigail switched the kettle on and Dot walked in, shivering. 'Cold, isn't it?'

'Yes, I suppose it is.' She hadn't noticed, had been too wrapped up in her worries.

'I need to tell you about Cynthia. She's staying with me at the moment.'

When she'd finished, Abigail patted her arm. 'You're a wonderful person, Dot Eakins.'

'So can Cynthia come and help me with the cleaning after she's had a good rest and eaten some healthy meals for a few days?'

'Do you trust her?'

'I think so. Don't worry. I'll keep a careful eye on her.'

'If she's working here, she deserves paying.'

'She'll be learning on the job at first. I'll tell you when to start paying her. Now, how's the library going?'

'It's going well. I'll have to ask you to help me out with it, though, because I'm going to go through the attic. When I have to leave the house, I —' Her voice faltered and she had to pause to pull herself together. 'Well, there might be things stored in the attic that I'll want to take with me.'

'What about Lucas? Won't he be coming in to help you do things like that?'

'Um, no. I can't let him put all his money into the house, so I'll be making a start on the attic alone and — and then I'll see how I go.'

'Your choice. I'd better get back to my guest. See you tomorrow.'

Abigail was surprised Dot hadn't protested more vigorously about her decision. Perhaps she was too engrossed in helping Cynthia. As the car vanished round the corner of the house, she locked the back door and went up to the attic. She didn't feel in the least like clearing stuff out, but then she didn't feel like doing anything else, either.

Juliana had been right. She had to do this, didn't want to lose everything her ancestors had hoarded as well as the house itself.

23

For over a week, Abigail waited to hear from Lucas, but there was no word.

Dot brought Cynthia round to see her and she'd apologised but Abigail wasn't really interested so just accepted her apology and let Dot organise things. She kept trying to decide where she would go if she had to leave Ashgrove. She even looked in the local papers at houses for sale. Sometimes she thought she should go far, far away; at other times she decided it'd be best to stay in the village, painful as that'd be in some ways. After all, her few friends were here, especially Dot. It all depended on how things panned out with Lucas, whether he still wanted her, whether he still wanted to stay in the village.

However, as the second week rolled on without hearing from him, she began to grow angry and was wondering whether to go round to his house and confront him. She didn't even know where she stood with him any longer and that was fretting her. She mentioned this to Dot.

'Didn't you know?' her friend asked.

She stiffened. 'Know what?'

'That he's gone off to London on business.'

'No, I didn't. He should have told me. One minute he loves me, the next he vanishes without a word.'

'That's men for you. Now, after we've done the cleaning today, can I have a dance round the house with Cynthia and make sure she still remembers the basics before I take her to my ballroom dancing club?'

285

'If you must.'

'It's important she make friends. I'm going to insist on you joining in as well. You need some relaxation. You're looking really peaky.'

'I don't think I'm in the mood for dancing.'

'Well, get in the mood. You can't languish like a silly Victorian miss. You're the one who drove Lucas away, after all.'

She felt hurt by that.

Dot changed the subject. 'How's the attic clearance going?'

'I'm finding all sorts of things that might have some resale value. I shall need to get them valued.'

'I can probably help you with that. I've got connections through working in a charity shop for years.'

'We'll see. I've found some more books which I need to have valued, really old, lumpy things, but in good condition. I never knew there were any others stored up there.'

'Give them to me and I'll pass them on to James Porfrey. You can trust him to get you the best price. And I'll bring Cynthia round this afternoon so I can see how well she dances. She might have attended classes as a girl but she hasn't done any dancing for years.'

'OK.'

'I'll find some bags to put the books in.'

Dot led the way upstairs, clutching a bundle of rubbish bin liners. The two of them brought four bags of books down and loaded them in Dot's boot, then she drove off to drop them at her house and fetch Cynthia back to help her for a while then practise their dancing.

* * *

286

Abigail was in the attic trying to open an old wardrobe that she'd found behind some boxes in a corner when she heard the music floating up.

Dot and her love of dancing!

She went back to trying out various old keys that had been piled in a cracked bowl in one corner. Why anyone would keep a damaged bowl was beyond her.

The music stopped and a voice called, 'Are you still up here?'

'I'm over in the corner, Dot.'

'Time to have a rest. We're all going to have a dance. I've found a record full of various songs from the era of twists. You don't need a partner to dance the twist.'

'I'm just in the middle of trying out these keys. You start and I'll come down to join you later.'

Instead Dot threaded her way across the attic and stared at the wardrobe. 'Stand back.'

She made a fist and thumped the wardrobe just above the lock, shouting, 'Ha!' when it jumped open.

'How did you do that?'

'It used to stand in one of the spare bedrooms in your mother's day. We never did find the key to that lock and the catch locks itself sometimes. What's inside it now?'

They opened the door as wide as it would go and peered inside.

'Paintings.' Abigail pulled a face as she looked at the top one. 'As horrible as the other paintings in the house. My ancestors can't have had any artistic sense whatsoever.'

Dot tugged at her sleeve. 'Well, leave them for now and come downstairs. I'm not taking no for an answer. We'll do the twist to warm up then do some real dancing.'

As Abigail started to shake her head, Dot folded her arms and said in *that voice*, 'I mean it.'

Abigail knew when to fight and when to do as she was told. 'Oh, all right. But you'll have to show me how to do the twist. It's not one of the dances Dad taught me.'

They went downstairs and she nodded to Cynthia in a cool manner, not ready to forgive her fully yet.

Then the music started and Dot began to dance, showing them how to move, joined almost immediately by Cynthia. Soon they were all three twisting their bodies from side to side in time to the music.

After that Dot put on a quick-step and danced Abigail round the house, after which she gave Cynthia a turn. Abigail was prepared to see an almighty muddle, but Cynthia seemed to follow Dot perfectly and they were soon executing neat corners and then went on to fancy patterns of half-hopping steps, which she could never have managed. When the two stopped, she applauded.

'You're a really good dancer, Cynthia!' Dot exclaimed.

'I'm way out of practice. It's been years.'

'If that's out of practice, you must have been very good indeed when you were younger.'

Cynthia flushed. 'I wasn't bad. I got all sorts of certificates and a prize or two. Then my parents ran out of money and I had to stop. My father had made some bad investments apparently. We had to sell the house and move.'

'Well, you're going to start dancing again from now on. You'll like our little club in the village.'

'Oh, but I —'

'No buts.' Dot folded her arms.

'When she looks like that I just say yes,' Abigail told Cynthia, her animosity just about gone now.

'I feel a bit the same way.'

★ ★ ★

At the end of that second week, Dot found Philip waiting for her when she went to clean the offices.

'Lucas wants to know if you can get Abigail away for the day — and lend him your house key. He's found someone to give a preliminary estimate of the value of the estate. But he'll need a full day to do it.'

'We'll go and visit old Martin. He used to be the head gardener at Ashgrove till he retired to Bourne-mouth. We'll take him out to lunch at the pub. He loves that.'

'Why don't you phone him now?' He gestured towards the phone.

When Dot put it down, she'd arranged for them to go the following Monday. She risked asking, 'Do you think she'll be able to keep the house?'

'I don't know. But Lucas is making an almighty effort to help her. Will she really go with you?'

'Oh, yes. She was always very fond of Martin.'

It was touch and go, but in the end, Abigail agreed to visit the old man who had once made her a little child's garden and taught her how to grow things in it. The trouble was he lived so far away now, it'd take the whole day.

But Dot had phoned him and said he sounded a bit down in the dumps, fed up of the winter, so Abigail couldn't refuse to go and see him, could she? She even agreed for Cynthia to join them.

289

Lucas picked up Keith Hammond early Monday morning at the station in Medderby. He drove over to Ashbury St Mary and parked further down High Street.

'Is something wrong?'

'I just need to check that the owner and her friends have gone before I take you inside. She's the one I'm trying to help by getting an approximate valuation. She's worrying herself sick about it because she loves that house. It's been in her family since the eighteenth century.'

Hammond's expression softened. 'That damned inheritance tax!'

'I doubt it's got any big-value items, but it's rich in everyday historical treasures.' Lucas grinned. 'You won't find any valuable old paintings. There are family portraits but they're badly executed and the sitters are mostly quite ugly, so no one but relatives would want to see them every day.'

He got out of the car and moved forward a few paces till he could see the front door. Dot's little red car was still waiting there, so he got back into his own vehicle.

'They'll be leaving shortly, I should think.'

They waited near the entrance till they saw Dot drive out of the gates in her little red car and vanish into the distance.

As the car waited to turn onto the main road, Lucas's eyesight was good enough to see Abigail sitting in the front passenger seat, looking anything but happy. Cynthia was sitting in the back, looking calmer than she had been a couple of weeks ago. Dot's magic hand, he presumed.

He glanced sideways. Keith Hammond was looking resigned rather than anything, but he owed Lucas a favour and would do an honest job simply because he was an honest person. He was well liked and regularly brought in by the taxation people as an expert on old manor houses.

'Right. Here we go. We'll park round the back, because I only have a key to the kitchen door.'

He led the way inside and showed Keith round the ground floor.

'If you've got something to occupy yourself with, Lucas, I'd be best left on my own.'

'I can always keep busy.'

Without thinking what he was doing, he walked into the drawing room, one of his favourite places. He glanced at the mirror and froze. Big mistake.

The three figures looking down at him were solemn today.

'Can you please explain exactly what that man is doing here?' Georgiana asked sharply.

Lucas did so quickly in a near whisper, not wanting to bring his friend to see who he was talking to.

'So the lower the value put on it, the more likely it is that Abigail will be able to keep it?' Juliana said thoughtfully after he'd finished.

'Yes. More or less.'

'Thank you.'

They faded from sight. He went into the library and switched on the computer he'd given to Abigail. She'd clearly been using it.

From then on he heard Keith muttering and sometimes sighing as he made his way round the ground floor. After a couple of hours, he re-joined Lucas.

'Can you show me the rest now, then I'll start going over that?'

So they went upstairs, then up to the attic till Keith had sketched the layout in his big notebook. He grimaced as he looked round the attic. 'They seem to have dumped all their broken stuff up here, and their old clothes. I haven't found anything that looks remotely valuable downstairs and I doubt I will up here, and it looks as if there's a leak in the roof over there.' He pointed.

Lucas looked but couldn't see any signs of staining. But the attic looked different from usual, darker, seedier. He didn't comment on that, just muttered, 'Pity this place has been let go. I think the family lost its money decades ago.'

As they went back down to the first floor, he said, 'I'll nip into the village and buy us some sandwiches. Won't be long.'

★ ★ ★

Keith walked round rooms where the hangings were dusty and badly faded, the furniture mostly battered, though sometimes not as badly as it had first appeared.

In one bedroom he stopped dead as a vase lifted up off the mantelpiece, wavered to and fro in the air, then settled in its place again. Had he really seen that? No, vases didn't lift up and down without assistance and he definitely didn't believe in poltergeists. It must have been a trick of the light.

On the other hand, he'd been in old houses before where there felt to be lingering echoes of the past, sometimes in a way that made people uneasy to stay there. Was this going to be one of those?

As he moved from bedroom to dusty bedroom, he found nothing of value, more signs of leaks and the paintings continued to be of very poor quality. And he became increasingly uneasy. More than once he felt as if someone had tugged his sleeve or the back of his jacket. He didn't think he'd ever been in a more uncomfortable atmosphere. When he went back up to the attic on his own, the feelings of unease seemed to intensify. He poked round here and there, finding mostly junk. And when he studied it he realised the leak must be worse than he'd first thought.

Lucas called from downstairs and he was frankly glad to be out of the attic.

He went down to the kitchen and ate half his sandwich then pushed it away. 'I shan't be much longer.'

'Oh?'

'It's in a very bad state and it's one of those places with a bad feel to it. Enough to make you believe in that feng shui rubbish — or in ghosts.' He forced a laugh.

'Not going to be as high in value as we'd expected, then?'

'Definitely not. Hasn't been cared for. Let the poor woman have it, I say. Another generation will probably see it crumbling around her descendants' feet.'

'Oh, dear. May I ask if you have any figure in mind for your valuation?'

The amount Hammond quoted astonished Lucas, it was so low. But he didn't say that. Was it possible? Had the family ghosts been taking a hand in this? If so, well done them.

'I think the old spinster lady who owns it will be glad if she can hold on to it for her lifetime,' he said.

'Yes. Pity it's so bad. It could have been a beautiful home if it had been properly maintained.'

They left before Lucas had expected to and he phoned Dot to tell her they had gone.

That was the first step accomplished, he thought as he waved goodbye to Keith Hammond at the station. He'd thought it wiser to catch the next train back to London, so he nipped into the nearby pub and ordered a glass of shandy to help him while away the hour that he'd have to wait for his train. He smiled as he wondered how on earth the family ghosts had managed to convince Keith that the place was in poor repair.

He now had to persuade his other acquaintance to play her part in the valuation process. For that he'd need an engagement ring, which he'd put to good use when he brought it back to Ashbury and confronted Abigail.

He wanted to find something beautiful and old, knew she'd not want a modern ring.

★ ★ ★

It was good to see Martin again. He always reminded Abigail of her happy childhood days before her mother died.

When Dot dropped her at home, she was pleasantly tired and glad to be on her own for a while. The house felt colder than usual and strange, as if someone had been there. But surely her ghosts would have let her know if there had been intruders. She watched the television news then prepared a simple meal in the warmth of the kitchen, yawning and going to bed early. She'd get up really early the next day and have another go at the attic. And maybe she ought to start planning how to celebrate Christmas. With Dot, of course, for part of the time, and she supposed Cynthia would have to be invited too.

It'd probably be her last Christmas here, so she wanted to make it rather special. She might even put up decorations, if she could find them in the attic. Edwina hadn't believed in putting up 'dust traps' but Abigail loved them.

24

Lucas invited his old friend Julia to have lunch with him and took her to his favourite restaurant.

'Are we celebrating something?' she asked when they got there. 'This place will cost you an arm and a leg.'

'I want to pick your brain. Let's sit down and order our meals then I'll tell you my news.'

As they waited for the shared seafood basket starter, she said, 'I must say, you look like your old self again.'

'Yes. I seem to have shaken off the dreaded lurgy completely now.'

'Well, take life more easily this time. You used to work far too hard.'

'I have a new venture I want to tell you about. And . . . I've met someone.' He reached into his pocket and pulled out the little box. 'In fact, I've just bought her an engagement ring and I'm going to pop the question on Christmas Eve. I've been dying to show someone. What do you think?' He flipped open the lid.

She took the box from him and sighed. 'It's gorgeous. Eighteenth century?'

'Yes. Or so the jeweller told me.'

'Is she into old things?'

'Very much so. She owns an old manor house, just a small one. Unfortunately she's going to have to pay death duties on it and she's scrabbling to find the money, or I'd have asked her to marry me sooner. She's insisting on sorting the house out first.'

She stroked the ring with a gentle fingertip. 'You

love her very much, don't you? Even your eyes go soft when you talk about her. Why are you waiting? You could surely afford to pay the inheritance tax for her even if she can't.'

'She's stubbornly independent, won't hear of me paying it, insists she's waiting to see how much it is. Trouble is, that takes months usually.'

Julia chuckled. 'I wondered what you were after when you brought me here.'

'I really did want to catch up with you again, but if there's anything you can do to speed things up, I'd be grateful. I sneaked Keith Hammond down to view it and offer a provisional valuation. It's not in very good condition and his guess is lower than I'd have expected, but she's one stubborn woman about not taking my money.'

'I'd never thought to see you so deeply in love.'

'Yes. She's my age so we may even, if we're lucky, be able to have a child or two. But the sooner we can marry and start trying, the better.'

'Wow, I never thought to hear you say that.'

'I never cared enough to say it about anyone else.' He stared down into his wine glass, letting Julia change the subject and genuinely enjoying a wide-ranging chat covering all sorts of subjects under the sun.

If she'd been twenty years younger, she might have been the one other woman he could have fallen for — if he hadn't already fallen for Abigail. He and Julia had become good friends almost as soon as they'd met and he was sure she'd approve of his choice of wife.

He hoped Julia would work out from what he'd said the way she could help him. He was rather counting on that. She was the only one who could do now. She had a lot of influence in certain circles.

That same day Sam Braxton cornered Dot and suggested they throw a Christmas party at their new 'library' to thank Abigail for setting it all up.

'What do you think? Would she mind us holding it here?'

'I'm sure she wouldn't. How about we tell her it's just a few drinks, but make it a real surprise party for her? She's had a lot of unpleasant surprises recently, so maybe it's time for a really good one. If everyone brought a plate, there would be no worries about catering, and I'm sure Lucas will be happy to supply some drinks. He's not short of money.'

'Good idea.'

'Can I leave the invitations and food in your hands? I'll set it all up here, with Cynthia's help.'

He chuckled. 'You've tamed that one. I used to think she was another Edwina Beadle, but she's actually rather shy.'

'She's another person who was bullied by that woman. I'm helping her sort her life out.'

'She's lucky to have you. Anyway, I'll leave Janie to do the organising. I just do as I'm told. There's nothing wrong with her brain, you know, and she'll really enjoy a job like that.'

* * *

Determined not to show how much she was missing Lucas, Abigail found the Christmas decorations, dusty old tinsel, glass balls and brightly painted figures for hanging on a Christmas tree.

Dot studied them. 'Not enough. Let's go and buy

a real Christmas tree, a big one, and have the place looking as it used to in your mother's day.'

'Yes, let's. If this is going to be my last Christmas here, let's make it a good one. We need to order a turkey too, just a small one.'

'Leave that to me. I'm a dab hand at cooking turkeys and your kitchen's got room for me to make all sorts of goodies. If I go too mad, we can put the leftovers in the freezer.'

Delighted to have her dear friend's approval, Abigail set out with her on a shopping expedition to the market, leaving Cynthia in charge of the library.

Dot waggled one finger at her protégée. 'Remember to be nice to all the people who want to borrow books.'

'I'm learning to be nice, aren't I?' she said with a touch of her old sharpness.

'You're improving.'

Abigail and Dot found what was needed, not only at the market but at a couple of the charity shops. In one of them Dot pounced on a big box of 'misc decs' that seemed to have been lying unnoticed in a corner. They were very old-fashioned but just what was needed at Ashgrove.

When they got back, they started decorating and that made Abigail feel a bit better. And when the Christmas tree was delivered later that afternoon, the three of them set about decorating it.

Cynthia stood back with tears in her eyes. 'I've never had such a magnificent tree in my whole life. My parents had a little artificial one, even before we lost our money because my mother said real fir trees shed too many needles when you brought them indoors.'

Dot winked at Abigail. She was pleased at how

299

Cynthia was coming on, communicating better, smiling and had proved a hard worker — which was a sure way to Dot's heart.

Dot watched her girl but could see that she was still missing Lucas. Well, that was out of her control. But where was he? Why hadn't he come back?

★ ★ ★

Lucas was feeling desperate. He'd staked so much on his acquaintances helping speed a valuation through the system for Ashgrove House. As he waited he bought presents for Dot and Cynthia as well as for Abigail.

He'd stayed until the day before Christmas Eve and still hadn't heard anything. He'd have to go back and find another way of convincing Abigail to marry him — all he knew was he wasn't giving up. Dot had phoned a few times to report progress, and Philip had phoned twice. He sat in his hotel suite feeling sorry for himself. He'd arranged to leave tomorrow. He'd done all he could. And failed. When his phone rang he picked it up, not recognising the number.

'It's me. Julia.'

'Oh, hi.'

'I've got some good news for you.'

As that sank in, he could hardly breathe, just pray that fate had been kind to him.

'I'll make this short. At my suggestion the taxation people got in touch with Keith about his valuation, which will save them money. They're very big on reducing expenses at the moment, fortunately for you. And since the place is in such bad condition, they've accepted his word for it. They know he doesn't fudge things. He's the most honest man in that area of work, some think.'

Lucas managed not to urge her to get to the point, but only just.

She did that next, telling him the valuation but warning him that this hadn't been formally ratified or made public yet.

'That low?'

'Apparently it's all it's worth. And the council are not intending to rezone the grounds of Ashgrove House, but keep it as a designated green space to help keep the village countrified. There are a couple of greenie types on it now and it seems they've been pushing this sort of thing through. It was made easier because it won't cost the council anything to maintain this particular green space.'

He took a deep shuddering breath. 'I don't know how I can ever thank you, Julia.'

'You can take me out for a posh lunch again, and this time bring your fiancée with you.'

'Done. But that'll be after Christmas.'

'Of course. Oh, and if you decide to do up that house, I want inviting down to see it.'

'I am going to do it up but it'll take a while, couple of years at least.'

'I'm not going anywhere.'

He had tears of joy in his eyes as he said goodbye. And afterwards he shed a tear or two. Who said men didn't cry?

He'd set off first thing in the morning and share the news with Abigail, then with Dot and Philip. If it wasn't too late, they'd plan a very special Christmas. And he wasn't going to let her say no to his proposal — a better, more romantic one, if he could manage not to open his mouth and put his foot in it!

★ ★ ★

Of course, his car broke down on the way to Wiltshire and he had to wait two hours for a call-out service to arrive and bring in a part to fix it. By that time he was going mad with frustration. He didn't phone them, though, was determined to make this a surprise, even if they only had cheese on toast to eat tonight. But when he got to Ashbury, he found a few cars parked across the area in front of the house and lights gleaming brightly from the front windows. Even as he watched from the street another car arrived and disgorged two elderly ladies. Was she having a party? Why? What had happened?

He drove into the grounds and went to park at the rear, going straight into the kitchen without knocking. He had the ring tucked safely in his jacket pocket and he took in one of the bottles of Prosecco from the box of them in the car boot and one of the bags of goodies.

As he looked round the kitchen, he was surprised to see platters of food set out ready.

Then the door opened and Dot came in. She stopped at the sight of him, beaming. 'Oh, I'm so glad you've come back in time!'

'I'm happy to hear that. Is Abigail home? And what's going on here?'

'She'll be home soon. Philip took her shopping in Medderby to buy some presents and supplies of drinks for Christmas. That got her out of the way while we set up the party. We asked her if a few of her borrowers could meet here for a quick Christmas drink and she said yes. She doesn't know it's going to be a proper party and she's the guest of honour.'

'What brought this on?'

'It's a surprise party for her from the people who borrow from the library, a thank you. The poor girl has had so few parties in her life, I encouraged it. I've been trying to contact you to tell you about it but my phone hasn't been working properly and I couldn't get through to you on the landline either. I was so worried you wouldn't be here on time.'

'I've set them out.' Cynthia burst into the kitchen carrying a big tray with a few crumbs on it. She looked flushed and excited, and hardly seemed the same woman he'd seen before. She was no longer quite as scrawny and she was smiling. She stopped and looked at him, the smile fading as if she expected him to throw her out.

Dot took the tray from her and put one arm round her. 'Turns out Edwina was bullying Cynthia too, but we won't go into details about that now. We want to finish setting up the party. I don't think it'll be long before Abigail comes back from Medderby. Do you want to bring anything else in?'

'Yes, quite a lot. I'd have been here sooner but my car broke down. I have some Christmas food in the car, but not as much as I'd intended to buy.'

'I'll help you carry it in.' When they got outside she asked in a low voice, 'Any news on the house?'

'Some really good news but I'll tell Abigail the details first, if you don't mind.'

He hesitated then thought, *In for a penny, in for a pound.* 'Look, I've bought a ring and I want to propose to Abigail. Can you leave me to do that in the kitchen, then spring the party on her afterwards?'

'Yes, of course.' She carried in a couple of shopping bags and set them down. 'Come on, Cynthia. Let's get everyone organised into the library then switch some of the front lights out so that Abigail doesn't realise how many folk are here.'

Lucas brought in the last of his things, all the time listening for a bigger car to arrive. That shouldn't be difficult to identify because it'd definitely sound different from the collection of small elderly vehicles currently parked outside.

Yes, there it was. He waited just inside the door for Abigail to come in, hoping Philip didn't stay with her. Then to his relief he watched Dot dart out from the front of the house and pull Philip away.

Thank you, Dot! he thought.

Abigail came in and stopped dead at the sight of him, looking annoyed.

'I can explain,' he said hastily.

She looked behind her, saw no sign of Philip and shut the door, leaning against it, arms folded. 'Go on, then. Explain!'

'You turned down my offer of financial help, so I made another plan to win you.'

'Oh, yes?'

He explained and saw the anger fade and its place be taken by first surprise then relief.

'That really is all I'll need to pay?'

'All *we* shall need to pay! I'm not being left out.' He moved across the room and took her in his arms. 'Darling Abigail, I'm not good at fancy words but I love you and I think you love me, so I want us to get married, and as soon as possible.'

He fumbled in his pocket and pulled out the small

box with fingers grown suddenly clumsy, so that he dropped the damned thing. 'Oh, hell!'

She was smiling now as he scooped it up.

'I knew I'd make a mess of it.' He managed to open the box and hold it out so that the beautiful amethyst and diamond ring caught the light and sparkled. In fact, it sparkled more than it should have done and he suspected someone was causing that. Probably three someones.

'You're supposed to slip it on my finger now,' she prompted, seeing how nervous he was.

He managed to do that without dropping it. 'I can have the size changed if we need to.'

'It fits perfectly. See.'

She held it out so he raised her hand to his lips and kissed it, then pulled her closer and kissed her too.

'You haven't given me your answer. Will you marry me?'

'Of course I will.'

He caught sight of three figures in the small kitchen mirror and heard them say, 'Congratulations.'

She turned round to smile at the ghosts.

'I don't mind them hanging around the house, but I want it making plain from the start that they're not to come into the bedroom,' he said.

'We never go into bedrooms of happily married couples,' Roderick said sharply. 'What sort of people do you think we are?'

Georgiana elbowed him in the ribs to shut him up. 'Congratulations, Abigail and Lucas.'

'You'll be very happy, I'm sure,' Juliana added.

He saw their images fade and sighed in relief before turning to his beloved again. 'I thought I'd have to nag you to let me help pay the inheritance tax and marry me.'

'No. You've performed a miracle and how can I turn that away?'

'Good. Now let's go into the library and tell Dot and her friends.'

* * *

As they walked through the door into the dimly lit library, the rest of the lights came on and a chorus of voices called, 'Surprise!' The brightly lit room came alive with sparkling decorations and smiling faces.

'We have a surprise for you,' Lucas called. 'We've just got engaged.'

Dot chuckled. 'It's not really a surprise. The minute you came through that door I could tell it had gone well. Abigail looked so happy.'

'Champagne, anyone?' Philip held out a tray full of little plastic cups. 'Sorry we haven't got fancy glasses to put it in, but it'll taste just as nice, and we do need a proper toast.'

He waited till everyone had a drink then raised his own in the air. 'To Lucas and Abigail!'

'Lucas and Abigail!'

For a moment the air seemed full of sparkling happiness, then it settled down and everyone started to enjoy the first party of this very special Christmas.

Dot was caught under some mistletoe by the brother of one member of the library and emerged from a kiss, ruffled and blushing.

Cynthia was danced round the ground floor by another man who proved to be a superb dancer and had been looking for a partner. Wine was drunk, food was eaten and books fell off shelves into the hands of people who'd been looking for just that title for ages. And when everyone except Lucas had gone home, the two lovers went slowly upstairs together, smiling happily. But we shan't go into details about what happened next. Not even the ghosts know the details of that.

Other titles published by Ulverscroft:

GOLDEN DREAMS

Anna Jacobs

Lancashire, 1895. Lillian Hesketh has taken a new name, and a brave step towards a happier life. Suddenly widowed after an unhappy marriage, and pursued by her unscrupulous in-laws, Lillian finds a fresh start in the beautiful Ollindale valley. Thanks to the kindness of her new neighbours, Walter Crossley and his family, she finally has a home to call her own — but the threat of discovery by her husband's family still casts a shadow over her new life.

Meanwhile, Edward Ollerton has returned to the valley to rebuild his ancestral home. Hoping to one day marry and start a family, Edward finds himself drawn to the shy, attractive widow — but not everyone is happy to see him reclaim his estate . . .

Will their dreams fade to dust, or can a golden future blossom on the shores of Jubilee Lake?

PAULA'S WAY

Anna Jacobs

An unexpected inheritance is most people's dream, but not so for Paula. She's happy and secure in Western Australia with her own business, a complete contrast to her rootless childhood, and has little interest in the minor stately home in Wiltshire of which she is apparently now the owner.

Persuaded to at least visit the property, she travels to the UK. But following on from the journey, complications personal, romantic, and financial abound — all of which will test the adage that home is where the heart is . . .

SILVER WISHES

Anna Jacobs

Lancashire, 1895. When her controlling stepfather suddenly dies, it seems that Elinor Pendleton finally has a chance of freedom. But her hopes are soon dashed when she learns that the thuggish Jason Stafford has inherited every penny, and is determined to have Elinor too. Forced to flee with her beloved maid, Maude, Elinor finds shelter with Maude's distant cousin in the remote village of Ollerthwaite, on the shore of Jubilee Lake. But Walter Crossley has troubles of his own. Having lost his closest family in a tragic accident, he needs one of his grandsons to return from America to inherit his farm — and when practical, kindhearted Cameron arrives, he appears to be the perfect heir. But is this young man everything he seems? And will Elinor's secret wish to have a family of her own ever come true . . . ?